THE FLIGHT OF HOPE

"Away in the winds..."

HJ Bellus

THE FLIGHT OF HOPE

Editor: Emma Mack, Ultra Editing

Proofreader: Julie Deaton @Deaton Author Service

Formatting: HJ Bellus

Cover Designer: Cassy Roop @Pink Ink Designs

Photographer: Perrywinkle Photographer

Model: Shailey Collier

Dedication-

Here's to the heartaches that didn't break us. You'll never know until you dive head first into the murky waters and pray you come out floating.

Prologue

"For me, there is only you." -Unknown

There are people. Rows and rows of cars. Black everywhere. I can't feel my feet as my high heels sink into the grass. My face is numb, as are my fingers. The searing pain burning my insides is alive and well.

Momma urges me down into a chair draped in velvet. It's front row. My view? Two caskets with flowers covering every surface. The sweet, floral smell is making so sick; to the point, I clutch my stomach.

"You okay?" Mom whispers in my ear.

I shake my head. If I open my mouth, a torrent of emotions will seep out. Sara screams in the background. I peer over my shoulder to see Maddie with tears streaming down her face, trying to soothe her upset toddler. She offers me a comforting smile, but I don't return it. I can't stand the sight of Sara, and her cries only infuriate me.

"Mom, shut that baby up now."

"Marlee, that's enough." She clutches my hand.

"Mom." This time my voice escalates to a scream. "I can't take it!"

"Okay. Okay." Mom rises, and it's only minutes later until Sara's cries fade.

I turn to see the backside of Maddie making her way to the parking lot. She glances back one more time before disappearing behind a row of trees. She's devastated, but I don't have it in me to care.

Silence. Caskets. Flowers.

The pastor welcomes everyone before the Military Honor begins. A muted bugle starts to play "Taps," the well-known song for a fallen soldier. I stare at the man in his uniform playing the song. He's only feet away. The song should be so much clearer, but it's not. I'm drowning.

Once the song is over, our country's beautiful flag is stretched before me and my family. The soldiers are meticulous as they present, fold the flag, and salute. Why couldn't it have been them? Anyone, but who God chose to take.

A soldier with bright blue eyes kneels before me. His pristine white glove is on top of the flag. Mom tries to get me to stand, but I refuse to. Dad's arm wraps around my waist, pulling me to my feet. He keeps me clutched to his side.

Nightmare after nightmare has played out in my sleep of this scenario and now I'm living it. My knees begin to quake, the effects of the pills wearing off, and I sob. The first, wracking my chest with a brutal force. I can feel my sternum crack under pressure then it becomes hard to breathe. The soldier's words are barely recognizable.

"This flag is presented on behalf of a grateful nation and the United States Army, as a token of appreciation for your loved one's honorable and faithful service."

Dad grabs my hand, holding it out to receive the flag. The red, white, and blue material burns my palm. My gut reaction is to let go of it in hopes of making this whole scene disappear. Dad won't let me. He's my rock right now.

***

The smell. The sight. Every damn element destroys me to the point it hurts to think about surviving. Once I'm able to pull in oxygen, a brutal force slams into my spine, reminding me of what I had. It was all taken away in a split second. The decision to run a red stoplight unraveled my past, present, and future.

My life flipped upside down. That doesn't accurately represent what happened. I died that day. My soul vanished, and my heart quit beating, yet, I'm still alive with blood pumping through my veins, but I was a casualty on the side of the road.

I had everything, and it was the idyllic American dream. Hell, some would label me as spoiled, and I wouldn't have argued. It was always my life. I was the center of everyone's attention. A girl and then a woman who had to be the best at everything no matter the circumstance. I had no friends. I had him. Then he was gone.

"Birdie, lunch is ready. Your favorite, sweetie, grilled cheese and tomato soup."

I peer up to my mom, regretting losing the scent of him once my nose leaves the sheets. His scent is barely there, and all it does is shatter the already broken pieces of my heart. I'm forced to bury my face back into the bed sheets. I do my best to shake my head. She knows I don't want to eat, but she's never given up on me.

Mom has made my favorite meals day after day. Grilled cheese and tomato soup used to make my world spin, and I'd squeal like a little girl. But, then again, I used to love life.

"Baby girl, you need to eat something." The bed

dips and then her familiar hand soothes trails over my dirty hair.

I shake my head again. My raw throat is sliced open by agony, making it sore, dripping with pain and blood. I'm unable to speak a word.

"Here, Birdie." She nudges my shoulder. "Take these, and when you wake up, I'll have another meal ready for you."

I hold my palm open and hear the crinkle of the water bottle placed next to me on the bed. These three little, white pills have been the only things holding me together. It's the magic keeping my shell of a body glued. But I'm tired, so sick of being numb, tumbling into slumber, and then springing right back into heartbreak. When the effects of the pills wear off, it's unbearable to open my eyes. I hear it, smell it, and feel death all over again.

My chest grips my heart. My vision fills with their caskets we buried in the fertile soil of the earth. The smell of fresh dirt was tearing me apart, and all the while, I sat there and watched their bodies sink down six feet.

"It's not fair, Mom. He fought for our country and then..." It hurts too much to finish my sentence. My words die off like they have since the doctors hit me with the news.

"I know, Birdie." Her tender lips pepper kisses all over the side of my exposed face. "You have to push on, baby girl; so many love and need you. You'll always have us. Always."

I remain silent, waiting for her to leave the room. The pills roll around in my palm. The silent clinking of them screams to the point of gifting me with a migraine.

It's at this moment I decide I can't stay here. I don't belong here any longer. The place I called home for so many years and then built a future with my husband doesn't belong to me anymore. I'm a foreign stranger trapped in the confines of a house.

The pills fall without sound to the sheets. I take one long inhale of his scent, branding it to memory forever. I'll never ever forget the man who was my first love and my only love who gave me everything. He was and always will be my best friend. No one will ever replace his force. It's too painful to stay. Death is screaming my name and clawing for my soul.

One slit of the wrist with the sharp edge of my fishing knife or a forceful stab to the heart. That's what I want. I hunger for the blood to drain from my body until my heart ceases. I won't have time to bleed out in peace before someone barges in, checking on me. My parents and his parents are enduring the same kind of hell I'm stuck in. I can't put them through more pain, but I can't breathe here. It's too damn much.

I have one option.

Run and never come back to my personal hell.

I take his shirt and the bag next to our bed and do just that, never looking back again.

Sorry, Mom.

Part 1
The Past
Chapter 1

"I'll never finish falling in love with you." – Unknown

"Momma, Bentley is here!" I dance in place, my fishing pole in hand.

"Just a minute, Birdie," she sings back with the clatter of the oven accompanying her voice.

"Mom!" I holler, knowing it's my rude voice and not caring.

I've been to so many new houses, but this one is different. It's gonna be my forever home like puppies get because Papa Wally is here. Momma and I get to stay with him at his homestead while Daddy stays on the base. It's all in the same town. I don't have to ever move again. No more new schools, making friends, and sick tummies.

Papa Wally's place has everything. He lets me do it all. And my new friend, Bentley, is here to go fishing. I stamp my foot feeling my temper coming on strong.

"Mom!" I stomp my foot again harder this time about to lose it.

"Birdie, enough." Her soothing palm pats my head. "You need to learn to control that temper of yours. You can go to the pond for two hours, okay? It's going to be your job to watch the time. Use your watch we bought in town the other day."

"Okay, bye, Mom." I swing the door open,

beginning to jet out the door.

I'm pulled back by the collar of my shirt. It makes me madder. I feel the heat on my cheeks and have to bite down on the inside of my cheek.

"Birdie, what did I just tell you?" Mom is in my face not joking around.

I pry my gaze to the side to shoot Bentley a grin. "Two hours and to check my watch."

"Do you cross the highway?" she asks.

"No, Mom." I roll my eyes annoyed.

"You do know I can keep you home, right?" she asks.

No, Mom. I think sarcastically.

"Yes, Mom. I'm just so excited. Papa Wally said fishing was gonna be good today and he's going to meet me and Bentley down at the pond. I'll be home in two hours and check my watch. We won't cross the highways. Okay, love you, bye."

This time I escape her grip. I don't miss her sigh and the slapping sound of her palms against her apron. I'm the only kid and just don't get why she's always so stressed and cranky. Laundry and cooking can't be all that bad.

"Be safe, Birdie."

"Love you, Mom."

Bentley nudges me with his free elbow while juggling the pole and worms in his other hand. He's such a fool. I only have a pole in my hand, and the can of corn is tucked in my back pocket. Papa Wally taught me well. I feel bad that I'm about to out fish my new best friend, but not that bad.

"You ready, Birdie?" Bentley drags out the damn nickname Momma always calls me.

"Don't be a jerk like P.J. at school or you can't go to my fishing hole!"

"Birdie, really? P.J., the biggest jerk of the class?"

"Don't call me Birdie. Only my momma calls me that." I elbow him right back in the ribs.

I growl at the thought of the dumb nickname. Momma always says it's because I flit and flutter everywhere and am always into everyone else's business except my own. She's crazy because that doesn't even make an ounce of sense.

"Okay, Birdie." This time there's no taunting in his voice.

We run side-by-side through Papa Wally's pastures, ducking under the fences we need to, and then racing each other to the pond. Our elbows fly and our arms swing as fast as they can.

We are breathless when we reach the pond. Both so exhausted we can't speak a word. Bentley is my first friend that I know will last forever. He's like my forever puppy friend.

I never have to move again because Papa Wally said so. He's tired of my family moving for the damn military, but he also loves the damn military, so it confuses me. All I know is Momma, Dad, and Papa Wally told me I don't have to go to a new school again because we are going to live here forever. It's a good thing because I've heard fourth grade is hard. I want to be able to stay in one place now. I need some turf in this area.

"Slowpokes."

Bentley and I both look up to see Papa Wally and Bill, Bentley's grandpa. His grandpa and mine with their poles cast in the pond. Their cooler lid is propped open with fish already on ice and their adult beverages fire up my competitive side.

Daddy is always telling me that my fighting side is gonna get the best of me. It's nonsense.

"Papa Wally," I scold him.

It barely comes out. I'm still bent over with one palm on my kneecap. Bentley recovers faster than me, and that just won't fly in my book. Still huffing, I stride over to Papa Wally and sit on the edge of his chair. He kisses me on the cheek. He's the only person whose kisses I'll never wipe off.

"Cast in." He points his hand. "For sure bite right there."

Remaining perched on the edge of the chair, I follow his instructions. I glance over to Bentley who's doing the same thing. My flare to be the best fuels right up.

"Got a bite!" we both holler in unison.

I reel in my line as fast as I can even though I know better. The excitement is too much. A beautiful, huge trout dangles on the other end of my pole.

"Yes!" I fist pump the air, nearly losing my pole all together.

Once my thundering heart calms down a bit, I glance over to Bentley and smile. Mine is way bigger.

"Baby girl, don't gloat when it comes to fishing now." Papa Wally pats the top of my head.

"Don't you see the size of this bugger?" I point, kneeling down, steadying my trembling fingers to get the hook out of its mouth.

His hearty chuckle is the only answer I get while prying on the hook. The thing isn't budging, so I give it one more go. White flashes of pain shoot through my hand; I pull it back, and it only gets worse.

A chorus of wails and cries fly from my mouth. "Ouch. Ow. Son of a biscuit."

Bentley's at my side crouching down next to me. "Don't move, Birdie."

Hot tears roll down my cheeks as the blood streaming from the tip of my finger comes into view. Bentley works the hook with gentle ease until it's out and then wraps my finger in the hem of his shirt.

I use the back of my hand to wipe away the tears and then fight to control my breathing. I'm riddled with hiccups and gasps.

"Nice fish."

I look up to see Bentley smiling down at me.

"Thanks," I whisper.

My heart and stomach both do a funny flutter, making me forget all about the pain and blood. It's the moment I fall madly in love with Bentley Foster.

Chapter 2
Years Later

"It's that heart of gold, & stardust soul that make you beautiful." -r.m. Broderick

Mom huffs, flopping down on the couch next to Papa Wally. He reaches over and offers his comfort by patting the top of her leg.

"I keep holding out hope, Birdie."

I quirk up an eyebrow. "For?"

"Just a glimpse of girly." She drops her head on the back of the couch.

"You love me." I lean the fishing pole against the door and then fly into her lap. I'm careful not to hurt Papa. Years of living have caught up with him quickly. He's still my all-time favorite even though he moves a tick slower and takes a few more pills.

"You're filthy. Get off me." Mom tries to push me, but I latch my arms around her neck, rubbing the mud from the fishing pond on her.

"I'm your little girl," I taunt.

"My little pain in the ass," she replies.

"You wearing those dirty jeans and boots to the dance tonight?" Papa asks.

"Dad, don't you dare!" Mom manages to get an arm out and point in his face.

Papa Wally and I erupt in laughter. We both know how to get her fired up, and it works every single time. The poor woman had one child and wanted nothing more than for me to be a girly girl, but it never happened. Don't get me wrong, I have my moments where I get all girly. But nothing can ever take the love and passion for the outdoors, fishing, and the homestead from me. I could live in the wilderness with Bentley for the rest of my life and be a happy chick.

"The red dress with rhinestones?" Mom squeaks out.

I roll my eyes. "Yes, Mom, I'm wearing that dress tonight."

"A shower?" She bites her bottom lip to keep the laughter trapped in.

I raise an arm and smell my armpit. "Nah, I'm good."

She slaps my ass, leaving a smacking sound reverberating around the living room. "Get going! I have to do your hair and makeup, and I want plenty of pictures before Bentley has to be on the football field."

"Yeah, yeah." I roll off her lap onto the floor with a thud. "We only went fishing today because it's Bentley's birthday and it's tradition."

"I'm not an idiot, Birdie. You two would go fishing any damn chance you got."

I wink at her as I stand up. "You're on to me, Mommy Dear."

"Go shower, Marlee." Mom does her best at her mean face, but it's never scared me. However, I know she's dead serious when she doesn't use my nickname. She's called me Birdie since I was young enough to remember. When she pulls out the real name card, I know shit is about to hit the fan.

"Okay, okay." I wave her off. "I'll be ready for hair and makeup in twenty minutes."

I take the stairs two at a time up to my bedroom. The walls are covered in snapshots of me and Bentley from over the years. It's a visual board of us throughout our childhood from our awkward toothless stage to our senior year of high school. Bentley's friend, Coy, is in a few of the pictures with us; besides that, it's just us.

I turn the shower to straight hot and wait for the water to warm up. I glance back into my bedroom, studying Bentley's football jersey from our sophomore year. He's been on the varsity team since our freshman year. He's the hometown hero who everyone loves, and I'm his girl. It's been that way since we met. It was our sophomore year he brought home the State title with the rest of his team. He gave me his jersey that same night when he got home off the bus.

I lean on the door jamb, crossing my arms, remembering that night like it happened yesterday. I can smell the steam in the air, but the memory is too powerful to ignore. It's the night we shared everything with each other.

Bentley: Bus just got in town. Meet me down at the pond in twenty?

Marlee: I'm here waiting!

Bentley: Love you

Marlee: Love you more

The quick hug and sweaty kiss weren't enough after the game. It was a nail-biter for the history books. Our team was down by a field goal with only a minute on the game clock. Bentley had done his best to lead his team down to the end zone, but they were exhausted, and the other team's defense was grueling. Wide receivers started dropping passes, and his running back couldn't break the line. Everyone in the bleachers chalked it up as a loss. Not me.

On a fourth and twenty, Bentley took off running. You could've heard a pin drop in the stadium as everyone from our town held their breath. I squeezed my eyes shut, praying and willing him to fly right down the field. It wasn't until the entire stadium erupted in cheers that I knew he had done it.

It's been three hours since our chaste hug and sweaty kiss. I've been dying to leap into his arms and celebrate with him. In moments like these, I wish I was a damn cheerleader so we could be closer even though we wouldn't be able to touch.

The crescent moon lights up the pond, sending off a shimmering glow. I run my hands through the tall grass as I start to run out of patience. Well, let's be honest, I've never been a patient person, so there's that. I leap to my feet when the low roar of his truck engine fills the air.

Two headlights bounce down the road in the darkness. Excitement like no other ignites inside of me. Bentley broke records tonight. Too many to count, but more importantly, he brought home the State title to our small town. It's been over fifteen years since we've had it.

The driver's door slams, long legs stride my way, and then his dazzling smile comes into view. I melt inside every single time I see him. It's a force I'll never be able to explain. My legs finally remember how to move, and I run to him. There's no warning before I leap into his arms. He always catches me.

I grip the sides of his face. "You did it, baby!"

"We did it," he corrects me before sealing his lips to mine.

Warmth spreads throughout me when his tongue glides into my mouth. His kisses are always tender and loving. It only takes a few seconds before this becomes something much more. I feel Bentley's body come to life, which only makes me ache with need.

I feel my body moving and then being laid down on the blanket next to the pond. Passion and raw love take over the situation. Our hands tear at our clothing until we are flesh to flesh. We've done everything, but this.

"I want you," I whisper in a raspy voice.

"Are you sure?" He props up on his elbows, staring down at me with rich brown eyes.

I nod with no doubt behind the action. Bentley kisses the tip of my nose and then reaches over to his jeans. My heart drums inside of my chest when I hear the condom packet rip. The anticipation is too much. I shiver in excitement and trepidation.

I watch as he readies himself then covers my body.

"I love you, Birdie." He kisses my cheek. "I've always loved you, and it will always only be you."

I nod, unable to speak. Thick emotions clog my throat, making it impossible to talk, so instead, I pull his face down to mine and kiss the hell out of him. The feel of him inside of me blindsides me until I grow dizzy with passion and so much more.

The slamming of a door downstairs snaps me out of my memory. A contagious smile dances on my lips. It's easy to get lost in the memories of us, and it's one of my favorite pastimes.

Steam fills my small bathroom off my bedroom. I hop in before Mom marches up the stairs with a wooden spoon. Tonight is more for her than me. When she heard I was nominated for Homecoming Queen, you would've thought she won the lottery. I left the dress shopping up to her knowing she'd nail it.

Even though the girly thing isn't my favorite thing to do, today is pretty damn exciting. My boyfriend's birthday spent fishing and fooling around at the pond, watching that same sexy cat play football, and then the chance of us being crowned royalty.

I don't have super close friends, but have lots of acquaintances. I'm not the most popular by any means, but also not a mean girl with a clan of bullies behind her. It will take a lot for me to swallow down some fear and stand next to some of those mean girls tonight during the crowning on the football field. I don't let myself get too flustered over it, knowing Bentley will be by my side.

"Are you ready?" A knock is on the door then Mom's voice streams in.

"Just a sec." I hop out of the shower, dashing into a loose sundress.

She doesn't wait, but barges in like she owns the place. I hide my smile, not wanting to let her know how much I'm loving all of this even if I bellyache about it.

Mom wastes no time whipping into her makeup

bag and going to work. It's her real passion and career. She complains she's the only woman who has to beg and plead with her teenage daughter to wear makeup. I'm a simple girl who slays eyeliner and mascara along with the occasional lip-gloss.

"I'd ask you if a smoky eye would be okay, but..."

I laugh at her comment then slap her ass while she's concentrating; it earns me a deep growl.

"Mom."

"Yeah." She doesn't stop applying a dark eyeshadow when she responds.

"How did you...uh...how..."

She stills, her hands falling to her sides. "Is this about sex?"

A bright flush creeps up my neck at her question. I guess Bentley and I have done a damn good job of hiding it. I shake my head.

"No."

"Then what?" The tip of her tongue peeks out between her lips as she concentrates on finishing up the eyeshadow.

"How did you handle it when Dad enlisted?" I intertwine my fingers, struggling to wring out the stress.

Bentley hasn't made it a secret he'll be enlisting in the Army after graduation. He's following in his father's footsteps. There's no way I would talk him out of enlisting. He's offering his life to fight for our freedom, and to me, that's the most honorable thing a man or woman could do. The selfish part of me struggles with the fact of having my best friend and love of my life taken away from me.

"I leaned on my family and prayed every single night he'd always be safe."

"I feel like I'm a spoiled brat by feeling the way I do."

Mom kneels down in front of me, propping up a makeup brush on my thighs. She clears her throat before she begins to speak.

"You're going to feel every single emotion during this journey. Some days will be easier than others. When he leaves for boot camp, it will devastate you, but you're going to have to dig deep, Birdie, because the pride and honor you'll hold for Bentley in the future is priceless.

I still find myself shivering with honor when Dad comes home from work. He gave all of this to us. He gave me my beautiful daughter, the opportunity to stay home with you until you went to kindergarten, and then my career. It will be hard, but so worth it."

Silence floats around the bathroom until I find the courage to speak up.

"The Army gave me Bentley. We moved here because of Dad, but now I'm struggling to give him to the Army."

"I know, Birdie." She grabs the back of my head, easing my forehead down to her shoulder. "It's not easy. You have the rest of your senior year ahead of you. Enjoy it, live every single day to the fullest, and never forget you. Plan your future right alongside Bentley's if that's what you want."

I sniffle, fighting to hold back the tears.

"If you even shed one damn tear right now, I'll beat your ass. Your eyeliner is on flick."

This causes me to burst out in laughter. I laugh so hard I'm forced to throw my head back to breathe.

"It's fleek, Mom."

"Flick, fleek, frick, fudge, frump. It's all the same to me." She stands back up, going right to work. "I shut down the salon today."

"You did?" I ask, trying to crane my head to look at her, but she pulls on my hair, keeping my head straight. "You have five other girls in there. I think it could survive one day without you."

"Nikki's mom called for an appointment, and when I told her I wasn't in, she wanted April. So, I decided to close the salon down today and send the girls to a hair and nail class. You know, professional development and all."

I groan. Nikki Miller is my arch nemesis. The battle started my first day of fourth grade. She didn't like a new girl on her turf. She tripped me, pulled out my pigtails, and stomped on my Captain America lunch box, smashing my lunch while all of the students giggled and pointed. I was saved by Bentley.

He held his hand out to me, picked me up, and dusted me off. From that day, no one else at school ever messed with me in such a manner. I was Bentley's. But that fact only made Nikki and crew despise me more. They've offered plenty of their snide comments when I'm the only one to hear them. They hurt. I won't lie, but I've risen above them.

"Mom!"

I feel her shrug as she pulls my hair through a

straight iron. "Those little bitches won't be on frick."

I don't correct her this time. Mom and I might not see eye-to-eye on everything, but we are best friends. I know that I can come to her with anything. I remain still while she straightens my wavy, thick brown hair then watch her put in soft curls.

When she's finished, I'm left with long, soft curls cascading over my shoulders and makeup that highlights my large brown eyes and defined cheekbones. It's straightforward and perfect at the same time. She eases me into my red dress. It wasn't her color of choice, that fact she made very clear. Mom's all about the trending color palettes and skin tone or whatever shit comes along.

I'm in the red today because it's school colors and Bentley will be by my side in his sweaty football uniform in the same exact colors. That's true love, and I've never been so excited in my life to stand next to him, girly shit or not!

The shrilling sound of the doorbell rings throughout the three stories of our house. I know it's him. It's way too early, but then again, he has to be on the field playing when all the other royalty will be picking up their date. Mom dashes down the stairs for her camera, all jacked up. I shake my head at her and go to the full-length mirror.

My palms smooth over the lacy material while the bling sparkles back at me as if it were giggling in glee. We have the rest of our senior year together before Bentley deploys. If I could look further into our future, we have the rest of our lives together. The present is too powerful and is scaring the shit out of me.

"Birdie, get down here." Mom's voice echoes into my room.

I take the stairs one at a time until I come face-to-face with Bentley. His hands are tucked into the pockets of his gym shorts, his t-shirt that's been transformed into a tank hangs off his broad shoulders, but it's his damn mullet he's been growing out with his team for their senior year championship playoff that gets me. It's hideous but is sexy as hell on him. The real game changer is his black snapback with his team logo on it. He always wears them backward, and I swear I fall even more for him every single damn time.

When his shy yet devious grin dances out on his face, I race down the steps until I'm bounding into his arms. He catches me like he has been doing since we were childhood friends. His scent of the most mysterious mix of woodsy, oranges, and all man envelops me before I have the chance to bury my face in the crook of his neck.

"Didn't even get a chance to look at your dress, Marlee." I feel each syllable he speaks parade across the sensitive part of my neck.

"Sorry," I whisper.

"What I did see was fucking amazing." Bentley's words come out so hushed I barely hear them.

Yeah, our parents think we are angels. We're not.

"It was all Mom."

"Don't think so." His arms wrap around me tighter. "It's all my girl."

"Enough, you two." Bentley's mom's voice interrupts us.

"Break apart! Or we won't have enough time for pictures." My mom's voice adds to the chaos.

It only causes me to giggle and to wiggle in even closer to my love. Papa Wally's voice soon joins the mix.

"Jesus, you two ain't going to get them to part. Bill and I told you that years ago."

Bill, Bentley's grandpa, passed last year, and it devastated every single one of us. The mention of his name still sends a shrill of pain to all of our hearts.

"I don't care. I want pictures," Mom hollers right back to her dad. And she claims she doesn't know where I got my sass. Yeah, right!

And then the picture taking commences. Bentley endures the wrath of his mom about his outfit. He indulges her, only offering me a few slight grins and winks. I told him it's how I wanted him dressed. Yes, we were nominated for Homecoming royalty, which is an honor in itself being seniors and all. This is the year to win it and the fact we won it the last two years is worthless at this point. But even bigger than all of this is it's Friday night lights, Bentley's senior year as quarterback, and squaring off against our rival, the Trojans.

Above all the glitter and excitement over being royalty, it's the game that matters. Bentley needs to be in game mode and not some dumbass suit. Although Bentley in a suit is a dream come true. Football isn't his end game, but the thing about

Bentley is he does nothing half-ass, and that includes loving me. Tonight is about him, and all the spotlight should be shining brightly on him.

"Gonna be able to get up in there?" Bentley winks, pulling open the driver's side door of his jacked-up truck. It screams badass, sex, and hometown hero all in one shout.

"Outta my way, man." I playfully shove on his chest, regretting it as soon as I do.

The red glam dress fits me like a glove all the way past my knees, making it impossible to leap up into his truck. Shit. I grab the steering wheel and the edge of his seat relying on arm strength to get the job done and pray no sounds of ripping material happens.

"Stubborn girl."

I can hear the smile on his face as he watches me struggle. Like always, he only lets me fidget for a bit before his two large hands grab my waist. I'm pulled back down until my heels hit the pavement. Bentley's large body presses into my back as his arms snake around my waist. I melt into him and tilt my head, giving him access.

"Mmmmm. My favorite smell. You." He kisses my neck between each word. "Sweet, sweet vanilla cherries."

"I love you," I whisper loud enough for him to hear me.

"This dress is going to be the death of me." Bentley pushes his hips into my ass, and I know what he's referring to.

"C'mon, number eleven. We've got a game to win, and then there will be plenty of time tonight to fool around." I spin in his arms to face him.

Big mistake. Our lips brush against each other's. We still for a moment drinking in one another's taste. It starts out as a slow burn, but turns into an inferno in only a matter of seconds. My hands roam through the back of his hair, clutching tight when he palms my ass, pressing further into me.

I groan in protest when he pulls away, instantly missing the feel of his lips on mine. Any other day I'd burrow down into his chest, clinging onto him for dear life. However, I refuse to stress Mom out by wrecking my makeup and hair.

"Don't forget we have some crowns to win as well." He smacks my ass.

I'm up in the air, screaming out in surprise before my ass lands behind the driver's wheel. A grinning Bentley stares up at me. Tricky little bugger he is.

I'm careful when I slide over to not tear any of the tight lace on my dress. I'm unable to straddle the stick shift like I normally do. Even though I have my car, we are always in Bentley's truck. Him behind the wheel and me right by his side and that's how we roll to the Homecoming of our senior year.

Chapter 3

Four and Half Years Later

"There is only one happiness in this life, to love and be loved." -George Sand

"Momma, quit it." I swat my hand over my head.

Her tears haven't stopped all morning. I've done my best to not let any of my own slide down my face.

"Okay, okay." She throws her arms up in the air. "I'm going to check on the men."

"Good. Go bother Daddy." I grin at her and throw my arms open for a hug. "I love you, Momma."

We hold each other for a long time. The first tear pricks at the corner of my eye. I refuse to let the waterworks even begin because I know they won't stop on a perfect day like this one.

"I love you, too, Birdie," she whispers in my ear before pulling back. She bustles out of the room, leaving me alone for the first time today.

The silence wraps around me in a gentle hug. I let out a long breath and look into the mirror. It's the day every little girl dreams about. My palms smooth down my white wedding dress. The intricate lace and beadwork make me smile. It's not a Cinderella ball gown, but rather fitted from the top all the way to the floor.

The front hangs higher than the back, showcasing my high heel cowboy boots. It's my twist on the day. Call it my added flair; it's what I'm known for. I twirl in a full circle and stop with my back to the mirror, peeking over my shoulder admiring the back of the dress or the lack of it. The diamond cut-out exposes the majority of my back.

Today is perfect. I'm marrying my best friend at the place I fell in love with him. We spent hours fishing at the pond when we were younger then it ended up as our go-to spot for making out, which led to more. Bentley Foster has been my one and only. He won over my heart before it even had a choice to decide.

The first tear spills over when I study our bed. The house Papa Wally had built for us on the hill near our pond is simple at best, but perfect. A two-level home with a wraparound porch and three bedrooms is our piece of forever.

I'm a girl on my wedding day that couldn't ask for a single thing. There's not one thing that's missing today. I run the scar on the pad of my pointer finger over my lips. The raised skin has been there for years and a simple reminder of my love for Bentley and life in general.

The creaking of the door lets me know I'm not alone anymore. "Squirt."

I turn to my Papa Wally dressed in his idea of a suit. He wasn't about to wear one of those damn monkey suits. Nope, he's in his fanciest dress jacket, white button-up shirt, blue Wranglers, and town cowboy boots. The only thing missing is his cowboy hat. He took the time to comb through his white hair. He's a handsome cat.

And just the presence of him standing before me on my wedding day is enough for the dam of tears to fall freely. Like every other time in my life, my Papa wraps me up in his arms and lets me cry. In the past, the majority of tears his chest caught were sad and painful, but today is so different. There's no emotional terror of having my dad being deployed, the agony of the day Bentley enlisted in the army, or heartache at all.

Everything is perfect. Each tear is a representation of how blessed my life is.

"Now, no crying little girl." Papa runs his hands up and down my back. "It's a happy day. It's not like you got out fished or anything."

The last part makes me crack up. Just because I fell in love with Bentley Foster, it doesn't mean my competitive spirit was wiped away. Everything we do ends up being competitive. It's who we are.

"Here." Papa takes a step back with each of his bones creaking and cracking. "Bentley wanted me to give this to you."

He hands me a blue, velvet jewelry box. I bite down on my bottom lip and shake my head.

"We said no gifts." I clutch the box in my hand.

"You know he would have to one-up you." Papa leans in and kisses my forehead. "You look beautiful, squirt. I'm sure proud of you."

"No more." I stomp my foot in a worthless effort. "I kept the tears back with Momma, and now they won't stop."

"Let 'em flow, squirt. It's a good day. A real good day." Papa creeps back over to the door. "I'll be downstairs waiting on ya."

Once the door shuts, I open the lid to the box. A scrap of paper covers the contents of the box. I recognize Bentley's handwriting right away from

. of the notes and letters we wrote each other back in high school. The sight of it always makes my knees weak.

Future Mrs. Foster,

Quit rolling your eyes and cussing me out; you know you love me! Yes, we agreed on no gifts today, but you also know I have to always one-up you. In romantic terms, that means I love to spoil my queen. This necklace is you. It's our love wrapped up in a piece of metal. You'll always be my Birdie and my one true love.

Forever,

Bentley

And the real tears fall hard and fast with no sign of stopping. The dainty silver chain swings back and forth, brushing my knuckles while I run my finger over the silhouette of the bird with its wings spread wide. Two milky white pearls dangle next to the bird along with each of our birthstones. M & B etched on the back of the bird. This is pure Bentley. He never ceases to amaze me and when I think I can't fall any further in love with him, I do.

My fingers shake, making it impossible for me to latch the necklace around my neck.

"Oh, dear." The bedroom door shuts with gusto. "Here, Birdie."

Momma grabs the back of the necklace, making quick work of clasping it. She rounds me, adjusting the pendant in place.

"It's perfect." She kisses my cheek. "Simply perfect."

All of her tears have dried up, leaving me a sobbing mess. Happiness. Elation. Sheer joy doesn't even begin to describe what I'm feeling right now.

"Sit down, baby girl." Momma's gentle hands guide me down into a chair while she goes about fixing my makeup. Her hands are natural applying makeup and styling hair. It's her profession, and she's the best at it.

"Momma?"

"Yeah." She doesn't stop what she's doing as she responds.

"Did you know you always loved Dad? I mean, how did you know?"

"I just did." She shrugs, touching up my eyeliner. "You know when you're in love, and your heart knows when it's the right one."

"I've always loved Bentley. God, I love him so much."

She chuckles lightly. "Oh, I know, Birdie. Dad and I used to swing on the front porch watching you two play, and we even knew it then."

I grab her hand, stopping her. "I love you, Momma. I don't tell you enough and know I can be a handful."

"God gave me the best daughter. I love you, too. Now and forever."

A loud banging at the door sounds before it blows open. Sergeant First Class Jones strides in with no introduction. My dad. The Army has been and always will be his first love. He's dedicated his entire life to it and sacrificed so much for it. I used to find myself hating him for loving the Army more than me when I was younger. But not now. It took me years to realize it's who he is, and I couldn't be prouder of him.

His sharp, crisp dress blues make my heart swell with pride. He's a handsome old man, aging well with a fit body and salt and pepper buzzed hair.

"I'm here for the bride." He holds out his hand to me while bending over to kiss Momma on her cheek. I don't miss the handful of ass he also grabs. Funny how things change as you get older because that gesture used to make me gag and cringe. It's not that I enjoy it now, but I view it more as a loving gesture that I can only hope to share with Bentley after thirty years of marriage.

Chapter 4

"If I had a flower for every time I thought of you, I could walk in my garden forever." -Alfred Lord Tennyson

The simple, exquisite atmosphere surrounding the pond takes my breath away. The crisp autumn air is firing all of my senses to life as I take each precise step down the aisle on the arm of my dad.

Most of the faces are a familiar blur. Bentley's mom, Susan, stands at the end of the first row with her hands clutched over her heart. She's a second mom to me and always will be. No monster mother-in-law here. Nope, scored in that department as well. Her husband, Frank, is at her side with a familiar, warm smile covering his face, and I know exactly what Bentley will look like as he ages right down to dress blues his dad proudly wears.

The damn tears come back when I make eye contact with my future husband. His bronzed skin, strong jawline, piercing brown eyes, and broad shoulders always punch me in the gut. His black hair is clipped in a tight buzz cut. His dress blues are my reminder of the career path he chose and the same that took him away from me during his first deployment.

I remember to breathe when his dimples light up. Bentley's eyes are full of unshed tears. His reverent stare as he takes me in is my final undoing. I unlace my arm from my dad's and rush straight to him. The laughter streaming from our guests is muted by the beauty and magic of the day.

The bouquet comprised of wildflowers falls from my hand. I can't get to Bentley fast enough. His muscular chest catches me like it has so many other times. I'm home in his arms. I don't pull back until Pastor Turner clears his throat several times.

When I do lean back, it takes everything inside me to not taste his full, bowtie lips. Bentley has the lips of an angel and knows how to use them. He's a fine wine that I'm always ready to devour.

We both stare at each other like lovesick fools. Hell, we are beyond lovesick fools. We've shared it all throughout our years. We survived the latter years of elementary, the awkward puberty stage, the judgmental trying years of high school, and a year of deployment convincing us we will make it through anything. Bentley breaks the moment with a sideways glance to Pastor Turner. He's always been the rule follower out of the two of us.

"I love it." I grab the pendant on my necklace.

He winks, nods, and takes my hands in his.

Dad is the first one to speak up. "No need to give this wild child away. Bentley has had her for years now. We love you, son."

This gains another round of laughter from our guests. It's muted again because all I can hear, see, feel, and smell is the man standing in front of me. Neither of us looks away from each other.

"Was it worth the wait?" Bentley whispers.

I nod.

"Told you I'd be home for you, Birdie. I'll always be."

"I love you, Bentley."

Pastor Turner gains control over the ceremony and proceeds. Again, it's all a blur in an echoing tunnel with Bentley and my future at the dead center. His grip on my hands tightens, keeping me grounded as each second ticks by. Rings and vows are exchanged with ease and grace. It's all as natural as our souls connecting years ago at the pond.

"You may now kiss the bride," Pastor Turner's deep, gruff voice announces.

Bentley doesn't miss a beat before pulling me into him. It happens so fast. I'm bent back in an earth-shattering, soul-seeking kiss. Bentley's arms keep me secure to his chest, not making the position awkward. Our tongues meet and even though we've kissed a thousand times before, it's like our first kiss. I'm his wife, and he's mine.

My hands wrap around his neck, and I kiss him back with everything I have. We ignore the cheers from our friends and family. The length of the kiss is far beyond the accepted time, but I've never been one to follow the rules. It's not until we are breathless that our lips part.

Bentley doesn't stand us up right. Instead, he brushes his lips against mine over and over until we are kissing again. We ignore our parents' threats, drowning in one another. His taste is always sweet and minty with the slightest taste of a cigar. It makes my insides melt every single time. I'm the luckiest girl in the world.

"I think we are about to be boo'ed out of our wedding," Bentley mumbles into my lips.

"So." I peck his lips. "Can we leave for our honeymoon now? Screw the rest."

His laughter rumbles against my love bruised lips. "Our moms would have our asses."

Bentley pulls me up into a standing position, but I don't stay here long before he sweeps me off my feet and not by a kiss this time. I squeal then wrap my arm around his neck. I peer down, making sure all of my goods are still in my dress.

"Boy, that's for the threshold," his dad hollers out, causing all of the guests to erupt in a roar of laughter.

"Yeah." I pat Bentley's chest with my bouquet.

"Couldn't help myself, Birdie." He nuzzles the sensitive skin in the crook of my neck.

It's a damn good thing we cherished our kiss because once Bentley reaches the end of the flower petal covered aisle, we are slammed with picture after picture then a long-ass greeting line. My face hurts from smiling, my body is exhausted, and my damn scalp is throbbing from the metal bobby pins.

I lean into Bentley's side. He's deep in conversation with an old friend from high school. He doesn't miss a beat in conversation, catching and pulling me into his side. He'd sweep me up in his arms if I asked him to without blinking. I lay my head on his chest, knowing I should be careful not to get makeup on him, but the excitement of the day has sucked all of the energy out of me.

"Doing okay, Birdie?" He kisses the top of my head, murmuring out his question once the majority of the guests have made their way under the enormous white tent.

"My feet hurt," I mumble.

"Let's go eat, dance, cut the cake, and then we'll be out of here."

I grumble, making him laugh. I was notorious for throwing fits and getting my way when I was a little girl. I've matured, but hey, still have to grumble once in a while.

I straighten out my dress, grab Bentley's hand, and begin walking toward the head table.

"Baby." I peer up at him. "Are you sad you didn't have any groomsmen?"

It's no secret Bentley has a ton of friends. Hell, the man's the hometown hero now and back when we were in high school. He talks to everyone and lends a helping hand whenever it's needed.

"No, I only needed one person there. The same one I need the rest of my life. Nothing else matters." He squeezes my hand while waving to someone with his other.

"I love you." I lay my head on his shoulder and let him guide me through the crowd.

I often pinch myself to make sure this man isn't a damn dream. He's been my best and only friend since the day he pulled the fishing hook out of my finger. Sure, I had acquaintances in high school, and some could be considered friends, but I never let anyone in too close because there was never a void to fill after Bentley.

It always drove my mom insane that I didn't have any close friends that were girls. Hell, I drove her nuts since the moment she realized I'd be forever a tomboy at heart. But it nearly killed her off when I refused to have a maid of honor or any bridesmaids. The only way I'd have girls stand behind me was if Bentley wanted his friends at his side. In the end, it was the two of us.

"You need to eat, Birdie." Mom places her hands on top of my shoulders and kisses my cheek.

I look up at her and smile. "I'm too tired."

"Another bite of your prime rib, it's delicious. Then it's your first dance."

"Okay, Mommy." I bat my eyelashes to match my voice.

Typically, she'd swat me in the back of the head since I'm sitting down, but she's too soon distracted by our neighbor, Shelly, who happens to be one of her best friends. I watch her flow away in her gorgeous yellow dress. My mother is the definition of elegance, grace, and beauty. I see glimpses of it in me, but I'm nowhere near her level. I love that woman.

"Bite." A warm piece of prime rib rubs along my lips. "C'mon, Birdie, do I need to use the airplane?"

I look over to Bentley who has a shit-eating grin on his face. It's his favorite pastime to harass me about my helicopter Mom. Bentley has two brothers, so he has never been able to understand my mom and her tactics. He claims his mom threw slop on the table and it was first come first serve. It wasn't like that at all, but it sure was a world different than how my mom raised me.

Puttering sounds begin to emanate from Bentley's vibrating lips. He pulls back the fork and starts circling it to my mouth.

"Stop." I slap his shoulder, barely able to get out

the word between my laughter.

"No dessert if you don't finish your meal," he taunts.

I bite down on my bottom lip, trying to stifle back my giggles. Bentley knows exactly what he's doing right now.

"Nom. Nom then you get your cake, Birdie."

I push my palm onto his broad chest, which does nothing to stop him. "I've had enough meat."

His eyes glow bright, his brows shooting up in his hairline, and then in a flash of a second, I see his determination grow. I open my mouth to protest, but he's faster than me. The bite of prime rib dangling from the edge of the fork lands in my mouth. Bentley leans in, striking me with his masculine scent. It's always a constant perfect mixture of citrus and a rich woodsy scent, and it makes me melt every single time.

He darts his tongue out, running it along the shell of my ear before he whispers. The evidence of my want for him races all over my skin in the form of goose bumps.

"You better not be full of meat, baby, we got a full night planned tonight." His hand snakes up the front of my dress. His large palm is burning my skin as it moves closer and closer to the apex of my thighs.

I hold my breath wanting so damn much more, but knowing we can't right here. Desire and frustration boil together, leaving me a mess. Bentley's eyes gloss over when he pulls back, and I can only imagine mine mirror his. It's clear what we both need and want.

We remain silent as he feeds me a few more bites of food. We never break eye contact, and you'd never know a celebration of our wedding surrounded us.

I lean forward after a long swallow of champagne. I do my best to mimic Bentley's actions before. My tongue darts out, tracing the shell of his ear. The problem is I have no self-control when it comes to this man. My body goes into overdrive. I nibble on his ear and then suck on the lobe.

"I can't wait any longer, baby. Can we go? Please." I beg.

Bentley pulls back, licking his bottom lip, and the look in his firing brown eyes leaves nothing to the imagination.

"Let me speed this shit up, and we'll get out of here." He stands and faces the back of the tent while he discreetly adjusts the crotch of his dress pants.

I giggle, and it soon turns into a full-on laugh. He rewards me with a glare that turns playful.

"Wouldn't be a laughing matter if one of our guest's eyes got poked out." He smirks and strolls away, leaving me in a mess of laughter.

It's an exhausted, giddy laugh that shows no sign of stopping. My belly aches after I'm able to get it under control. I use the napkin with our initials monogrammed on them to wipe away the happy tears. I collapse back into an exhausted heap in the chair.

My body feels like it's been weighed down by a ton of bricks, but it's also more at peace than I've experienced in a long time. It's not the fact I married my best friend. It's more than that. He's home. He survived his first deployment and returned the same man he left. I watch him across the tent, throwing back his head in laughter, deep in conversation with his best friend Coy.

Bentley tips back the bottle of beer, taking a long gulp. The man is so damn sexy and everything else between. My life.

"Marlee, you look stunning."

I look over to see Maddie standing next to me. I smile brightly at her. We never went to school together. Her and Coy met online.

"Hey, girl. Thanks." I stand up and hug her.

"Your wedding is stunning. I love everything about it."

I shake my head. "Thanks, but that was all my mom and Bentley's mom."

She laughs lightly. "Well, they did a fantastic job."

A shine catches the corner of my eye, and then I see the large diamond on her hand.

"Congrats." I point at her ring. "Bentley told me the other night that Coy popped the question."

Her eyes go dreamy, and her cheeks flush with a hint of pink. "He did. I was beginning to think it would never happen."

"I knew he would. That man is in love!" I gesture for her to take a seat next to me. I'm not lying about being dead ass tired. She sits where Bentley was before, and the conversation comes easily and natural. None of it the forced small talk. Maddie is down to earth and friendly as all get out.

I've picked up on this fact on a few times we hang out, but today it's different.

"Didn't you guys get in engaged in high school the end of your senior year?" Maddie asks.

I nod and roll my eyes. "I think we took ten years off our parents' lives."

"Yeah, mine would've locked me up in a tower."

I chuckle. "Our families are really good friends. We eased their tensions after letting them know Bentley was enlisting in the Army and I was getting my realtor license. Then he got deployed..."

My voice trails off. Even though he's home safe and sound, it's still a subject that guts me to talk about. All of the what-ifs and, even worse, the possible deployments to come. I swallow down the fear and pick up the conversation.

"The day he returned, I begged him to take me down to the courthouse, but in the end, he won. Our mothers would've beat our asses and probably disowned us."

Maddie chuckles lightly. "Coy has told me your parents and, hell, the whole community have been planning your guys' wedding since you were in middle school."

"He'd be right there." I smirk, wanting to get the attention off me. "So, have you guys set a date yet?"

"With Coy just enlisting, I'm not sure what's going to go on."

I grab her hands to calm her fidgeting fingers. Coy didn't sign up right after graduation like Bentley and chose to do so now. I could pin down the emotions she's going through with a fine toothcomb. There's not one single thing anyone can tell you to make it better. It's the oddest mixture of pride, honor, selfishness, and fear that attacks your core.

"What kind of wedding do you want?" I slap my chest with my free hand. "Now, I'm abnormal when it comes to wedding shit. Like I said, I would've married that man in the courthouse. All of this shit is pretty, but I don't need any of it. So, on a scale from one to ten, ten being bridezilla, what are you?"

Maddie nibbles on her bottom lip and cringes a bit before squeaking out her answer. "An eight."

"You're killing me here, but I think I can work with an eight."

Maddie's final walls tumble down to the ground as she goes on about plans for a wedding. I don't miss the hints she drops about the timing with enlisting and other stress factors. She doesn't have a helicopter mom or even a mom at that. She claims her dad won't handle a wedding well either way since she's his baby girl.

"What about Vegas?" I throw up both hands. "Now, give me a second to explain here. I looked into it when the moms were planning this one. There are so many options, not just Elvis you know? But I'll throw this out there, too, Elvis would be kick ass."

A stern look covers her face, then a finger in my face. "No Elvis. Not ever, but Vegas, I'll think about."

She cracks a smile, and I relax.

"Dude, I thought you were about to kick my

ass."

We both laugh and then at the same time look toward our men. Maddie groans. I don't have to ask what's wrong. It's the same picture that's been before me since high school. The popular girls, aka the cheerleaders and sluts, surround the two men. There is shoulder petting, lots of fake laughs, and even more fake titty action going on.

"Just watch, Maddie."

"Uh?" She doesn't make eye contact but stares at Coy.

"Each time one of their fake ass nails touch them, the men step back."

She looks over to me and holds up her hand, displaying her very fancy fake nails adorned with gems.

"Well, you can have fake ass nails because you're not fake, but seriously watch it. I've dealt with this shit for years. At one point or another, they all pretended to want to be friends with me. Didn't take me long to realize it was just to get closer to Bentley and Coy. It didn't even matter that Bentley and I were head over heels for each other."

"I hate it. We can't go anywhere around town without this shit happening."

"You'll get used to it. Trust me."

"How?" she asks with genuine wonder dancing in her deep chocolate brown eyes.

"Like this." I stand to my feet and gesture for her to do the same thing.

We both pluck a flute of champagne from a table as we pass it. Bentley smirks when he notices me coming his way. He knows damn well what's about to go down. I've had to refine this tactic over the years. It started as me beating the shit out of the women to berating them with every evil word I could come up with to my mere presence that makes them run. Persistence is key when it comes to this game.

"There's my gorgeous wife. Mrs. Foster." Bentley pulls me to his side and kisses the top of my head.

"And my sexy husband." I look up to him and plant a lingering kiss on his lips, leaving no guessing to what my tongue is up to.

On cue, it's now the group of bitches start groaning and clearing their throats. I hear Coy greet Maddie, but continue to kiss my man. When I pull back from Bentley, he's left me breathless with swollen and bruised lips.

"I was telling our old school friends how damn sexy you are."

"Ahhh." I pat his chest and then turn my gaze to the group of women. Pathetic. They're dressed up for a nightclub in a big city and not a wedding. I have to admire their dedication to digging their claws into Bentley one last time. "Thanks for coming today."

Odd. They're not so friendly to me, so being the better person I make conversation to help them feel more relaxed. I mean, it's the nice thing to do.

"Nikki, did you ever find out the paternity results on your newest child?"

Bingo! Game over.

Her face grows a bright red, her fist clutching

around the stem of the flute before she opens her mouth. "Some things never change, do they, Marlee?"

I cut her off. "No, they don't. Always running you away from my man. It's an old game between us and I always win. Thanks for coming today."

I gift her with a finger wave. Not another word comes from her before she's spinning on her heels and marching away. The rest of her gang follow suit. Bentley doesn't even try to hold in his laughter. This may come across to an outsider as being rude or even edging into bullying. But after years upon years in a small town dealing with the same shit, I've been forced to stand up for myself. It was evident from my first day at school that I didn't fit into the small town's box of ideal. I never apologized or tried to fit because I found Bentley before the town got to me. We fit together.

"Oh my God!" Maddie hops from foot to foot. "That was freaking awesome."

Coy groans, burying his face in the top of her head. "I knew once you two had time to sit and chat that you'd hit it off."

"Don't ever back down from them bitches. They sense fear, and they'll attack."

"You have no idea how snotty they are to me at the bank where I work."

Bentley spins me around and pulls me to his chest. "Bet they won't anymore. Run with my little gal here, and you're good as gold."

I wrinkle my nose up at Bentley, admiring the sparkle in his rich whiskey-colored eyes. His palms glide down my sides then reach around to cup my ass. The built-up passion from earlier sparks right back to life.

"Maddie, you better close your eyes. Marlee initiated a sex ban once Bentley refused to take her to the courthouse. They're like frustrated rabbits at this point."

I bust out in laughter. Coy always has a way to be downright crude, but funny at the same time. He's made me laugh more than I can count at indecent comments.

"Alright. The time has come for Mr. and Mrs. Foster to take the dance floor. Gather around."

I clutch Bentley's strong shoulders all of a sudden feeling giddy for this moment. A second wind has brought my energy levels right back up. I'm certain it's from hearing the DJ announce Mr. and Mrs. Foster. I'm not worried about escaping the reception early as Luke Bryan begins singing, "Play It Again."

Bentley never lets go of me as he drags me out on the dance floor. Our bodies are intertwined together, swaying to each word. We never break eye contact and share a few kisses. Bentley Foster is my song that I want to play on repeat for the rest of my life.

"I love you, Bentley."

Chapter 5

"Her eyes held an endless kind of love for him."
-Karen Kingsbury

"Can I open my eyes yet?" I whine, dangling my legs out of the passenger door of his truck.

"No, give me five more minutes."

"Bentley, it doesn't sound like we are at an airport."

It takes all my discipline not to rip off the bandana tied around my face. Bentley knew there was no way in hell I'd keep my eyes covered. He had the blindfold secure before we left our driveway. I did get a glimpse of him in khakis and a white button-up shirt after he changed. He's been hell-bent on keeping the honeymoon a secret.

"Two more minutes."

"Bentley, if we are at Motel Six I'm going..."

His lips shut me up. I didn't even hear him near me. The bottom of my wedding dress flows in the evening wind, my boots dangling out of the door as I wrap my arms around his shoulder and spread my legs to make room for Bentley.

"Are you ready for your big surprise?"

"I'm a bit nervous," I mumble into his lips.

"Nah, no need to be." He kisses me again then pulls back, grabbing the pendant of the necklace he gave me. "This is us. It's how I see us, and when I sat back and thought about our honeymoon I wanted every minute of it to be us. There's no other place I could think of spending the first night with my wife. It's where we fell in love."

"The pond," I whisper.

"Yes."

He carefully pulls back the blindfold. It takes me several long seconds to adjust my eyes and when I do, I gasp in shock. We are at the pond, but tonight it's lit up with dainty white lights, a huge tent with a plaid blanket in front of it. Bottles of wine and beer flow out of the top of a cooler. Our two-childhood fishing poles are leaning up against the tent.

Even though I thought I was too tired to cry, tears spring to life. It's amazing.

"It's not Hawaii or the Caribbean..."

I place my finger over Bentley's lips to stop him. "It's more and perfect."

The glowing lights of the dying down reception are off in the distance next to our house. It's serene. So simple, yet extravagant down to each detail of us.

His warm palm cups my cheek. "I know the wait was hell on you, Birdie. My deployment was the hardest thing we've overcome, so I wanted everything about tonight and the next week to be perfect."

"Honestly." I lick my bottom lip. "Motel Six would've been perfect as long it was with you."

I pull him closer, clutching the back of his neck. "I want you to kiss me every single day like you did in front of all of our guests."

"I can do that," he growls into my lips.

And he does. I grow greedy as the kiss intensifies, wanting and needing more and more of him. I do my best to tug him up into the cab of the truck. I lost my virginity here, so it seems perfect to have my husband make love to me here as well.

"C'mon, baby, we have all night." Bentley pulls back and turns around, offering me his back.

I grumble and moan my disapproval at this, but eventually, wrap my arms around his neck and do the same with my legs around his waist. Bentley begins striding over to the tent with his hands around my calves.

"Remember when you used to pack me around like this all the time?" I ask while kissing up and down his neck.

"Do you remember begging for piggyback rides our entire junior year?"

"Me? Never! It was you begging to pack me around when you were all sweaty and worked up after football practice."

His deep chuckles echo around the pond, warming me from head to toe. Once Bentley sets me down on my feet, I fall backward on the blanket splayed out like a starfish. Not one ounce of lady manners in sight. I kick up both feet, pointing my fancy boots at Bentley.

"What's this?" He crooks up an eyebrow.

I spread my legs apart that are up in the air. "Please, baby, take the boots off then devour me while I lay here."

"You're such a little shit." Bentley eases each boot off and tosses them over his shoulder.

I'm about to scold him when he begins unbuttoning his shirt. I watch in silence as he strips down to a sleek pair of black boxers.

"You're overdressed, my lady." Bentley slinks

down on top of me, cupping my face with his hands.

Even through the thick material of the dress, the heat of his body makes my core sizzle.

"Son of a bitch!" Bentley rolls off me, howling in pain. "Your dress bit me."

He points to a dribble of blood on his torso, and I lose it. I should not be laughing, and the more I think about that, the harder I laugh my ass off. It takes Bentley no time to recover before he's pulling me by the ankles toward him. His nimble fingers strip me out of my dress and then toss it to the side.

"If this is a biting bra, I'm going to smack your ass." His body covers mine again.

"Mmmm. I like it when you spank me." I pull his face down to mine, darting my tongue out to lick the seam of his lips.

"Naughty girl."

"Kiss me like you did at the wedding and make love to your wife."

My words do something to him. I can see it in his eyes and the rise and fall of his chest pushing into mine. The tenderness of his lips swiping over mine makes me melt back into the blanket. There's nothing to stop us this time. Our hands tear away the rest of the clothes until it's our two bodies pressing together.

Bentley dips his head, swirling his tongue around my nipple before biting down. He pays the same attention to the other one. My hips buck up into him, begging and pleading for more.

"Bentley, I need you now," I beg.

He comes back up to my face, settling between my legs. His muscular arms cage me in; we are nose to nose, the intimacy of the moment one for the record books. I squeeze my eyes shut with his first push in. My breath vanishes at the fullness, and my heart squeezes with so much love it's about to burst.

"Open your eyes," Bentley whispers, running the pad of his thumbs up and down my face.

I do. He begins moving slowly in and out of me. I wrap my legs tight around his waist. The stare of my husband's brown eyes piercing me sends me over the edge. My nails dig into the top of his shoulders while I ride out the waves only he makes me experience.

While I fight to catch my breath, it becomes hard to do so with this man giving me the world. I struggle to extinguish the thought of him never coming home when he was deployed. It still haunts me and is the one thing that could take me down at the knees.

Bentley grunts and the pace picks up. It's my favorite part to watch. The sharp features of his face is so damn intense while our sweat-slicked bodies glide together. His features tighten as he bites down on his bottom lip and then collapses down on me.

We lie in silence, holding onto one another. Our heartbeats are steady, and my thoughts are screaming out loud. I know he can hear them without even having to ask him.

"You do know kids can do the math."

I laugh, running my hand up and down the back

of his head.

"Then you'll be the one explaining to them it happened on our wedding night."

"I can do that." I kiss his cheek.

We both want a baby and even tried for one before he was deployed and right up until the wedding sex ban. It's not a common thing for a young couple to want, but then again, we aren't your typical love story.

Bentley pulls back a tick and stares down at me. "Love you, Birdie."

I tap the tip of his nose with my finger, rubbing my scar along it. He knows as well as me it's as good as an I love you right back. Bentley rolls off me to the side but tugs me right along with him. He bobbles us around for a long time before his head is propped up against a tall stack of comfy pillows with a blanket wrapped around us. A bag of Jalapeno Cheetos and a jumbo box of Milk Duds balance on his abdomen with me tucked tight into his side.

"Good call on the juice box wine instead of glass." I pop a spicy Cheeto in my mouth.

"I know you and glass, baby."

I feign glare up at him, studying the way he takes a long pull from his beer.

"Are we going to fish tonight?" I climb up his body without knocking our snacks off him.

"Later. I have other plans."

"Like?" I ask, trailing my lips along his jawline while sneaking a hand under the blanket.

"You're getting hotter." Bentley winks.

I change the direction of my hand up toward his

armpit.

"Colder. Freezing."

I quirk an eyebrow, continuing to his armpit.

"Freezing. Ice-cold." He rolls over to the side, sending our snacks up into the air. His large body crunches on them as he rolls over trapping me. "Speaking of cold, you better be ready to pull out your winter coat."

"Uh?" I push on his chest, trying to figure out where this sexual joke is heading.

"We are going to Alaska tomorrow. Two weeks of fishing competition, my dick, and your..."

I burst out in laughter about the dick part and can only imagine where he was going with the next part. I cup his face in my hands after my giggles die down.

"You do know I'll kick your ass every single day in a fishing competition, right?"

"Yeah, yeah, we will see about that." Bentley moves between my legs, making me forget all thoughts about any competition.

Chapter 6

"Let us always meet each other with smile, for the smile is the beginning of love." -Mother Teresa

"Babe, people don't renew their vows after six months," I reply for the tenth time while studying a brochure of the strip.

"But it's Elvis, Birdie."

"I don't care. It's a waste of money."

A hand wraps around my ankle, yanking my body to the bottom of the bed. The loose towel that had been wrapped around me falls to the side. Bentley is on me within a blink of an eye, trapping me to the mattress. His low-hanging swim shorts are rubbing against my sensitive skin.

"I want to marry my wife again with Elvis." He dips his head in the crook of my neck, nipping and kissing.

"One, you are insane. Two, this weekend is about Maddie and Coy." I push on his chest, not budging him at all. "Three, the answer is hell no."

Bentley pops up, placing his palms down on the bed. He does his best to glare down at me, but the man is too damn carefree and loving to pull it off.

"Are you in a ball busting mode this weekend or into crushing childhood dreams?"

I bite back the smirk. "All of the above."

"Permanent sex ban until our vows are renewed by Elvis," Bentley declares.

I cock an eyebrow up at him. "Bullshit."

"Bullshit?"

"Yeah, I'm calling bullshit. You haven't gone one

day since we got married, and it's been well over five months. Shit, most days you get it two or three times."

"Are you questioning my discipline, baby? I'm a US soldier."

"When it comes to sex? Yes. You took me in the damn closet at your grandma's ninetieth birthday party."

"I was horny, and there was chocolate cake, dammit."

I refuse to laugh at his antics even though it's damn near impossible. It's what gets me in trouble with him every single time and more than not the reason he gets his way every single time.

"You know that chocolate cake was begging me to eat it from your tits and pu..."

"Stop," I warn him.

My husband knows how to get to me every single time, and that's with his dirty mouth. I love it when he talks dirty to me, which means I'll be begging him for sex any minute and with his permanent sex ban in place until I agree to renew our vows, all of it equals me being screwed well and truly and Bentley getting his way.

He thrusts his hips into me, weakening me by the second. Of course, Bentley Foster would take advantage of my naked state. I can't complain when his teeth sink down onto my nipple. Lord, only if I had more willpower when it came to him.

***

I'm convinced Bentley did way too much research before coercing me with his talented body to have our vows renewed. He's like a kid on

Christmas morning walking down the strip. I ended up begging him to take me and knew it was the final nail in my coffin. Bentley always gets his way.

Oh, and let me say it's not only getting our vows renewed by Elvis. In true Bentley fashion, he had a whole scheme planned out. I swear this man lives for moments like these. I would never admit it to him, but these are the moments that I will cherish forever. The goofy ones that make you laugh your ass off and fall even deeper in love when it's not even possible.

After he dressed me and dragged me out of the hotel, it was then he told me exactly how it was going to go down. We went down to Fremont Street and found the cheapest souvenir shops. It was then he laid it on me that we would be dressing each other for our renewal ceremony using eight dollars each.

A part of me was relieved because I wasn't looking forward to wearing a skimpy dress that hundreds had squeezed into before. The primary mission of the shopping trip was to pick the most God-awful outfit we could find. Las Vegas has the cheese factor, so it wasn't too hard to find my outfit for Bentley.

It took me fifteen minutes, and ten of those was standing in a long ass line. I snagged a neon yellow t-shirt with the saying on it, *Cat Hair is Lonely People Glitter* with Las Vegas bedazzled below it. I have no clue why or how in the hell the two things go together, but then again it was two dollars. I blew most of my budget on the neon pink spandex shorts. The ass is covered with Welcome to Vegas, Baby. I had one penny left after throwing in the patriotic old-school sweatband.

After an additional fifteen minutes of standing on the sidewalk in front of the store, I become a little nervous wondering what in the hell the man is up to. I mean, he only had eight dollars to spend.

Standing out on the sidewalk, I watch him through the window and like always he has the attention of a group of store clerks helping him out. It's cute watching them tail my husband as he scours the racks. He stands out in a crowd. It's not only the fact he's over six feet tall with broad shoulders and a rock hard body, no it's more than that. His smile is welcoming and would make anyone feel like a champion. And he graces it to everyone he comes across. Not to mention, his dimples and strong jawline and those damn dark honey colored eyes that get me every single time.

I'm about to go in and pull him out of the shop when he comes out smiling like he won the lottery. I should be scared right now, but deep down I'm more intrigued to see what the hell he came up with. No way it could be worse than the outfit I slapped together.

"You're going to look gorgeous in this." Bentley grabs me by the hip, tugging me into his chest.

I lick my lips and smirk up at him. I love seeing him so happy and carefree. It's a rare sight since his career is so intense. He always makes time for me at home, but I see the stress always weighing down on his shoulders. If I have to stand through a damn renewal ceremony to give this to him, then

I'd do it every single day for the rest of my life.

"I have a feeling you outdid yourself, Mr. Foster."

"I'm getting hard thinking about it." His hand sneaks down to my ass, and he squeezes it hard.

"Food." I pat his chest with my free hand. "I'm going to need food before we do this."

"I've got something for you to eat." He winks.

This time I playfully slap his chest. "I swear, you only have one thing on your mind twenty-four seven."

"Not my fault." He throws an arm up in innocence. "It's all yours. You do this to me every single day."

I roll my eyes and shake my head with an ear-splitting grin covering my face. Everyone told us we were too young and this crazy love would fade away in time. There's no damn end in sight for us.

Bentley leans down, licking the shell of my ear, and then whispers. "That smile on your face is what got me through the endless days of my deployment. It was that and your giggle, your gorgeous body, and the love I knew I had waiting on me at home."

Tears sting the back of my eyes. The deployment will always be an imminent threat to our marriage. It's not a topic I care to talk about. It hurts too damn much and frankly scares the shit out of me. Bentley has never skirted the issue, and I know it's because he needs an outlet.

"I do what I can." I wink and walk toward a strip of restaurants.

We go to a little shop and buy some street tacos

for lunch. I take my time eating them, and of course, Bentley devours his then orders more. I barely have the last bite down before he's tugging me off the stool and rushing us out the door.

"Are you sure Coy and Maddie are okay with this?"

He tugs on my hand, picking up his pace. Both of our plastic shopping bags are swinging in the air. He ignores my question, so I plant my feet on the sidewalk stopping us.

Bentley turns to me. "Yes, remember Coy scheduled a spa day for Maddie and his sister, so they have to bond or some shit like that."

"Coy?" I ask. "You are his best man."

"He's golfing with his dad. You know golf and I don't mix."

"How could I forget the golf cart accident heard around the world?" I smile, remembering the day Bentley was banned from our local golf course for life.

He cups my face. "Are you going to marry me again or keep stalling?"

"Take me to the chapel, you hound dog."

I continue to tug on Bentley's hand as he walks the few blocks to the chapel. It shouldn't surprise me he knows the most precise route and gets us there in no time. The Little Neon Chapel lives up to everything you'd imagine a Vegas chapel to have. Tacky material is hanging in the windows and there's color everywhere.

An overzealous couple exits as we enter. Their enthusiasm is contagious even if they may be a bit tipsy. The inside of the chapel makes me smile with its cheesy décor and Elvis music playing softly. I guarantee this place owns stock in the velvet industry. Dark red, crushed velvet lines everything. I almost lose it when the Oompa-Loompa colored Elvis pastor rounds the corner. His white bedazzled Elvis suit is making his skin glow, not to mention the buttons bursting at the seams.

There's no way to conceal my reaction to him, so I bury my face in Bentley's shoulder while he checks us in. A female voice joins the conversation, and I don't dare look up. I can tell by the rasp the woman has smoked one too many packs of cigarettes in her days.

"You can change over here and your little lady over there."

I look up in time to see the Elvis impersonator dry hump the air. The man puts his all into each movement. He is dedicated to the mission, and I'm right back to nearing the edge of a fit of giggles. It would be rude to slap my hand over my mouth to fight them back, so I bury my face back into Bentley, focusing on his scent.

"We'll change in the same dressing room." Bentley tugs me over to the open room, and once locked away I erupt into laughter until tears roll down my face.

"This was the best idea." I use the back of my hand to wipe away the tears.

"And to think I had to convince you with my cock." He grabs his crotch.

"Easy there, tiger." I shove the shopping bag in his chest. "Just wait until you see what you're going to be wearing. And who says I didn't play you to get some action?"

I pop a hand on my hip and stare him down. We both know I'm lying, but it's all I got and the closest I'll come to admitting he had a fantastic idea. Bentley tosses his clothes off until he's left in a pair of boxers then begins digging in the bag as if there was a pot of gold at the bottom of it.

"Hold on." I grab his wrist and take a step forward. "These, too."

I tug down his boxers until they hit the floor and he steps out of them. He keeps hold of the bag, stepping toward me until our chests are pressed together. I feel him harden in an instant. A slow, evil grin plays out on my face before I deliver the blow.

"There's only going to be one layer between you, me, Elvis, and the world."

"Damn." He throws back his head. "Talk about a chub killer."

I pluck the spandex shorts out of the bag and dangle them on my finger. "Your bottoms."

Bentley holds his poker face, not showing an ounce of reaction. He jumps into them then pulls his shirt over his head. He takes time to study himself in the mirror as I place the headband on his head. The whole concoction is a hot freaking mess, but it doesn't stop Bentley from flexing and posing in the mirror.

"Damn, you're a lucky lady." He winks at me in the mirror.

"Sure am." I slap his neon pink-clad ass. My heart warms seeing Bentley so relaxed and having fun.

"Close your eyes. I'm going to dress you."

I roll my eyes and shake my head. Bentley never gets tired of surprising me. I indulge him without arguing because I know it wouldn't do any good anyway. The sound of the bag rustling fills the dressing room. His knuckles brush up my torso as he takes off my clothes. It's not meant to be erotic, but I swear with the brush of his hands on my skin, it turns me on.

"I hope you're not done since it feels like I have a sports bra on."

He ignores me, adjusting what I think is a skirt around my waist. His hand is sneaking up underneath my lacy thong a few times while he gets some ass action. He does the same thing to the front until I'm nearing the point of taking him right here and now with Elvis as our witness.

"Baby, stop." A throaty whisper escapes me.

"Stop, what?" His hand cups my sex taunting me.

I refuse to move my hips encouraging him on. He brushes his thumb over the perfect spot, and it undoes me. I want more. Need more. Right now. Before I can beg, his hand is gone. My eyes fly open while a growl escapes me. He has the nerve to laugh at me.

His hand covers my eyes while I'm chewing his ass out for that little tease.

"Just a few more seconds, Birdie."

"What the hell was that?" I demand.

"Couldn't help myself, but my dick was about to punch through these shorts."

"Damn spandex," I grumble to myself.

"Keep your eyes shut."

I feel him move his hand from my face.

"Okay, open your mouth." I feel a kiss on my cheek.

"Excuse me?"

"Quit being a pain in my ass and open your damn mouth."

"If you stick your di..."

This time he slaps a hand over my mouth. Bentley places a finger on my bottom lip, prying it open. Since I'm standing, I guess there can't be anything too dangerous he's about to do. My jaw unclenches in slow motion then Bentley places something plastic in mouth, pushing it up against my teeth.

"Dude. Epic." I hear him clap his hands together and can picture the smile on his face and gleam in his rich chocolate brown eyes.

I can't even ask if I can open eyes from the foreign piece of plastic that is currently hugging my lips, so I open my eyes.

"Are woo widding me?" My hand flies up to the flashing grill in my mouth. I push it further in place.

"You're so sexy." Bentley tries to grab me, but I sidestep him, taking in my outfit.

A leather mini skirt, sports bra, and flashing LED grill in my mouth. How in the hell did he get a mini skirt? Holy shit! My tits read She Wants The D! with Las Vegas printed in tiny letters underneath it. I shake my head and then erupt into a fit of laughter. This time Bentley joins me. *Who would've thought renewing our vows only after six months would be this fun?*

"Selfie before Elvis dry humps us into our renewed vows," Bentley announces.

He holds up his phone and snaps several shots of us. For the last one, he makes sure plenty of cleavage is up and out, then kisses my cheek, and snaps the final picture.

It only takes two steps down the aisle before I realize laughing during this ceremony will be inevitable as the glowing Elvis stands at the end next to Bentley. I don't even try to hide the giggles as the ridiculous ceremony goes on. And if I never see an Elvis impersonator or the act of dry humping air again, I'll be a happy girl.

Bentley, of course, paid for the full meal deal that included a photo session in front of a hideous backdrop. I soaked up the entire experience, flashing grill and all. We decide not to change and make it make down to the strip in our ceremony clothes. The Uber driver didn't even flinch. I guess the saying is true, What Happens in Vegas, Stays in Vegas.

Bentley checked in with Coy and then it was to our room. Our clothes flew, and we consummated our renewal. I'm not sure that's even a thing, but we did it with a bang. My head rests on his heaving chest. Our bodies are exhausted and coated with a thin layer of sweat.

"What made you want to do that today?"

He's quiet for a long time before answering. He clears his throat before speaking. "Burnett."

"Baby." I prop up on an elbow. "You don't have

to."

Even though it's dark in the room with a sliver of moonlight from outside peeking in, I can see the shimmer pooling in his eyes.

"No, it's fine. You know he was a funny jackass, but in love with his high school sweetheart. He had big plans of taking her to Vegas and marrying her the moment he got home." He throws his arm over his forehead. "The ass would walk around base camp, singing Elvis songs non-stop. He never made it back."

I kiss up and down Bentley's jawline, hoping to ease up some of the pain he's feeling. He's kept the ugly side of deployment to a minimum, only sharing bits and pieces, but I'm not an idiot and know he protects me.

"You're living it for him," I whisper.

He nods and clears his throat one more time. I'm able to catch one of his tears with the pad of my thumb before it hits the pillow.

"Lost a lot of brothers over there and made a promise to them and myself that I'll never take another day for granted. I want to do it all and all with you."

This time it's me rolling up on top of him. My body is covering his, lining us up perfectly.

"I'll renew our vows anywhere and anytime you want, baby."

Chapter 7

"Keep love in your heart. A life without it is like a sunless garden when the flowers are dead." - Oscar Wilde

"I'll put one hundred dollars down they go balls to the wall." I glance over to Bentley. It's been one full year since I became his wife, and he still takes my breath away. He keeps his vision on the road ahead of us, giving me time to admire his sexy as hell profile.

"Naw, I say a family barbecue with lots of desserts." He pulls down his aviators and sends me a quick wink before focusing back on the road. "And there better be chocolate cake."

"Mmmmm. Chocolate cake. I do hope for that." I squeeze his hand resting on top of my thigh. Like years ago in high school, we are in the same truck and same seats. I still ride smack dab in the center. I often think what we'll do when a baby comes along. Knowing Bentley, he'll take care of it and still make me feel like his queen while being the best daddy ever.

Thoughts of a baby make my stomach spin. The butterflies are real this time. I'm three weeks late. I've been late before, rushed out to the store to buy pregnancy tests to only be disappointed. It's a tender topic for us. Bentley's ready to go to the doctor to find out answers. We have plenty of sex on a daily basis and have toyed with counting the days for the best ovulation.

None of our family understands our concerns.

They claim we are too young and all that other shit. I'm nearing twenty-three and was having unprotected sex before we were married...I know something isn't right.

But three weeks late is the biggest sliver of hope we've had yet. I'm determined to give it one more week before taking a test, and even then I feel like I may be jinxing it.

"Where did you go there on me?" Bentley kills the engine of his truck and leans over, running his nose up and down my jawline.

"Just thinking about work," I lie. I never lie to Bentley, but this is different.

"The big Anderson Ranch sale?"

I nod. Because yes, that's weighing heavy on my mind, too, just not in the forefront. The papers are in the final stage, and with this sale, it will set us up for a full year off the commissions.

"They're complete idiots if they don't buy from you." He forces me to look at him. His lips crush to mine. When he's done kissing the hell out of me, he whispers into my lips. "You've got the deal."

He's so sure of himself. Bentley has no idea if the deal is going to go through or not, but it's his demanding reassurance that calms me on that front. The other not so much. I manage to smile against his lips, picturing his face the day I tell him we are pregnant.

"Thank you," I whisper.

He swings open the driver's side door, keeping his gaze on me. "Now, let's go see if this shin-dig has any chocolate cake."

The country club is packed. I was so right and

should've bet a lot of money and favors on this one. Our moms did, in fact, go balls to the wall with this party. As much as this scene isn't my style, it's well needed. If it were up to me, Bentley and I would've enjoyed a quiet evening at the pond. Only the two of us.

Tensions have been high the past couple of weeks with threats of another deployment. To me, I consider them a threat, but that's not how Bentley views it. It's the one thing we always fight about if we allow ourselves to. It's inevitable but doesn't make it any easier to process and accept. I wish I had his courage. A night out with our family and friends is what we need.

We are swarmed by those same family and friends in the blink of an eye. It takes me right back to our wedding night. I've always hated sharing my Bentley. He keeps my hand laced in his as we weave through the crowd. As much as I hate to, I let go of his hand and make small talk with some clients of mine. It's an empowering feeling knowing they want to speak to me and respect me as a realtor. I'm the star of the show with Bentley cheering me on from the grandstands.

I spy Papa Wally sitting at a table all by himself and excuse myself from the current conversation. Each day the years of wear and tear on my Papa becomes more and more evident. He's always been healthy as a horse, but he's tired.

"Papa." I bend down and kiss his cheek.

His eyes light up, and his familiar, gentle smile wraps around me like a hug.

"No white dress?" He grins. "Surprised your

momma didn't force you to wear it."

"Trust me, she tried." I fall into the chair next to him and throw one of my legs up on the table. "Wore the boots."

"Atta girl." His husky chuckle warms my soul. "Your momma will kick your ass if she sees you sitting like that."

"What?" I look down. "I'm wearing skinny jeans and not a skirt."

He shakes his head. "I swear since the day you were born, you were determined to test your mother's patience on a daily basis."

"Someone's gotta do it." I shrug.

It hits me hard when no laughter escapes Papa Wally. There are bags and dark lines under his eyes. His wrinkles are more pronounced. My favorite man isn't going to be here forever. I reach over and grab his hand. Those hands that have endured so many years of hard work, love, joy, and heartache and they're still silky smooth between the wrinkles. This man taught me what life is all about.

"You busy in the morning?" I ask him.

He shakes his head.

"Wanna go fishing?"

"Do you even have to ask?" He flashes me a smile. It takes me right back to my childhood.

I lay my head on his shoulder and study the crowd from the corner table. There's laughter, conversation, and lots of booze going down. My heart sings observing it all by the side of Papa Wally. Bentley soon joins us with two plates of food. One is heaping, damn near spilling over. I know it's ours. The other one has ribs, mashed potatoes, and vegetables. It's the one he places in front of Papa Wally.

"Thank you," I whisper and kiss his cheek once he's settled into the seat next to me.

"You okay, Birdie?" Concern plays out across his face.

"I am now." I smile and kiss him.

I've become well adapted to getting my fair share of food knowing Bentley will devour the rest of it. I moan when I sink my teeth into one of the ribs. The best around and I know right away Dad cooked them. It's his specialty and rare because of his rigorous work schedule.

"Making me jealous of a piece of meat," Bentley whispers into my ear.

"You should be. I'd leave you for these." I take another bite, cleaning the rib right down to the bone.

"You're killing me right now for so many reasons," he growls.

I continue to clean the already meatless bone in a fashion that's not acceptable at the dinner table. Bentley buries his face in the palm of his hands, and Papa Wally roars in laughter. Another memory to store away in my treasure chest along with a thousand other cherished memories with these two men.

"Marlee Jo!" We all glance up to see Mom with her hands planted on her hips and a scowl on her face. "You are sucking on a bone with barbecue sauce all over your face."

"Baby, let it go." Dad wraps his arms around her

middle from the back. "She's almost twenty-three years old and isn't going to change."

"I hired a professional photographer, and you are..." She falters, stumbling over her words, struggling to get the next one out. She gives up before erupting into laughter. "I can't wait until you have a little one giving you as much hell as you have given me."

They sit down at our table, and we all dive into conversation with me being the focal point. Not something you'd typically brag about, but Mom loves to go on about me and how I drive her insane. Each word is spoken with deep and true love, making it a perfect night.

The only chocolate cake enjoyed was the top tier of our wedding cake from a year ago. It was stale, dry, and freezer burned. The worst shit I've ever tasted, but at the same time the best ever. Bentley made it memorable and the best cake ever later that night at home.

Chapter 8

"We are made of all those who have built and broke us." -Atticus

"Smells amazing." Arms wrap low around my waist, my head tilts on automatic, and searing kisses pepper my neck.

I'm able to get out a light moan while continuing to chop up vegetables.

"What are you cooking?"

"Grilled salmon, twice baked potatoes, and a green salad."

"And?"

"Brownies and vanilla ice cream for dessert."

"And?"

"Hefeweizen beer for the guys and raspberry beer for us girls."

"And?"

"Babe!" I set down the knife, frustrated.

I'm whirled around in his arms until our chests are pressed together. Bentley reaches down, palming my ass, pulling me up to him. I wrap my legs around his waist, hooking my ankles above his perfect ass.

"And?" He quirks an eyebrow.

I run my hands up and down his muscular neck, missing his mullet from years ago. I'd give anything to be thrown back to our high school years where we were carefree with no worries of deployment, having a baby, or bills. Our only concern back then was spending every single second together embraced in each other's arms.

"That's it," I reply.

"You're missing something."

I cock my head to the side, having no clue where this is leading. It only takes a few beats until I understand right where it's heading. Bentley whirls around, takes two steps, and then my back hits the cold surface of our sturdy dark cherry walnut dining table. He lays me down with ease and then steps back. I perch up on my elbows, watching him strip down. His fingers are steady as he unbuttons his shirt. It's slow and seductive, and I feel myself heat up for him with the simple action. My shorts and panties slide down my legs and Bentley's knuckles graze my skin.

His body covers mine and all thoughts of cooking timers and guests coming over disappear. The table creaks as our bodies connect. His lips are on mine, and his hands go to my hair as he evaporates every single one of my thoughts and worries.

"This is what I was asking for." His brows scrunch up as he works in and out of me. "It's all I need every single damn day."

"Faster," I beg. My hands lace around his neck, pulling him closer. My legs wrap around his waist, grinding up against him.

His teeth sink down on his bottom lip, and it's my final undoing. I come undone around him. He follows, collapsing down on me.

"You're a very naughty boy." I run my hand up and down his back.

The sound of a truck roaring down our lane snaps us both back to reality.

"Shit," he hisses, pulling me up as he stands up.

He races to the guest bathroom with me in his arms. We clean up and throw on clothes like teenagers who've been busted by their parents. We erupt into a fit of laughter when I pull on his boxers not realizing it, and he's left standing with lace panties dangling off his fingertip.

"Honey, I'm home." Coy's voice echoes throughout the house.

"Shit," I hiss, pulling off Bentley's boxers. "Bentley, do something."

The panic in my voice cannot be masked. Bentley, on the other hand, laughs. All the while still dangling my lace panties off one of his fingers. I snatch them from him and give him my best stern look without cracking a grin.

"You better get your ass dressed and get out there right now." I slip into my panties as fast as possible, catching my heel in one of the holes and toppling forward, landing face first right where Bentley wants to keep me all night, which makes Bentley's entire body vibrate from his laughter.

I reach around and slap his ass so hard it leaves my palm stinging. I should know better by now because this will only fuel his fire. I look up at him, pleading for help and for him to get his ass in gear to cover up our sexcapades. He gets my drift and begins dressing with ease. How the man can make it seem so easy to slip on all of his clothes, brush his hand over his hair, and walk out of the bathroom is beyond me.

I take my time making sure my shirt is forward and my pants are zipped. Everything was perfect for tonight before Bentley distracted me. I might add it was one of the best distractions to come my way, but I won't spill that secret. Lord knows, Bentley Foster doesn't need an ego booster.

Maddie and Coy's voices seep into the bathroom from the kitchen, and I know Bentley has them distracted. I pull up my hair, placing it back into a sloppy bun, making sure all the stray hairs are smoothed back. Even though it looks like nothing happened, I guarantee the look on my face when I walk out there will give it all away.

When I round the corner, Maddie and Coy are sitting at the dining room table with the appetizers they brought. I cringe, knowing what we did on that table and can't seem to break my stare on Maddie's palms face down on the table. I send Bentley a sideways stare, and he shrugs.

I guess you can't have it all; at least we got covered up and out of the danger zone before our guests arrived. Bentley winks at me. There's nothing we can do about it, and this will no doubt be one of our best inside jokes to date.

"What did you bring for appetizers, Maddie?" Bentley leans over the tray of food in the center of the table we banged on, eyeing each of them.

Maddie, being her quaint little self, gives a shrug and then offers up all the delicious appetizers she brought. The woman can cook like no other. I'm not a slob when it comes to ninja skills in the kitchen, but Maddie? Now that girl has it down. It doesn't even offend me anymore when Bentley begs to go to their place for dinner instead of ours.

Bentley pops an appetizer in his mouth and then stares over at me, cocking an eyebrow up. "Very delicious. Must be something with this table."

Coy and Maddie both stare at Bentley with a questioning stare, silently wondering what in the hell he's talking about. I can't help the little smirk that plays out on my face and the giggle that escapes. He's quite the bragger when it comes to me and would have no problem spilling the beans. I'm forced to step in before that happens.

"I'm grilling salmon, have twice baked potatoes, and a green salad for dinner. It will be ready in about fifteen minutes."

Coy perks up at that announcement, super excited about what's for dinner.

"You catch those fish you cooking, woman?"

I have to laugh at his antics because only Coy could get away with calling me woman and not getting slapped upside the head. Okay, Bentley could, too, but he owns my heart and soul.

I stand up tall, beaming like a child on Christmas morning and answer him. "Yep. Papa Wally and I've been fishing every morning since our anniversary party. We've been catching some big ones."

Maddie's shoulders sag in defeat because I've confided in her with all my worries about Papa's health and the men at the table don't seem to catch on. Coy pipes right back up super excited for dinner.

"That Papa Wally, he's the best fisherman in the state; ain't nobody going to deny that. Just glad he could teach you some of your tricks."

This time I do smack Coy upside the head for his comment because by damn Papa Wally did teach me everything, but I'll stand next to any man claiming to be the best fisherman around.

The night goes on a lot like this; banter, good friends, and even better food. We all have a good time and enjoy several laughs. It's nice having Coy home. It was hell on Maddie when he was away at boot camp. She hasn't missed a minute with him since the several months he's been home. *Damn newlyweds.* Maddie and I have been dedicated to our weekly coffee dates and staying in touch. It's nice to have a friend like her around where she's genuinely interested in me and not getting closer to Bentley or my family, specifically my dad to climb higher up in the army ranks.

It's been a fact of my life all through the years and has never really bothered me because of the close-knit bond I have with my family and Bentley. I'm so happy for Maddie and Coy that they're back together and for the time being, it looks like he will be stationed here at the home base for a while.

All of us army wives know anything can change in the blink of an eye, but we embrace the present, the now, and everything we have in between. Our men serve our country and their families. It's an honor. But the heart doesn't always see it that way.

We clean up the mess from dinner. All the food has long disappeared, not because of Maddie or myself, but mainly our men. It really doesn't matter if it's burned, charred, or even an identifiable pot of slop, these men will finish it off.

They know the way to a woman's heart, and that's by eating their cooking; the ugly, the pretty, and the delicious meals.

Once everything is cleaned up, we all sit on the front porch. The men with their Hefeweizen and us girls with our raspberry beers. We sit in silence for a long beat of time. Maddie isn't in the mood to drink. She hasn't even sipped on her drink. I'm on my second one, but also made mine a virgin, not letting anyone else know.

"Well, since I returned from Boot Camp it didn't take us long," Coy announces, taking a long pull from his beer.

Bentley shoots him a questioning stare, urging him to finish on with his weird ass statement. Maddie slaps Coy's chest, and at that moment I know what's coming.

My heart sinks and my skin prickles with fear and excitement. I know I have to be happy for them and I am happy for them, but it doesn't lessen the sting.

And on cue Coy pipes up

"We're pregnant! Man, I did it! There's a Coy junior coming. My goddamn swimmers were so good, knocked her up the first time we banged after coming home from Boot Camp." Coy takes a long celebratory pull from his beer.

Maddie giggles and I force a laugh right along with her. Coy isn't disrespectful; he's being himself among good friends. Doesn't make it hurt any less. Bentley's hand in my hand grips a little tighter, letting me know he's here for me.

I make everything disappear, swallowing down

the pain and congratulate them. I am happy for them and will be happy for them. I want the same thing, and it doesn't seem to be happening. I've often wondered if I want this too much and that's why Mother Nature is telling me to be patient and wait.

I still haven't taken the pregnancy test, but I will tomorrow. And we will go from there. I'm able to focus myself and concentrate on the positive side of this because of Bentley's hand gripping mine. He doesn't ease up but only grips my hand tighter. As long as I have Bentley Foster, everything will be okay. We can get through anything and will.

"When are you due?" Bentley clears his throat before asking.

Maddie beams with excitement as she gives us all of the details. Their families don't even know yet. Coy and Maddie put us under strict instructions to keep it a secret because they don't want to share with others until after their first doctor appointment. It's an honor to know they chose us to share the new good news with.

Without conscious thought, I run my free hand over my lower abdomen, sending up a silent prayer to God. I know it's our time, and this time it will happen. Everything is perfect. I have to keep faith it's the only way I won't drown. I have so much to be thankful for, and that's what will keep me going.

I feel his warm breath on the shell of my ear before he whispers. "I love you, Marlee Foster."

I turn my head slightly until our lips meet and mumble right back into his lips. "I love you more."

"Get a damn room you, two horndogs," Coy hollers out.

I don't look over to him, but hear the resounding smack that undoubtedly Maddie whomped him with. It makes me giggle, but just for a few seconds. Bentley grips the back of my head, pulling me closer, and he kisses the hell out of me. This right here is what will keep me grounded forever no matter what our future does or doesn't hold.

Chapter 9

"Sometimes the heart sees what is invisible to the eye." -H. Jackson Brown, Jr.

A serene sensation dances over the pond this morning. It's quiet, eliciting a sense of peace nothing else could ever offer up. A tug on my line alerts my attention back to my fishing pole. I give it a light yank and begin reeling it in.

The sunrise is as tranquil as they come, but I still have a restless feeling in my bones. Papa Wally was too tired to go with me this morning. I can't recall a time when he ever refused an opportunity to spend time at the pond fishing. I continue reeling in the fish until a beauty of rainbow trout splashes out of the pond. The natural high and shot of adrenaline courses through my body.

Papa stocks the pond and the river that feeds into it, always providing us a wide variety of fish. Rainbow trout are his favorite to catch, and that's why I unhook the beauty and toss him back in. I spend the rest of the morning doing the same thing. I have a meeting around one to close a deal on a ranch house style home across town and later tonight family dinner at Mom's house.

I finish up early and head home to clean up. The house is quiet and empty. I hate it when it feels like this. It's only a home when Bentley is here with me. I ignore the hollow feeling and get ready for work. My fingertips graze over the sealed pregnancy test in my makeup drawer. I can't do it right now even though I promised myself. Tonight. I'll take it tonight, or at least that's what I tell myself.

***

"Are you kidding me?" The toe of my designer boot slams into the wall of the flat tire. "I don't have time for this."

My day has gone from perfect to shit in a matter of seconds. The sale fell through on the house on a technicality coupled with the owners not willing to work with the buyers. And now a flat tire on the highway a good fifteen miles from home.

I reach for my phone in my purse and am greeted with a blinking red battery icon.

"Shit!"

I'm notorious for never charging my phone. My family and Bentley are regularly riding my ass about it and love harassing me on the subject. I live up to my stubborn self and try to dial Bentley's number. Before it even rings, the phone dies.

I send it into the asphalt out of rage. Dumb, dumb decision, but all rationality has vanished. I pick back up the tire iron and try to loosen the lug nuts with no success. Yes, I know how to change a tire, and this one wouldn't be my first, but whoever in the hell rotated them last time wrenched them so tight I can't even get it to budge.

I am screwed. I slam the tire iron down on my cell phone to make me feel good at least for the damn moment. I'm resigned to being stranded after a shit day. The only thing going my way is the slight breeze keeping the damn mosquitos at bay. I fling open the driver's side door and flop into my

SUV. I don't bother to shut the damn door, propping my foot up through the driver's side window, letting it dangle out and slouching back in my driver's seat.

I feel each minute as it ticks by. I'm bored beyond belief, and there's not one damn thing I can do about it. I try to close my eyes, willing sleep to come along like when I was a child and wanted time to pass faster. I'm so livid, sleep isn't even an option. Finally, I turn the key and glance at the digital numbers on the radio. It's been almost two hours. Okay, an hour and fifteen minutes, but it's felt like every single second of two hours. I've peeled off all the nail polish on my nails and chewed the last stick of gum in my purse.

I've resigned myself to start walking. I throw all the items back in my purse that have been entertaining me and ready myself to hoof it home. I won't have to do cardio for weeks, hell, possibly even a year. And if I'm realistic, I'll more than likely die on the trek. I'm normal body size, but not into being fit, gym clothes, and packing a water bottle at all times. I'm more of the Diet Coke in hand, limiting carbs so that I can indulge in sweets once a week kind of girl.

As soon as my boot hits the pavement, I hear it. I'd know that sound anywhere. It's his truck. The same sound that used to make my heart go pitter-patter in our high school days and now the one to save the day. My knight in shining armor, my husband, the man known as Bentley Foster.

I use my hand to shade my eyes from the sun beginning to set. The black truck slows down. I can hear him gearing down as he pulls in behind me. He's not alone. My other hero is in the passenger seat. My daddy. The doors to the truck open in unison, black boots step out, and they stride to me in their fatigues.

My shoulders slump in relief, knowing my day has been saved. I bite down on my bottom lip to keep the tears held back. I don't cry often and when I do it's out of frustration or anger.

"Looking for fun, sexy?" Bentley reaches forward, grabbing me by the hip, tugging me to him. "Because if you are..."

I bury my face into his chest, inhaling his scent, gulping it by the lung full, ignoring all of his cheesy ass pick-up lines he's throwing my way. I know he's trying to melt away the shitty day even though he has no idea about any of the details. It's the way we work.

"Bad day, Birdie?" Dad walks past us, ruffling up my hair.

"You could say that," I mumble into Bentley's chest, relishing the last few seconds of his embrace.

"Phone dead?" Bentley whispers in my ear.

I do my best to nod.

"Guess you lost the bet."

This makes me giggle. Of course, he'd remember. Bentley's always riding my ass about keeping it charged and threw out a bet one night while we were lying in bed.

"Daddy gets butt sex tonight!" Bentley bites down on the lobe of my ear.

I gift him with a punch to the gut, which only

makes him throw back his head in laughter.

"Not a damn chance." I shove off his chest and turn to the flat tire and my dad.

"A bet is a bet," Bentley sings out.

I know he'll never let me live this one down. Hate to break it to him, but it's never ever happening. He smiles like a loon the whole time helping Dad change the flat. They make it look easy, which pisses me off even more. I need a huge ass bottle of wine tonight. That thought takes me right to what I'm preparing myself for when I get home. The test. No adult beverages for me until I know.

I was certain last night that everything was perfect, and it was our time, but after the events of today, I'm losing that sliver of hope.

"You're ready to roll, Birdie." Dad tugs me into a hug. "I'd chew your ass, but those lug nuts were a bitch to get off. Drive slow until you get to a tire shop in the morning."

"Telling her to drive slow is like telling Santa Claus to not love Christmas." Bentley brushes off the front of his pants.

"Ass," I chime back, climbing into my car relieved to have been saved.

"Race you home." Bentley slaps the top of the car and leans in for a quick kiss.

"I never lose," I whisper into his lips.

I take it easy on peeling out, spraying gravel in the grill of his truck, but make sure I'm the first to pull into our driveway. Dad shakes his head at me, knowing it's worthless to chew my ass for not following his advice. He disappears down the narrow trail that leads to my childhood home.

"See you in a bit for dinner," I holler to him. "Love you, Dad."

All I see is a wave of his hand over the tall pasture grass. Then a stinging slap lands on my ass right before I'm pulled into a tight hug. Bentley bends down, running his nose through my hair, inhaling my scent.

"Coconut and oranges. My favorite."

"You say that about every scent on me."

"So." He holds me back by my shoulders staring at me. "Who or what pissed in your Cheerios?"

"Shit day. I'm worried about Papa Wally, the deal fell through, the flat tire, and now we will be late for family dinner." I try to shrug under his palms. "And I won't have time to make my famous sour cream, cheese, bacon dip."

"I'm sorry, Birdie." He pulls me back to his chest. "But you get to come home to a stud of a husband."

I chuckle into his chest, wrapping my arms low around his waist. He begins walking me backward to our house. I trust him enough that I don't decide to look up or squeal. When the back of my legs hit the stairs, Bentley pulls me up into his arms, carrying me the rest of the way into the house.

"No matter how shitty of a day you've had, there's no excuse not to make your Dorito crack dip. None."

"It's too late, Bentley."

"Nonsense."

He keeps walking through the house until we are in the master bathroom and I'm sitting on the countertop right next to the unopened pregnancy test. Bentley glances at it but doesn't say a word. He goes about starting a hot bath. Like always my sexy husband juggles three Lush bath bombs in his hands. He's like a damn four-year-old when it comes to them. It doesn't matter how many times I've explained how expensive they are. Bentley claims you can't put a price tag on little balls of fun. He tosses all three in then begins to undress me.

In a matter of minutes, I'm in the tub surrounded by a field of varying scents and fizz. Bentley bends down, kissing me with force and a promise of so much more before whirling around on his heels, stripping off his white t-shirt that was underneath his fatigues earlier.

"We are going to be…" I'm cut off.

"I'm going to jump in the guest shower, make the dip, and then we will head over." He winks at me. "I got you, Birdie."

"You just want that damn dip."

"Damn straight, woman." He rounds the corner, whistling the tune of "Patience" by Guns N Roses.

Through the shitastic day, the sound makes me melt. I let the hot water wrap around me, melting away the worries of the day. A few cuss words and clanging come from the kitchen are making me giggle. If I were a betting woman, I'd put money on the fact Bentley cut himself slicing the green onions. I lay my head back, close my eyes, and let my mind go blank.

It's not until the water grows chilly that I force myself out of the tub. I'm immediately saddened by the fact Bentley didn't get to join me. Long, hot baths are one of our favorite pastimes. He links up his Bluetooth speaker, playing his favorite old rock and roll songs; I light candles, we enjoy drinks, and relax.

I begin toweling off the droplets of water running from my body when I spot the yoga pants and Army t-shirt laying on the counter. I didn't even hear Bentley when he delivered them during my zone out session. An idea strikes me, erasing the remorse over not sharing a hot bath with him.

I reach up into the vanity and pull out his bottle of Pi cologne. I'm addicted to the scent and spray our sheets and some of my clothes when he's out of town. I went through cases when he was deployed. I spritz the shirt to ensure he'll surround me all night.

"Ten minutes, Birdie."

"Okay, baby," I holler back, reaching for my plum berry body lotion.

I go about lathering up my skin before reaching for my clothes. I freeze, slam my eyes shut, and will away the dread. No. No. No. This can't be happening. I refuse to open my eyes facing reality.

It doesn't work. The warm liquid continues to flow down my legs. After long moments of my heart not beating and my shallow breathing, I pop open my eyes to see dark, crimson red liquid trailing down my legs. My body gives out on me. I collapse on the bathroom floor.

I hide my face in the palms of my hands unable to shed an emotion. I knew for sure it had happened this time. My body is telling me otherwise. I'm numb, so damn numb I don't even feel the pain. The sound of my heart shattering is deafening.

"Birdie, you ready?"

Bentley's voice comes from off in the distance. I open my mouth, but no words come out. I rock back and forth, fighting for the courage to move on. I struggle to focus on everything I have and not the loss I'm experiencing. I don't know how many more times it will take to learn my lesson. Every single time I will myself to not get my hopes up because they only get obliterated.

"Baby."

Bentley's voice is louder this time nearing me. I fight to sit up and move, but there's so much blood underneath, taunting me to run. Slide and slip around in my misery. The first sob escapes me, cracking my chest wide open. Once it starts, it doesn't end.

I hear myself crying in pain and misery, but am unable to believe those sounds are coming from me. I grab a towel, clutching it to my chest, continuing to rock back and forth willing time to halt.

"Baby..." Bentley freezes in the doorway when I peer up. He covers his mouth, and when I see his eyes fall in horror, I lose everything I was battling to keep control of. Shrill screams escape me one after another. I study his bare feet as he nears me. Soon his arms wrap around me. His hot, wet tears tumble down onto the top of my shoulders.

"I've got you, Birdie, I've got you." He rocks back and forth, holding me nearing a painful point.

"I thought..."

"It's okay." He kisses the top of my head, continuing to soothe me by keeping up the rocking motion. "We will be fine."

I believe him. Each letter of every single word as if they were the gospel because I know we will be okay.

Sobs and silence wrap around us as Bentley holds me, letting me get everything out. He doesn't offer any more comforting promises or tell me it's going to be okay. He simply uses his strong arms to keep me tight to him. When I grow numb from crying and my eyes are close to being swollen shut, Bentley picks me up.

He wraps the towel around me and starts the shower. When the water is hot enough, he strips off his clothes and climbs into the tub. He holds his hand out for me, waiting for me to take it. I drop the towel moments later and step under the hot stream with him.

In silence, he washes away everything that's transpired in the last thirty minutes or however much time has lapsed. I have no clue how long I was crumbled on the tile floor devastated. He washes my hair and my body, and then we relax underneath the streams of water. It's symbolic of the loss we are experiencing together.

He never takes his hand off me. His strong, dedicated arms stay wrapped around me as they catch my tears for the baby I thought may have been coming our way. He leaves the shower with a quick kiss on my forehead. I watch through the glass door as he grabs a towel and slips into a pair of black boxers.

I close my eyes and let the water spray down over my hair. It's not meant to be, and that may be the most devastating thing I've had to face to date. Often late at night, I wonder why I want a baby so damn bad. Anyway, I analyze I've never been able to figure it out. There's a gigantic scenic puzzle laying before me with one missing piece from the center.

I have to focus on what I have in my life. Some people never find true love, and I have that in spades. The shower turns off, and I open my eyes to see Bentley holding a towel. He grabs me from the shower and places me on the rug right outside of the shower. He towels me off and points to the clothes and feminine products for me.

And then leaves the room.

I hear him talking loud enough on the phone in the hallway. I don't focus in on each of his words, but I know he's talking to my parents. Pregnancy, bleeding, and we are not going to make it tonight, are the only words that scramble around in my brain.

I'm exhausted after getting dressed. Hell, I don't even have the energy to walk myself out into our bedroom. All I want to do is crumple on the floor, close my eyes, and forget all about this day. But I don't have the chance to before I'm lifted up in Bentley's arms once again. He carries me to our bedroom, pulling back our comforter, placing me on the bed, and pulling the blankets up. I roll over to my side defeated and hopeless and ready for sleep. The bed dips behind me, and all too soon I feel his muscular chest up against my back. His arms wrap low around my waist, his nose in the crook of my neck with his lips peppering light kisses on my chilled skin.

It's what I need. Silence, peace, and my husband. I lace my fingers in his that are now draped over my hip and squeeze them, hoping to let him know that I love him and I'm thankful for him being here right now.

"Go to sleep, baby." He kisses my neck one more time. "I love you, Birdie. I know you don't want to discuss it right now, but maybe it's time to see a doctor."

I know the answer deep down in my gut and don't have to think about it before responding.

"I don't want to go to a doctor, baby. I can't stand any more devastating news and to have a doctor tell me that having a baby isn't possible for us would crush me more than words. I'll be okay because I have you. Let's be us, be married, and enjoy our days together."

I want the pain to go away. He runs his hands through my hair, each movement soothing.

"It'll happen. I'm not going to say give it time because I know you're tired of hearing that. But it will happen one way or the other. The day I married you, I promised you I'd give you the world and that's what I'll do every single damn day of my life."

I roll over in his arms until we're nose to nose. "It makes me feel like a failure."

His finger goes over my lips before I have a chance to finish the rest of my sentence. "Marlee,

I'll let you be sad, upset, and whatever else you need to be. But I refuse to let you sink into that train of thought."

I kiss his lips and pull back. "If you would've let me finish my sentence, I was going to say I do feel like a failure deep down inside, but it's your love that always pulls me back along with my family."

He rubs his nose along mine for long beats of silence. "Do you want me to get into yours and Maddie's secret stash?"

It takes me a minute to catch on, and when I do, I feel like a kid busted by their parents. I tilt my head and raise an eyebrow.

"How did you know about that stash?"

He pulls me into his arms tighter, hugging me to the point where I can barely breathe.

"I'm no idiot, Birdie. I knew what you were doing to get Maddie through those dismal days when Coy was gone. I let you girls have fun."

Of course, he would know exactly what was going on and not say a word.

"Well, I guess it's a good thing you were unable to get into my stash, soldier. More for us."

"Do you need to indulge right now?" He raises an eyebrow.

I shake my head from side-to-side. "I don't need to get high right now. I've got everything I need right here next to me."

And that's all we say until I fall asleep once I've grounded myself in Bentley's embrace. My eyelids grow heavy, and I'm able to relax. I know beyond a shadow of a doubt that this man is my home no matter what life throws our way. He spoke the truth when he reminded me about his promise. Even if I'm never able to ever have a baby, I guarantee adoption would be the next course if I want that. Bentley would have an appointment made for me first thing in the morning to see a fertility specialist if that's what I also wanted.

In my core, I know I'll never have enough courage to see a doctor. It would be another blow to my soul when I hear that it's me that's the problem.

I dream of Bentley and me growing old together and bracing the future and being happy no matter what life throws our way. It's the sweetest of sweet dreams a girl could have. The rhythm of our life is ever evolving. I embrace it because it's all part of the game. I choose to thrive in the game of life.

Chapter 10

"The greatest healing therapy is friendship and love." -Hubert H. Humphrey

The morning I woke up after having my period or a miscarriage, I'm not sure which happened, knowing I had to put on my big girl pants and move on because I have too much in my life.

The days drifted by and with each passing one, it became a little easier to breathe and enjoy life. The days added up to weeks only showing me life always goes on no matter the ache in my chest. Papa Wally and I continued to fish for a week or so afterward until it became too much for him. The old man only has enough energy for him to go once or twice a week nowadays. It hurts my heart to know the end is coming soon and my days are numbered with him, but like in any other challenging circumstances in life, I've chosen to embrace the good and enjoy and relish every single second of it. I had an early meeting this morning, so my hunk of burning love and I have a dinner date at the pond.

I place the last piece of freshly, fried chicken in the picnic basket and check my phone to see a text from Bentley.

Hottest Hubs Ever: I'll meet you at the pond. Running late.

Me: Okay. Want me to bring a change of clothes for you?

Hottest Hubs Ever: Naw, I'm good.

Me: Are you sure?

Hottest Hubs Ever: Yep, get your sexy ass down to the pond, woman!

I chuckle at his response.

Me: See you soon.

Odd, but I've decided to not overthink anything when it comes to Bentley. He's strict with self-discipline for days. I mean, he's a well-trained soldier in the United States Army, but the way he can divert plans and go with it is something I'll never understand. I shake my head and grab the picnic basket. I decided against taking the Razor down to the pond and walk instead.

The crisp autumn breeze blows across my face. I tug up the collar of Bentley's favorite Penn Con hoodie. The woodsy, basil, and somewhat fruity scent of his cologne washes over me. Some girls want diamonds, big mansions, and extravagant vacations around the world, not me. This is my idea of perfection.

I look up to see Mom helping Papa into his fishing chair on the hill by the pond. I chuckle seeing Papa swat her away. He grumbles about us girls being on his ass too much. If Mom isn't at his side, I am. We are greedy like that, soaking up every single moment with him.

It's his heart, and Papa refuses to have another open-heart surgery at his age. None of us can blame him, but it doesn't make it any easier on us either. Papa has taught me so many lessons. Looking back through the years, my life didn't truly start until I moved here the summer before my fourth grade year. Papa gave our family a home, built a legacy, and gave me Bentley.

I walk up the hill with a smile playing out on my face even with the impending doom looming over our family.

"Birdie," Mom chirps, opening her arms wide for a hug.

Not only has she been mother-henning the hell out of her dad, but I'm next in line. She didn't give me her typical talks about being too young to have a baby or that it will happen. Nope, she has become my rock and has been cooking up a storm for me and Bentley. It's all eased my stress since work has been insane. The real estate market is booming right now, keeping me on my toes. The amount of houses on the market and potential sales is at an all-time high record. I'm determined to take advantage of all of it.

"Momma." I give her a one arm hug, clutching to the basket in my other hand. "Want to join us tonight? I have lots of chicken."

"Smells amazing." She pulls back from me. "And like you finally nailed down my recipe."

I shrug. "It is Bentley's favorite after all."

"And took how many years to get it down?" Mom raises an eyebrow.

"If he dare mentions it doesn't taste like your mom's fried chicken, I swear I may throw him in the pond and walk away."

That earns a hearty chuckle from Papa Wally who's already busying himself with his fishing pole. Mom beams with pride. That woman loves cooking for her family.

"It's not that hard, Birdie." She takes a seat next to her dad.

I place the basket on the ground and throw my arms up, pulling back the sleeves of the hoodie. "Tell my damn forearms that."

Mom and Papa both share a good laugh. He finally leans over and pats Mom's leg. "Your momma looked like that way back when. It took her much longer to master my momma's fried chicken."

"Roasted," I sing out.

Mom swats at Papa, screwing up his cast out. He grumbles at her, but it doesn't stop her from giving her opinion. A familiar roar of a truck engine that sets my body to life fills the air. I look toward the sound and see the dust rolling behind a sexy truck, and I know my husband has arrived.

Bentley pulls up to the pond, and I notice he's in a Penn Con t-shirt. Weird, he must have packed a change of clothes to work. He's late. Guess his day at work was a full one as well. I tuck the basket behind Mom's chair and bounce over to the truck.

Bentley is out and heading my way before I even make it halfway. He has me up in a hug, kissing me. Even though I want to sit here and enjoy the moment even with the witnesses, I pull back, eyeing his outfit.

"You're changed."

Busted! I can read this man like a book. He shrugs, tilts his head, and mumbles about a long meeting and wanting to have fresh clothes for fishing. I swear a light yip comes from the truck. It's not a squeaking sound, but I swear I heard it. The noise happens again, but this time Bentley kisses the hell out of me before I have a chance to pepper him with questions.

I indulge in the kiss for long moments before I hear Mom clear her voice and that mysterious sound again. It takes all of my resolve to push Bentley away and give him a cross, inquisitive stare.

This time he shrugs, furthering his damn guilty state.

I lean back in, brushing my lips against his. "What are you up to?"

"Kissing my wife." He takes advantage of my lips.

"You're so full of shit."

This time a full bark comes from his truck. It's a little yippy bark like a puppy trying to do its best to let out a full one. It hits me. He bought us a puppy.

"Bentley, what's in your truck?"

He must think I'm a fool and his lips have magical powers to distract me. He's partially right on the lip front, but my curiosity is piqued, and now nothing will stop me.

I push back on his chest with a light shove and then juke to the side. My long legs dart to the truck. I hear Bentley on my tail and know damn well he can catch me without much effort. His hand wraps low on my hip as I pull myself up the driver's side door and peer in the window.

"Oh my God, Bentley." My voice echoes around the cab. "Is it ours?"

His chest presses to my back, his legs frame mine on the running bar, and his hot breath tickles my neck as he talks. "Meet our baby."

Tears well up in my eyes until they spill over. The level of my voice from before frightened the tiny puppy, and now I feel horrible about it. He peers up to us with big blue eyes, his tail tucked between his legs and a shivering body.

"Come here, baby." I pat the driver's seat.

It takes some coaxing until he pads over to my hands. My instinct is to swoop the precious pup up in my arms, but I have to take it slow.

"A litter of puppies was brought into the animal shelter. They were rescued from a car wreck. The owners didn't survive, but the paramedics were able to save a crate of puppies that were in the back."

I gasp, and now the tears running down my face aren't from joy but rather heartache. Bentley reaches around, drying my tears, and he continues.

"I was on a wait list to adopt one of them. Got the call today. I've visited the animal shelter a few times and was hoping for this one. I mean, they were all cute, but this little guy just belonged to us."

"He's a boy?" The puppy begins sniffing my fingers, growing comfortable with me. "I feel like an ass spooking him earlier when I shouted."

"It's all good, baby." Bentley kisses the outside of my neck. "It will take him a bit to adjust. The little guy has been through a lot."

I can relate I think to myself. He's perfect for us.

Bentley goes on giving me all the details. "He's an Aussiedoodle. Doesn't shed, will grow to be a full-size dog, and will have the Aussie protective instincts. He'll be your guy."

"As in an Australian Shepherd Poodle mix?"

Bentley nods his head.

The little bundle of wiry, fuzzy fur steps into my arms. With ease, I bring him to my chest. His wet nose sniffs around the side of my cheek until his pink tongue darts out kissing me. Bentley steps down from the running board, taking me with him. I keep our new addition clutched to my chest.

"He's gorgeous," I whisper, running my hand through his brindle colored fur. It's a mixture of gray, white, and peach colored spots, but it's his piercing ocean blue eyes that melt my heart and steal my soul with one look.

"He is my guy." I peer up to Bentley. "You never cease to amaze me."

Bentley leans forward, kissing the top of the pup's head.

"Meet your daddy, Guy."

"Guy?" Bentley asks.

"Yep, he's our little Guy."

Mom doesn't give us long to bond with our puppy before she's pushing her way in, and she doesn't treat him like any old puppy. Nope, she introduces herself as his Grandma. I've read all the motivational sayings that pop up on Facebook and posts on Pinterest, talking about enduring the dark days before you experience the light of life. I never believed in them until now. The saying rings true; life doesn't have to be perfect to be wonderful.

Dad pulls in thirty minutes later, appearing as if he held up the local PetSmart at gunpoint. Every puppy item you can think of fills a large periwinkle woven basket. They even bought him doggie outfits.

"Good lord, Dad." I keep digging to the bottom of the basket.

He holds his hands up in surrender. "Wasn't me. Your husband here sent me with his Visa with strict orders."

We all settle onto a worn, plaid blanket, playing with Guy and eating the best chicken of my life.

Chapter 11

"A dog is the only thing on earth that loves you more than you love yourself." -Josh Billings

"Birdie, your turn."

A wet tongue runs up my cheek, forcing me to grumble and bury my face in a pillow.

"No, it's yours." My words come out muffled.

A strong paw comes down on my back. Guy taps away in a rhythmic motion.

I turn my head, pressing my cheek into the heaven of my pillow. "Blowjobs for a week, any time you name it, if you take Guy out."

Just like that, Bentley is up and out of bed clothed only in his black Calvin Klein boxers that do a poor job of concealing his morning wood and a damn excellent job of showcasing his ass. I'm not a morning person. Never have been and never will be, so I let my eyes flutter shut and dream about that beautiful ass.

It feels like five minutes of sweet slumber. My ringing cell phone tells a different story. It's well past ten a.m. Guy is curled up in Bentley's spot out like a light. Even though he's nearing a year old, it's still like having a damn puppy. It's completely our fault because he runs our life and owns us. We've been told by the perfect dog parents it should be the other way around, but screw that. Guy is the king of our house.

My phone dings with a text and I know it's Maddie reminding me of our weekly coffee date. I've never been late or even required a reminder.

It's the Maddie way. She's type A personality on steroids since sweet Sara was born. The woman makes it all look simple and never breaks a sweat.

It was immediate, undeniable love the first time I held Sara. I'll never forget the happy tears that welled up in Bentley's rich brown eyes when he held his best friend's daughter. Jealousy and longing for my baby evaporated the day we became her family.

Even though we aren't blood-related, Sara is our niece through and through. And of course, we are the cool kick-ass aunt and uncle. We made sure she was stocked with onesies that had borderline sayings printed on the front.

Maddie: Noon at Wicked Brews. Don't forget.

Me: I had us down for tomorrow.

I can't help but chuckle, picturing Maddie scurrying around the house, tidying it up and now panicking over my text. It's been Wednesday for nearly a year.

Maddie: Funny girl.

Me: Seriously, closing a deal, can't talk right now.

Guy rustles around until his nose is right up against my cheek and his long body is parallel with mine. I run my fingers through his curls. He has long outgrown the precious puppy, zoomed right through the lanky, awkward puppy stage right into a momma's boy. His coloring is the same with pops of gray, white, and peach spots, and his piercing ocean blues eyes are more dazzling than ever.

Maddie: Seriously, Marlee, we've had the same date and time forever!!!

Me: Gotcha, sucker. I'd never miss an opportunity to spend time with my favorite person.

Me: That would be my Sara Bug! See you in a bit.

Even though Bentley let me sleep in and took care of Guy before he went to work, it's still a struggle to climb out of bed. I swear sleep and my comfy bed are truly my best friends. I smile when I smell the aroma of coffee dripping into my favorite mug. It has Bentley's face plastered on it with "Husband of the Year" printed above his face. Best birthday present ever.

Guy licks my fingers dangling at my side. I pat his head. "Just a minute, boy."

It took me forever, but eventually I nailed a doggy treat recipe I found on Pinterest for Guy. It doesn't matter the time of day or night when I walk into the kitchen, he's on my heels ready for one. Never in my wildest dreams did I think baking epic doggy treats would make me smile.

"I better shower and get moving." I place Guy's treat in front of him and pat his head then pour more creamer than coffee into my mug.

He ignores my affection and devours the treat. It's then I spot a note on the counter. Bentley's sexy as sin handwriting fills the half piece of white printer paper. His writing has always been blocky yet delicate in an odd way, and it's always had the power to put a smile on my face no matter the circumstance. The infatuation started way back in fourth grade.

Birdie,

Be home around five. Don't forget your coffee date with our Goddaughter. Yes, I can see you rolling your eyes from here. Guy needs more rawhides and could you pick up a bottle of Old Spice body wash for me?

Enjoy that coffee, sexy momma, and get your lips ready for me tonight.

Love,

B

I hide my stupid grin behind my coffee mug while reading his note. I fall harder and deeper in love with the man every day. I could stare at his letter all morning, but know I need to get my ass in gear. If I show up late, Maddie will never let me live it down. Everyone in my life lives to ridicule me about my timely fashion. It's just that I've learned life is too intriguing to show up on time. No one buys it.

Guy nips at the bottom of my booty shorts. His pleading sapphire eyes gaze up at me. I'm a damn sucker, not even thinking twice about dipping my hand in his cookie jar. The treat vanishes in a flash. The sound of his paws trail behind me and echo down the hallway. As the loyal companion Guy is, he circles around on the bath rug several times before curling up in a ball. He knows my routine even on my days off.

The steaming hot water taunts and coaxes me to run a bath instead of a quick shower. Bentley still hasn't overcome his fixation with bath bombs, and I'm not going to complain. He's even dedicated a large drawer in our bathroom to store them. It's essentially a mini-Lush store on steroids.

There's no way I'm going to miss any snuggle time with my Sara Bug, so I rush through my shower. Guy snores lightly when I step out and towel off. It's insane how mellow, loveable, and calm he can be, but when a threat or anything foreign nears our home, Bentley, or myself, his Australian Shepherd tendencies come out strong. I don't fear anything or get spooked when home alone.

No sooner than I turn off my blow dryer and flip my hair up from being bent over, I hear the front door shut. Guy stands to attention but doesn't bark. He hears Bentley's voice and sprints down the hallway. He's long gone, skittering, and skattering on the hardwood floor. For as fast as he's moving, he covers no ground at all.

I round the corner in time to see Bentley pat his chest, signaling his boy to hoist his two paws up. It's their thing. His dad has chewed Bentley's ass several times, telling him it's a bad habit. Guy only does this with Bentley and only on command.

Guy's Australian Shepherd influenced ears flap up and down as Bentley scratches him in his favorite spot. Dad clears his throat, and it's then I realize there were two sets of footsteps. I make my way to him and open my mouth to greet him when I freeze dead in my tracks. His look says it all. I don't even have to ask them why they're here in the middle of the day.

I begin shaking my head from side-to-side. Tears appear without effort and I back away from the men, as if it would make the impending news disappear. Of course, it doesn't.

"Birdie." Dad's soothing voice shatters my heart. "Have a seat, darling."

"No," I repeat the word over and over, shaking my head in sync until my back hits the wall.

Guy's at my side the same time Bentley steps in front of me. His strong hands cup my face, trying to reassure me. I stare right into his whiskey-colored eyes but don't see a thing. My world has gone blank.

"Let's run. Leave. They'll never find us."

His jaw ticks with tension. I know I'm not making this any easier on him. The Army and his loyalty to it come before anything; it's what makes him a soldier. And that passion is why I'm so madly in love with him. But right now, it's crumbling my world. My head spins so damn fast dizziness settles in, my vision blurs even though not a single tear has rolled down my face. It's not his first deployment and more than likely not his last, but the terror is real.

"I've got you, Birdie." He leans forward and kisses my forehead before he pulls my stiff body to his chest.

I can't move. I should be hugging the hell out of this man, knowing now our time is limited. Guy nudges my leg, sending life back into me. In slow motion, I wrap my arms low around his waist. He tugs me closer, and I fall into his firm chest that's always been my home.

I feel Bentley kiss the top of my head several times before he speaks. "I'm so sorry, Birdie. I have to go."

"I know," I mumble, my cheek pressed against

his chest.

"Twelve short months. It will fly by, baby, and I'll be back here pestering the shit out of you."

"Where?" I squeeze my eyes shut, hoping like hell it's not the one place I already know deep in my core.

"Afghanistan," he whispers into my hair. Each sound and syllable seals the deal, making my knees quake.

It takes everything inside of me to hold it together when all I want to do is lose it in his arms. I refuse to let my greed and emotions take over. It's the respect the man I love is owed. I adore his service to our great country, but it will never make it easier handing him over to the Army.

Once my breathing settles down and I'm able to move, Bentley guides me over to our dining room table. Dad has a seat pulled out for me. He kisses me on the cheek before guiding me down. The two men follow suit, giving me all of the details.

All I pick up from the conversation is Afghanistan and one year. There's other information they throw my way to settle my nerves, but none of that registers. I'm losing my husband to the war our country is in. I choose right then and there to stand by his side and to never waiver. I'll write and send weekly care packages like I did on his first deployment. I will also be the first one to tackle him to the ground when he returns. It's my duty as an Army wife.

"Shit." I slap the table. "Maddie!"

Bentley reaches over, grabbing my hand. "Coy is with her."

"He's going, too?" I ask.

Both men nod their head in unison. My beating heart bleeds for my best friend. Pain and hurt long gone by now with terror left behind. I gasp, and the tears flow down my cheeks.

"Sara's daddy."

I vowed not to break down, but this was the final straw for me. Dad nods to Bentley, rounds the table, and kisses my cheek before striding out the door with his head held high.

My body moves through the air. My toes catch on a corner before I realize Bentley is packing me in his arms. I fight to control the torrid storm exploding inside of me. Bentley places me in bed, mirroring the night we lost our baby or the idea of it. He strips down to his boxers in a quick beat and is in bed, pulling me back to his chest.

"You can cry, Birdie. You can be angry and pissed beyond belief. Let me have all of it while I'm here. I don't get to crack, but, Jesus." Each word comes out slashed and sliced with pain. "I want to break down and run so bad you couldn't even begin to understand. I can't. I won't. You can, baby, do it for the both of us. Let it go."

A sob breaks free, rattling my chest, radiating pain throughout my entire body. The bed bounces and soon Guy nestles his massive body between us. He licks Bentley's face and then my ear. It repeats over and over until the darn dog has both of us bursting into laughter. I roll over, coming face-to-face with my husband. My hand goes to his jaw, tracing the outline of it.

Guy bounds off the bed and returns with

squeaky toy slobber and all dripping down. He drops it between us, his tongue sticking out and ears perked up as far as they can go. It brings a smile to both of us. Even my dog is stepping up to the plate being my own personal hero. It's the perfect remedy, keeping me from spiraling out of control with thoughts and worries I have no control over.

I throw the squeaky toy and Guy has it back to us within seconds. Bentley throws it next. The process repeats itself over and over again until it feels like a lazy Sunday afternoon. It's the furthest from our reality, but therapeutic all in the same. He tires out after a solid twenty minutes of playing fetch with us.

My tears have dried up, leaving the brewing pit of anxiety low in my belly. It dulls to a low simmer when Bentley's lips touch mine. My beating heart skitters as passion fuels me. I tumble head first into him, adrenaline coursing through me as my tongue sweeps into his mouth. Bentley rolls on top of me, covering me. He grinds his hips into mine, feeling the same as me.

He slides down my shorts and panties. I help him by pulling his oversized t-shirt over my head. His chiseled, perfect chest collides with mine as he pushes inside of me. I gasp, relishing each movement. We spend the rest of the night like this, and I plan to spend the rest of our evenings the same way. Bentley Foster will be branded and inked so deep in my soul, I won't be able to forget him even if I tried.

Chapter 12

"Our lives may have not fit together, but ohh did our souls know how to dance." -K. Towne Jr.

I'll never get used to waking up to cold sheets on Bentley's side of the bed. It leaves a sliver of me hollow, vacant, and cold. Guy was depressed the first seven weeks, moping around the house. It tore my heart out of my chest. He's remained by my side, making it hard to leave him when I go to work and he has become more protective.

I received my first call from Bentley yesterday. His voice came across the line exhausted and defeated. I pried a bit, but he sidestepped each of my concerns. I winced every time there was a bang in the background. It was complete chaos, not doing anything to help my already fraying nerves.

I sit up in the bed, throwing off the blankets. A whiff of Bentley's scent floats around the room. It's faint and fading way too damn fast. A bottle of his cologne sits on the nightstand next to his side of the bed. I squirt his pillow every night in hopes of keeping his smell in the room. It's not the same scent when it's not mixed with skin.

All ten of my toes touch the chilled hardwood floor. I pull them back up to my chest, wrapping my arms around my knees and rock onto my back. The swift movement makes me dizzy and nauseous. The dizziness never disappeared and has stuck around since the bad news was delivered. I chalked it up to anxiety, stress, and worry. It's getting worse coupled with the threat of puking. I'm also late.

I had to bite down on my lip to not spill my guts to Bentley. In the end, I know he doesn't need any more worry on his shoulders. He'd take on that burden and my own worry. It would distract him. I've been known to be stubborn in the past. I'm not brave enough to even begin that game.

The doorbell rings in rapid succession. I smile, picturing my Sara Bug pushing it as fast as she can. She's figured out how to push buttons, pick up toys, and squawk in delight. Her wild blonde curls, chubby cheeks, and bright baby blue eyes pretty much allow her to get away with anything.

I open the door to see the little chunk leaning over Maddie's arm, poking the button. She giggles every single time the doorbell lights up, and the shrill of the bell goes off. When she spots me the doorbell is forgotten, her arms fly up, and bare feet kick against Maddie's side.

"Ya-Ya." She waves her arms in the air.

"Sara Bug."

"Me." She pats her chest with all the pride a year and half old toddler can muster up.

"Get over here." I hold out my arms.

Sara leaps into them with gusto like she does every single time. If you're not ready, it could turn into a disaster real quick. Maddie rubs her swollen belly and walks in. She's six months pregnant. Yep, Coy has deemed his swimmers gold medalists.

It's Maddie's strength that keeps me glued together. She not only gave up her husband to the Army, but also the father of her babies. I've seen her shed a few tears in weak moments, but the woman is my rock. She pushes through everyday life with the same gusto her little girl has.

"Woof. Woof." Sara reaches down toward Guy. The two are partners in crime. Last week, we caught Guy bringing Sara pieces of his dog food. She'd slap her palm over her mouth and gobble it down. I panicked. Maddie laughed. I place Sara on her bottom next to Guy. It doesn't last even a second before she's standing up and climbing on his back. I swear Guy smiles. He doesn't move from his laying position, letting Sara run her fingers through his curly coat.

"Go pee on that stick, woman." Maddie plops down in a dining room chair, kicking her feet up on the table.

"Nice to see you, too." I pop my hand on my hip, offering up some sass. It's opposite of what I'm feeling inside. Fake it until you make it, right?

The door bursts open, letting in a delicious aroma of fresh baked blueberry muffins. Mom's frazzled, rushing in, setting the muffins down, and then clapping her hands together.

"Did I miss it?" Mom takes three strides until she's in my face. "Well, did I?"

I shake my head unable to speak a word.

"Go!" Maddie pushes me down the hallway until I'm in the same bathroom I bled in last time. The door clicks behind me, and I'm alone. With shaky fingers, I pull out the pregnancy test, reading the directions even though I have them memorized by now.

Once finished, I place the test flat on the countertop and go to the kitchen. Sara Bug is in the high chair, shoving bits of blueberry muffins in her mouth with one hand and sipping on her milk cup with the other.

Mom rattles on about nonsense while Maddie watches her cell phone, biting on her nails. These two give me the strength to go on. If I had it my way, I'd avoid all of this until it was so obvious I couldn't. I guess some would claim two missed periods would be pretty damn obvious.

"Go." Maddie stands up, trying to guide me back to the bathroom. "It's time."

I shake my head side-to-side, refusing to face reality once again. I can't stomach anymore heartache. I refuse to.

"Yes." Maddie is determined and adamant. "You have to face it. Pregnant or not. Baby or miscarriage you have to face it, and we are here by your side. I'm not going to blow roses and rainbows up your ass. Whatever that tests says, we will get through it."

We will…those two words bounce around in my head. I finally nod my head, letting her know I'm ready, but I don't move toward the bathroom. Sara has all of Mom's attention. Maddie takes it upon herself. Each of her footsteps sends out echoing screams in my home. With each sound, my heart slows down. I can't handle this.

Maddie reappears, but I refuse to look at her, instead staring at Mom, plucking Sara from her high chair.

"I'm looking now." Maddie reaches down and grabs my hand. "We are here for you every single step of the way." A pungent pause fills the air, causing my ears to sting.

"Holy shit," she squeals.

It's then I open my eyes and peer over to see two perfect, bright pink lines in the window indicator. Hope has always failed. Kicked me in the soul leaving me gutted. But this time I choose to believe. A slow smile spreads out across my face.

"I'm pregnant." The two words ghost my lips in a whisper.

"You are." Maddie wraps me up in a hug.

Mom soon joins with Sara in her arms. I feel her petite little hands tug my hair. I turn and grab her. She plays patty cake on my cheeks with a toothy grin then begins babbling.

"Shit. Ho shit. Shit."

We all erupt in laughter. The amount of joy, trepidation, and excitement is so intense it's crippling.

Chapter 13

"Courage, dear heart." C.S. Lewis

"Stop it." Mom reaches over, grabbing my fingers.

They've been in steady movement since sitting down in the waiting room. Two weeks is only fourteen days, but when waiting on an OB/GYN appointment it feels like a lifetime. There has been no bleeding, lots of exhaustion, and some nausea. All positive signs are in sight, but there's always that little reminder in the back of my head screaming at me.

Of all things that make me throw up on command, fish and cheese are instant triggers. My fishing pole has been put up for some time now coupled with Papa Wally's death over eight months ago and now the threat of puking.

Thinking of Papa causes tears to spring to my eyes. I brush them away, refusing to let them fall. We all saw it coming and were at his side when he took his dying breath, but it doesn't make it any damn easier. Thank God, Bentley was still here by my side.

"Don't cry," Mom whispers in my ear.

I'd tell her it's not what she thinks, but then I'd have no control over the tears. We've spent hours holding each other missing his presence. Man, to see his reaction when and if I get to announce I'm pregnant would be priceless. He is always my biggest fan.

The door leading back to the doctor's office

swings open, causing me to tense up. “Marlee Foster.”

Mom is up and out of her seat before I even move. She drags me up and leads me to the nurse. It’s like the days when she’d have to pull me back for immunizations. So many different emotions are racing through me as I get all checked in and pee on a stick. I remember Bentley’s words that he tells me all the time…there’s no such thing as a broken heart.

The paper crinkles as I take a seat and wait for the doctor. I tug up the blanket covering my naked lower half and fidget with the shoulders of the gown. “I’m happy, Mom.”

She looks up at me with a questioning stare.

“I’m so damn happy right now. I want Bentley here so bad, but if this is our time… I’m not even scared to be happy this time.” I beam at her.

“About damn time. This is your time; I know it. You’re such an amazing woman, Marlee. I mean, a pain in my ass, but an amazing one.”

“You love me.”

“If it’s a girl, I’m dressing the shit out of her in pink, tutus, and any other frilly shit.”

I shake my head. “No, we will let her decide what she likes.”

“Bullshit! I carried you for nine months, pushed you out, changed your shitty diapers, and I swear you refused to wear pink from the moment you were born.”

The door opens before I have a chance to respond. I can see I’ll be on the anti-pink campaign for a while with her. Hell, I love flipping her shit.

Bentley and I will raise our baby like our parents raised us to be respectful and allow them the room to make their own choices.

"Marlee, I'm Dr. Kinsley Hilton." She extends her hand.

One, I'm surprised the doctor is female and immediately feel comfortable with her. Two, she's beautiful with pinned back raven hair and pronounced features that would intimidate me in any other circumstance, but not here.

"Hi." I take her hand, shaking it, my voice shaky and trembling. "Guess you already know who I am."

"Yes." Her warm smile comforts me even more as she grabs the rolling stool from under the counter. "We are going to become quite good friends over this pregnancy. I'm going to read over your notes, and we will see how far along you are."

She props her laptop on her lap, reading through some medical charts. "Looks like your first pregnancy, Marlee?"

I fill her in on the entire backstory which she's more than likely already read in my medical notes.

She peers up from her laptop. "This is more common than you think, Marlee. Most women in your same shoes don't talk about it much because it's so painful."

"I can relate to that." My fingers begin fidgeting again.

"I'm guessing this is mom?" Dr. Hilton stands to shake Mom's hand. "Nice to meet you."

On cue, I blurt out. "I'm married. My husband is deployed in Afghanistan."

"I see." She pulls out an extension to the table, easing me on my back. "There are several support groups in our area for women in your circumstance. I'll send you home with the information."

I dig my fingertips into the paper on the table. The sound of the crinkle and crunch is much louder than I expected, echoing around the room, flaring my nerves to an all-time high. My happiness is quickly morphing into trepidation.

"Just relax, sweetie." Her hands roam over my abdomen. "Since you've missed two periods, I want to do a vaginal ultrasound to determine how far along you are. It's not the most comfortable thing in the world, but you'll get to see your little peanut. How does that sound?"

"Perfect," I croak out. The well of tears that have been building up begin to spill. "Mom."

She's at my side, holding my hand, brushing away the hair on my forehead. "I'm here, Birdie."

"I want Bentley here," I whisper, choking on each word.

"I know. I know." She squeezes my hand. "Your dad missed your birth due to his deployment. Papa Wally was there the whole time holding my hand. I remember wanting your dad so bad."

She tells me the same story she's told me several times. It eases my nerves. My mom did this, so can I. Dr. Hilton joins in on the conversation, offering up her encouragement intermingled with what's about to go down. It's similar to a coffee date with girlfriends except me lying on the table, legs spread, and yeah, nothing like a coffee date except the way they make me feel.

"A bit of a cold sensation, shouldn't be uncomfortable. Let me know if it is."

The lights have dimmed in the room, and I sense the nurse in the background, but can only stare at the fuzzy screen in front of me. She's right, it's cold, but not uncomfortable. Swirls of gray, white, and black fill the screen. There's movement, but nothing identifiable. It feels like an eternity before Dr. Hilton speaks again.

"And there's your baby." She reaches over with her free hand, freezing the frame and dragging lines over the object. "Strong and steady heartbeat. Let's see here."

A silent pause cracks through the room. I grow numb as I stare at my baby with Dr. Hilton's words on repeat. A vigorous and steady heartbeat. It's all happening so damn fast, and it's real.

"Hope," I whisper. "There's hope."

I squeeze my eyes shut, picturing Bentley and growing excited to share the news with him. The next phone call will be the best we ever have.

"Okay, you're measuring around eleven weeks pregnant, Marlee."

I gasp. "That's almost three months."

"Yes." The cold sensation vanishes. Dr. Hilton rolls back on her stool, pulling her gloves off, and is by my other side, grabbing my hand. "There's no way ever to promise everything is going to be perfect, but, Marlee, you're pregnant, and everything looks perfect. It's time to embrace and enjoy it."

"Thank you." I squeeze her hand with all I have. "Thank you so much."

At this moment, I know I'll get through this with the support team I have. I'm determined to take her advice to the fullest.

"When can we find out if it's a boy or a girl?" Mom asks. "It's been way too long since I had Marlee that I can't remember."

"Typically between sixteen and twenty weeks, we will do an ultrasound. It will be up to the mom and dad if they want to find out the gender of their baby."

"Oh, they do," Mom replies, answering for me.

"The keywords were mom and dad," Dr. Hilton replies with humor lacing her words.

"We do want to find out," I answer with confidence. Bentley and I have never been known for our patience.

We set the next appointment, go over insurance and all the cost before leaving the office. As Mom and I walk down the hallway, my steps are light like floating on a cloud.

"Marlee."

I turn back to see Dr. Hilton, leaning on the entrance to another room. "Congratulations and enjoy the ride."

"Thank you." The grin on my face is contagious and downright ridiculous. Cue the happy girl moment.

***

Days turn into weeks, drifting by with no call from Bentley. I've begged and pleaded with Dad, but all he does is reassure my raging anxiety. The weekly care packages have been sent every Monday with the letters to Bentley.

With my feet kicked up on our coffee table, I laugh at Guy who loves to lick my baby bump. It's become his favorite resting place over the last weeks. He knows he's going to be a big brother. I chalk it up to his dog instincts and not the big brother sweater I bought him for the holiday season.

"This one is my favorite." Mom settles next to Dad on the loveseat with a large bowl of popcorn.

"You say that every year." Dad rolls his eyes, rubbing his tightly clipped salt and pepper hair.

Every night is much the same. They made sure the holiday season was as normal as could be. Considering we're missing two significant men, it's been damn near impossible. Even though it's two days past Christmas morning, Bentley's presents remain wrapped underneath our tree.

My parents are worried about me. I've done my best to conceal my fear, but I guess they see right through it. It's been two months with no word from Bentley. Dad acts funny around me or at least that's what my wild imagination thinks.

The ultrasound to find out the gender of the baby came and passed. I had to put the sealed envelope in the safe to keep Mom from it. She's about to stroke out over the fact I won't let her peek at it. That envelope will not be opened until I'm on the phone with my husband.

I feed Guy one piece of popcorn and then stuff my mouth with a handful. Mom's popcorn is the best. She always dumps a large box of peanut

M&M's to the mix. I make myself sick on the combination every single time, pregnant or not. The morning sickness finally faded, and my appetite is in full force.

The doorbell chimes throughout the house. I look down at my cell phone, seeing it's well past nine.

"You expecting someone?" Dad asks, standing up.

I shake my head.

"Probably a desperate salesman," he replies.

"Damn desperate at this time," I add.

I follow Dad to the front door and when he swings it open, my world crumbles. A Causality Notification Officer. Everything is a blur, leaving me unable to process a single word. Mom's arms wrap around me, pulling me to her chest. Dad takes the conversation outside. His voice is booming with wrath, shaking the inside of my house. He's outside for a few minutes but it feels like an eternity in a fiery hell.

Dad steps back in, slamming the door. "He's alive. There's been an accident, but Bentley is alive just injured."

Dad paces around the room, his arms roped with tension, and veins throbbing in his neck. His words soak into my brain, and I collapse in Mom's arms sobbing.

"Birdie." Dad pulls both of us into his arms. "It was out of respect. They knew I was here and have been demanding information on his whereabouts and the exact location of his squad. He's okay and coming home."

My body trembles with no hope of stopping. My parents hold me tight until I'm able to control my breathing and the shuddering ceases. They guide me back to the couch.

"It was a roadside bombing. Men were killed during it. His brothers, but Bentley is injured."

"How bad?" Mom asks.

"We don't know. He's in transit on his way out of Afghanistan."

Chapter 14

"Love isn't something you find. Love is something that finds you." -Loretta Young

My voice trembles as I answer my cell phone. Unknown number.

"Hello."

"My wife. Birdie." Bentley's voice is scratchy, but the sincere, familiar timbre soothes away my fears.

I sit down on the edge of the bed. "Bentley!"

"Yeah, baby girl, it's me."

"Oh my God," I cry. Mom and Dad race into my bedroom.

"Calm down, sweetie. I'm okay. I'm okay."

The inflection in his voice tells me another story.

"I love you." It's the only three words that I want to repeat over and over again.

"Marlee." His voice cracks and there's some beeping in the background. "I miss you."

"Where are you?"

"Hospital in Germany."

"Are you okay?"

A pungent pause fills the line. The bed dips on either side of me. Dad takes my free hand and Mom places her hand on the top of my thigh. My hand clutching the phone begins to shake to a point I can barely hold it. Dad takes it from my hands, lays it in my lap, and pushes the speakerphone.

"He was my friend."

"Who?"

"Sam. We'd been training soldiers. He was my favorite. Young and so full of life. His name was too damn hard to pronounce, so I called him Sam. He loved Snickers and other snacks you sent. He made himself sick on them to the point of puking.

"We were out on a sweep through of town..." Bentley's voice cracks and sobs fill the other end.

"Baby, you don't have to."

"There was a bombing, and Sam was hit the hardest. I went to him, held him, and tried to get him back to safety. He was so hurt. The gurgles and smell of searing skin I'll never forget."

Dad squeezes my hand, dropping his head.

"He died in my arms, Marlee. Took his last breath. He told me to go home to my sexy woman and thanked me. It was Christmas morning."

I slap my hand over my mouth, aching and hurting for him. I want nothing more than to hold him, run my hand over his hair, and kiss away the pain.

"Son, it's Jones."

Dad begins talking to Bentley. His voice echoing around our bedroom feels right as rain through the turmoil. I focus on him being alive and coming home. I don't feel selfish at all over that fact. Dad gets Bentley to share about his condition and his orders to come home. It will take a week or so before he arrives in the States. He suffered a laceration to his neck and second-degree burns on his torso.

God had his arms around my man, keeping him safe. Without thought, my hands go to my protruding belly, rubbing light circles. It catches Dad's attention, and he gestures to me. I shake my head. I want more than anything to tell Bentley he's going to be a daddy, but it's not the right time.

"Sir, can I talk to Marlee?"

"Yes, son. Can't wait until you get home. We love you. Call your parents."

"Yes, sir."

Dad takes the phone off speaker and hands me the phone. I'm able to hold onto it. Dad leaves the room and I know damn well he's going to call Bentley's mom. My mom helps me lay down in my bed, tucking me in. She flips on the lamp, turns off the bedroom lights, closes the door giving me privacy.

Guy leaps up on the bed. He hears Bentley's voice and begins whining, getting as close to the phone as possible. Bentley's hearty chuckle fills the line, sending excitement throughout me from head to toe. It's the first sign that everything is going to be okay.

"Is that my boy?"

"Sure is. Talk to him." I hold the phone out to Guy.

Bentley begins his doggy talk with him. Guy's tail is out of control as he throws his head up in the air, barking. I laugh. Bentley laughs.

"My turn." I bring the phone back to my ear. Guy circles around on the bed several times until he settles down, his head propped on my belly like he's showing his daddy he's taking care of me and his soon to be sibling. I smile again and, damn, it feels so amazing.

“Sorry for breaking like that.”

“Bentley, stop. You’ve always protected me from the stuff you’ve experienced. It’s the way you cope, but I’m here and always will be. I want to know everything and anything you need to lay on me.”

“Fuck, I miss you. Tell me everything. Did you can this year with your mom? Did she make her potato casserole for Thanksgiving and Christmas? How’s the fishing?”

I do what he asks, telling him everything, not leaving out a single detail except for the fact he’s going to be a daddy. We talk and talk until his voice begins to fade off after a nurse interrupted us, giving him pain pills. I don’t stop talking. Soon his rhythmic breathing fills the line, and he doesn’t answer back. I stay up for hours, listening to it until the phone call disconnects.

Chapter 15

"True love stories never have endings." - Richard Bach

I've never denied it. I'm a brat. Spoiled rotten, always getting my way. Some things never do change. I wait for the soldiers to exit the plane, standing in the front row. Our parents are not far away at our house, preparing Bentley's favorite meal for his homecoming. They gave me this.

Families are scattered everywhere. Posters, balloons, little kids on their uncles' and dads' shoulders, all eagerly await the arrival of their loved ones.

The plane landed a few minutes ago. I keep my hands clutched over my stomach, unable to mask my excitement. Our little one is feeling the same way, spinning and rolling around excited to hear her or his daddy's voice.

Soldier after soldier exit the plane. Families surround me in a happy homecoming. I don't recognize any of the soldiers. My impatience grows by leaps and bounds as each one steps from the plane back on US soil. The elation and gratitude is so profound and thick it's intoxicating. The sun high and bright shining overhead forces me to shade my eyes.

Then it happens. My husband steps from the plane. One bandage covers the side of his neck. His stride is full of grace and powerful as it always has been. Not one single piece of evidence that he's endured the darkest hours of his life. I wave like a lunatic. He doesn't see me through all the joyous chaos.

I cup my hands around my mouth and shout his name. His head whips up in my direction. I break through the crowd as his pace picks up. Tears, the happiest of happy tears, roll down my face. My home and world is here running toward me. I jump into his arms, not considerate of his condition at all.

We both ramble between stolen kisses. My hands roam over his face, relishing in the familiar lines. His hands move on my ass, keeping me clutched to his chest.

"Marlee." He tries to peer down at us.

"I love you. God, I love you. I'm never letting go of you again."

"Marlee." He looks back down. I'm juggled around in his arms, and I giggle. With caution, I climb down his body until my feet are safe on the ground and step back. Bentley drinks me in as if I'm a chilled glass of sweet tea on a hot summer day. His eyes grow wide. He wipes his hands over his eyes a few times before blinking to realization.

"We are having a baby." My hands go to our baby.

"How?" He steps closer, lowering to his knees.

I plant my hands on the top of his shoulders. "You see when a boy loves a girl and they..."

His lips are on our baby bump. His trembling fingers raise my shirt. His lips pepper kisses all over my skin. I reach into my back pocket and pull out the tattered envelope.

"This is for you." I hold the envelope between

us.

"What is it?" He gazes up, happy tears cascading down.

"Open it if you want to know if you're going to have a daughter or son."

He doesn't hesitate tearing it open. He unfolds the paper, scanning the paper with urgency. I witness the moment he sees the gender. His attention goes back up to me.

"Do you know?"

I shake my head, holding back my eagerness. He folds the paper up, tucks it in a pocket in his fatigues, and rises to a standing position. His familiar, strong hands cup my face, and he kisses me like he never has. It's raw and intense in front of the crowd. He pulls away, leaving my lips swollen and bruised with his imprint.

"We are going to be parents." Kiss. "And it seems a whole lot of pink is in our near future."

"A girl?" I ask.

He nods.

It's my turn to kiss the ever-loving hell out of him, clutching to his neck.

"Hope. We held it for years, and now our own little Hope is on her way." Bentley uses his thumb to brush away my happy tears. "Hope Marlee-Ann Foster."

"It's perfect," I mumble into his lips, going in for another kiss.

We make a detour to the pond on our way home. Our hands were all over each other on the way, never letting go. We revert to our high school ways, easily driving out to the pond with our headlights off. There's no blanket tonight, fancy lighting, or tent, it's just us. It's all we need. The windows fog up as Bentley lays me across the front seat of his truck.

"You were thinking ahead when you brought my truck to pick me up, weren't you?" he asks, covering my body, peeling away each piece of clothing.

"Maybe." I shrug, tilting my head to the side.

Bentley takes full advantage kissing, licking, and biting at the tender flesh. Nothing about our frantic motions is romantic. It's raw desire and longing coming full circle. Soon we are stripped bare, writhing against each other. Passion pools, controlling every single part of me.

"Is it...um safe?"

"Don't be an idiot and take me," I respond.

"Seriously, Marlee."

"Yes, and God, I've wanted you forever. Seems like an eternity I've gone without you. I need you, Bentley." I pull him down to me by the back of his neck.

"I'm going to smash the baby."

"Good hell." I reach down, guiding him into me.

His eyes slam shut, and he stills inside of me. I take it upon myself to begin the movement. Bentley's veins pulse as he keeps most of his weight on his arms as he moves in and out of me.

"Jesus. I thought I was going to vanish away in the wind without you. Hardest days I've ever endured. This. All of this is my home, my heart, and everything." Bentley picks up his pace, our skin slapping together, creating a beautiful melody.

“Ditto.”

Chapter 16

"A flower cannot blossom without sunshine, and man cannot live without love." -Max Muller

A set of deft hands brush over my protruding belly. Our little girl begins to kick and roll, not only can I feel it, but when I peeked open my eyes, I can see the tumbling motion.

"Does she ever stop?"

I wipe the sleep from my eyes, covering my mouth with my free hand as I yawn. "Yes. I remember the first time I felt her move. I thought it was nerves or gas, but since that day she's never stopped."

"Tell me exactly what you were doing." Bentley leans down, peppering our baby bump with kisses. "I want to know it all. It still seems so surreal to me."

A pang of guilt hits me for not telling him the night he called from the hospital. Bentley has reassured me over the last few days that I did the right thing, but I still feel like shit for it. He was in an active war zone the last few months, and that's the reason there was radio silence. He's talked about Sam a few times. It hasn't gotten any easier. I know it's scraping away at his soul, but Dad has reassured me it's something he'll have to work through on his own time.

"The first time it happened I was at work. I was finishing up some paperwork, bending down filing some papers, and I felt it. My first instinct was to grab for the trashcan because the puking was horrible at the time. I stayed over the trashcan for long moments and then it passed.

"I chalked it up to gas pains and kept on going. Well, a few days later, it was one of the nights I finally went back out to the fishing pond. I was all set up in my chair and had cast out a few times and hadn't caught anything. The sun was about to set, you know that time Papa Wally always said was best for fishing?"

I wait for Bentley to nod his head and continue telling my story.

"I cast my line out one more time, and the same sensation hit me. Again, I thought I was going to puke. Which was odd because it seemed the morning sickness had faded away."

I run my hands up and down his shoulders.

"And you know I don't know why they call it morning sickness because those first four months were brutal, but the three month mark it hit with a vengeance. It didn't matter the time of day, the smells, or where I was; I would up-chuck without warning.

"So you can see I became a little cautious. I sat back in the chair and then all the sudden my stomach kept fluttering. At the time, I was steadying myself to lose my cookies. But it never came. However, the fluttering sensation low in my belly continued.

"Right when the sun dipped below the horizon, it happened again, and I knew without a doubt it was the baby moving. It was such a crazy experience, Bentley, I have no idea how to explain it, but I knew Papa Wally was there. He was by my side smiling wide, enjoying the moment.

"It was silly, but I cradled my abdomen hoping to feel something, but of course, it was too early in the pregnancy to feel from the outside. On the inside, it was chaos and she's never stopped."

Bentley pops his head up and looks at me with tears in his eyes. "I'm so sorry I missed all of that, Marlee."

I reach down, running my hands through his hair and smile. "There's no reason to be sad or apologize because you're home safe and sound, I'm in my third and final term of pregnancy, and we have each other. I couldn't be more thankful."

He inches up my body until he's at my face, peppering kisses all over my jaw, chin, eyelids, and forehead.

"I still can't believe this happened to us. Who would've ever thought especially after everything we've gone through? I guess it's true what they all said; we had to be patient and our time would come."

I grab his hand, squeezing tight, letting him know I agree with him. "Today's the day you get to hear your baby's heartbeat and see her on a 3-D ultrasound. It's incredible because you can see everything. I swear she's going to be a thumb sucker. The two times I've had ultrasounds, she has her thumb nestled in her mouth."

Bentley liesdown against me, listening to my excitement. I called Dr. Hilton's office, letting them know Bentley was home and asked if there was any way we could have a 3-D ultrasound so he could experience the same thing I did. They didn't hesitate and got us in as soon as they could. And even told us it was on the house. I'm thrilled for Bentley to meet Dr. Hilton. He is going to love her.

I fidget with my fingers, trying to bring up the next topic. It's not going to be easy on him. The few days he's been home, I've noticed how this deployment has changed Bentley. It's not his fault, and I know it's typical for soldiers who return from a war zone. But he did not come home the same man. It's crushing to see the love of your life go through that.

"So we have your coming home party tonight. I figured before our doctor appointment we could spend some time at the pond, head to the doctor's appointment, and then head over to your welcome home party. How does that sound?"

He shrugs, showing no excitement, and it's exactly how I thought he would react. I cup his cheek and stare into his eyes. "We can call and cancel. Both of our parents are very supportive and know how hard this is on you, babe. If you don't want to go, we don't have to go."

He shakes his head and thinks for long beats before clearing his throat. "It's not that, Birdie. I'm not sure how to explain it. It's almost like I've been trapped in an intricate mousetrap maze for the last several months and now I found the exit out. I'm always looking over my shoulder even in our own house. It makes my own skin crawl. The counselor said it'll dull over time with coping mechanisms and also mentioned there's medication for it. I'm okay with the counseling, but I'm not good with taking medication. I need time, you, and my family."

I roll over, pressing him back into our mattress. I'm not as quick or swift as I used to be with this big ol' baby bump in the road. It takes some time and leaves me gasping for air, but I manage to get him pinned down to the bed with me straddling his center, our hands interlocked over his head. Bentley grows playful, nipping at my full breasts dangling in his face

"I'll be your damn rock, Bentley. Hell, consider me your boulder. God knows you've done it for me for enough years. I'm so happy you're home. And I know I sound like a broken record, but I swear to God, I'll be repeating that for the rest of my life."

We spend the rest of the morning down at the pond like old times before marriage, the Army, and war. Before any fishing happens or we even unload tackle and poles, we fool around on a blanket. It brings back so many old memories that I'll never forget and also gives the promise of so much more to come.

Bentley rolls off me with his chest heaving and lies at my side, pulling me to him. I stare up at the clear, electric blue sky, letting my eyes flutter shut, picturing a little girl out here with us one day learning how to fish. She won't have a Papa Wally to teach her the way around a fishing pole or the ways of the world. She'll have us and two sets of grandparents who will adore her.

We eventually make our way to our poles only to find the fish aren't biting. I'm happy about this, so I don't have to clean and cook them. The smell of fish still isn't easy to swallow, and the mere thought has me gagging. Which is odd as hell seeing as I grew up fishing, cleaning, and cooking them.

There hasn't been one minute since Bentley's return, granted it's been a handful of days, but we haven't been separated. I called into work canceling all my meetings and showings. The old me would be petrified another realtor would make a sale over me, but right now nothing else matters but my Bentley and spending time with him.

He's funny, washing me in the shower like he used to. The only difference is that he spends extra time on my belly. I'm pretty sure his hands haven't left our baby bump since he's returned. He's quiet on the drive to the doctor's office, and I know it's because he's analyzing and going over in his mind mentally preparing himself to be around people.

It hurts like no other to see a dedicated, strong man like Bentley struggle to make his way back into society. I've been around the Army my entire life and know it's a long, grilling process. He grips my hand as we walk toward the glass doors leading into the office. As Bentley reaches for the door on the left, the one on the right flies open nearly knocking me off my feet.

A young man comes flying out, knocking me to the side as he strides by. He's either not had a very good day or is pissed off at the world. He doesn't stop or apologize for shoving me out of the way. Everything happens so fast, Bentley's hand shoots out, grabbing the man by the upper arm, jerking him back. The man's head whips to the side with a vicious snap.

Bentley lets go of my hand, getting right up in the man's face. I've never seen Bentley so pissed off and raging in my life. He's bloodthirsty and has lost all control. I wouldn't even categorize his voice as yelling; it's a downright growl that would come from a rabid animal.

"What the fuck, man?" Bentley jerks on the man's arm. "You almost knocked my wife on her ass. And she's pregnant with my goddamn daughter. I think you need to have a fucking lesson in respect, you little shit bag."

Bentley rattles the man again expecting a response. All former anger radiating from the man has long disappeared, transforming into pure fear.

"Bentley." I grab his arm, squeezing it. "Baby, it was an accident. Come on, let's go we will be late."

I know my words will do not a damn thing to pull him out of his rampage right now, but there's also no way in hell I'm going to watch him go to jail for assault. This isn't Bentley. This isn't my husband. He would never react this way. The Bentley before his second deployment would've called him a shit bag, shook his head, possibly threw up his middle finger, and walked away.

"He almost hurt you, Marlee. Step back."

The boy manages to get out a word with his chin quivering.

"Sir, I'm sorry. I shouldn't have done that. I was in a rush."

Bentley gives the stranger another terrifying shake, rattling the teeth in his head before he lets go.

"Next time you think about supermaning a door

open like that maybe picture your little sister, your mom, or someone you care about if you care about anyone, you scumbag. I better never see you around again."

Bentley drops his arms to his sides. The young guy takes off rushing down the sidewalk. I let go of Bentley's arm and step back from him. I'm not scared, and I know he would never hurt me. But he needs to cool down right now. I watch him pace back-and-forth running his hands over his tightly clipped hair for several seconds before he sits down on the metal bench in front of the entrance.

He collapses down, defeated and disheartened. It's the last thing I wanted for this day. He leans over, elbows on the top of his knees and buries his face in his palms. After a few minutes of letting Bentley calm down, I go to him. I'd love to kneel down before him and make him look me in the eyes, but the truth is I couldn't get back up. So I step to his side, wrapping both of my arms around him. Leaning down inhaling his scent and kissing the top of his head for a long time. My hands run rhythmic circles on his back, helping him ground himself.

"I saw red. When there's a threat, I can't control myself, Marlee. I've survived in mass chaos where threats meant death. The adrenaline and reactions were immediate when that threat was focused on you."

"Babe, I get it. This is expected from what you just came from. Not that I'm saying it's okay what you did. But right now your whole system is adjusting back to life here at home. You have a choice, you can keep talking to me and working it out and leaning on me. Or give in to those threats, reacting like you would when you were deployed and ruin your life. I'm here for you; you know that."

He sits up, leaning back on the bench, spreading his legs and grabs one of my hands, pulling me around until I'm sitting in his lap. His arms wrap low on my waist, settling right under our baby girl. My arms lace around his neck and Bentley buries his face in my side boob, and I let him be.

"I'm going to counseling, Birdie. I will continue going to counseling because when that baby girl of ours comes, she's going to have a healthy dad. And above that, you deserve a healthy husband forever and always."

I kiss the top of his head and smirk.

"You don't have much convincing to do with me because I've always known I have the best husband in the world."

"God, I'm a wreck," he mumbles.

"Enjoying that boob action?" I chuckle, kissing his head again.

"Yeah." He sinks his teeth into my flesh. My thick winter sweater is doing nothing, I swear I feel every part of his mouth and teeth playfully sinking in.

"We will get through this." I grip the back of his neck. "Through anything."

"It's what keeps me going," he murmurs.

I force myself to stand, adjusting my dress sweater and hiking up my thick leggings. Maternity clothes are heaven and don't even get me started on the underwear. I'm going to need an intervention to quit wearing them after I have Hope.

"Are you ready to go see your little girl?" I hold my hand out to Bentley.

I'm home the minute he places his palm in my hand. We get through the doors this time with no incident. Walking down the long corridor, a medical cart crashes into the wall. The ruckus causes Bentley to jump and go on high alert. I squeeze his hand, continuing to walk like nothing happened. It takes him a few beats to calm down.

We settle into familiar waiting room chairs after I check in. Bentley's reaction as he takes everything in is downright comical. The expression like a fish out of water explains him perfectly.

"Marlee Foster."

"It's our turn." The giddiness in my voice and the way I pop up out of the chair is downright ridiculous. I can't hide it. I've waited days and ended up coming to terms that Bentley would never get to experience this.

He remains in awe as the nurse weighs me and takes my vitals. I squeeze my eyes shut like I do every single time avoiding the topic of gaining weight. I may regret it later, and I deal with it then.

Just like I expected, Bentley hits it off with Dr. Hilton the moment she walks into the room.

"So nice to meet you, Bentley. I've heard nothing but good about you."

"Thanks." He nods, stepping back to me after shaking her hand.

Dr. Hilton explains the process of ultrasound. Bentley stands, hands on his hips, eyes wide with excitement soaking every single detail and even cracking a few jokes about knocking me up. I, in turn, soak it all in. It's always surreal sitting in this room hearing Hope's heartbeat and facing my reality. I'm going to be a mom.

"Is your wallet empty yet?" Dr. Hilton asks, squirting the warm liquid over my belly. "Babies tend to do that."

I clutch Bentley's forearms. "Our moms have that taken care of it. Drove them nuts I wouldn't let them peek in the envelope, but it didn't stop them. We pretty much have everything from a crib, bassinet, swing, high chair, vibrating chair, and even a Keurig for bottles."

"How did they manage to keep everything neutral colored?" Dr. Hilton asks.

"They chose to go with a farm animals theme, but I wonder if they used a light or something because it's pretty damn girly."

"Those two would." Bentley bends over, kissing my forehead. "I could picture them holding it up at a light pulling out all stops."

"Or it could be Grandma's intuitions," Dr. Hilton offers, pressing the wand against my belly.

That action stops all conversation. Hope's vigorous and steady heartbeat fills the room. I don't stare at the screen like I normally do, choosing to study Bentley. His jaw goes slack and tears well up. Proud, happy ones that have been rare for us. I squeeze his arm.

"She's beautiful." He covers his mouth.

"I think she was excited to show off for her daddy." Dr. Hilton begins pointing everything out on the screen for Bentley. Hope has her thumb up to her mouth melting my heart. My knees will get tired thanking God every day for this miracle.

Dr. Hilton's voice cracks. She even has tears in her eyes. The moment is magical. She prints off several pictures of Hope for us and by the time we leave the office, Bentley has worked his magic on all the nurses and even Dr. Hilton. His natural charisma is charming their scrubs off, only proving some things never do change.

Chapter 17

"You can't blame gravity for falling in love." - Albert Einstein

"I know there will be a shit ton of food at the party, but I want to go out to dinner with you." Bentley stares straight ahead at the road. "That way I can focus on talking to people and then we can sneak out early."

He turns to me, waggling his eyebrows. Dirty boy.

"If that's the case, I say we claim you have diarrhea and head home now."

"Why is always me who has a case of the massive shits?"

It's true I always blame it on Bentley to get out of events we don't want to attend. At one point, his mom was determined he had irritable bowel syndrome. Our family caught onto us after that.

"Because it's the right thing to do, like taking one for the team."

Bentley's stopped at a red light, leans over, trailing his tongue along the seam of my lips. "Sounds like I'm going to have to punish you, Mrs. Foster."

"Oh, do tell."," I moan, writhing in my seat.

Bentley picks up on what he's doing to me. His hand glides down between my legs. Christ on a cracker, all things holy, and God bless leggings, letting me feel the strum of his fingers. It's almost enough to send me over the edge of ecstasy. Just a few more strums, my hips buck to help him, and then a car horn blares behind us, snapping Bentley's attention back to the road. He takes his damn talented fingers back to his side.

"Jerk!"

"Punishment," he taunts.

We go back and forth engaging in playful banter. Bentley doesn't ask where I want to eat. He pulls into our favorite pizza place, Maxie's. My stomach growls on command. This pizza may be better than what was about to happen in the car. Okay, not better, but a very close runner-up in the game.

We order two large pizzas and settle in a corner booth by the fireplace. I urged Bentley to order a Coors Light draft in hopes to take the edge off the impending nerves. He finally gave in after I told him I'd drive us to his party since he's the celebrity and all. That earned me a grand eye roll.

I take a long pull from my lemonade, snuggling into Bentley's side. "Do you think there's any married couple in the world that both like pineapple on pizza?"

My question catches him off guard. He stares down at me, shaking his head then raising his eyebrows. "I often worry about your thought process, Birdie."

"I'm serious. There's not one couple I know of that both love or hate pineapple on pizza. It's always split down the middle. I love pineapple, but it's a crime on pizza, and you love pineapple, sausage, and green peppers on pizza."

"I'm sure there are plenty of couples out there who have mature taste buds enjoying the exquisite delicacy of pineapple on pizza."

"I think you're wrong and I said married couples. I think plenty of dating couples might agree on the horrendous topic, but the ones who commit to marriage are another story."

"You're not going to give this up, are you?"

"Nope, not until you tell me I'm right."

Our server places down a pizza rack followed by the two piping hot pizzas. My mouth waters.

"Anything else I can get you?" she asks, wiping her hands down the front of her apron.

A large crowd fills the abandoned section of the restaurant we're nestled in. Bentley tenses, surveying his surroundings.

"Another beer please." I grab his hand flexing on the top of his thigh, gently squeezing it.

She bee-bops off not picking up on the tension, and I decide to do the same thing, grabbing the spatula and serving up pizza. I put two on Bentley's plate knowing the man will have it down within seconds. With my free hand, I pick up a slice of thin crust pizza biting into the cheesy goodness.

Seconds later, Bentley does something that shocks me. He begins humming the tune of "I Love Rock N' Roll." I've always loved it when he mindlessly hums, and oddly it always has the power to ground me. He picks up a slice of pizza from his plate and has it down in three bites. He finishes off his first beer and takes a long pull from the fresh one. After half of his pizza has disappeared, he relaxes back in the booth.

"That was delicious." He leans over, kissing me on my cheek.

The noise level in the room is a dull roar, but he's managed to fight through the anxiety of it.

"Look." I point to a table where an older couple sits.

"What am I looking at?" He squints.

"Two pizzas. One with pineapple and one without."

He shakes his head. "Coincidence."

We box up my pizza and one slice of his nasty one. Bentley leaves the server a generous tip. The three beers did the trick relaxing him just enough. The server offered him a fourth, but he waved her off. I think he was reassuring himself when he explained he wouldn't become dependent on alcohol.

"Quit over-analyzing everything, baby." I shrug into my winter coat. "You're being too hard on yourself."

He grabs my hip, pulling me to him. "I know I'm scaring you and I don't want to. I have to talk it out."

"You're not scaring me. I hurt for you. It's not fair."

"It's not," he agrees, dropping his forehead to mine. "Let's get this welcome home shindig over with, so I can go home and sink balls deep in you."

I swat his chest, pushing him away. "You dirty, dirty talking man."

"You know you love it."

"I do." I wink at him and turn, walking to the door. Bentley keeps his chest pressed to my back all the way to the car.

He hands over the keys, waiting until I'm settled

behind the wheel adjusting the seat.

"Damn, Larry Long Legs." I tap his chest once I'm buckled in and ready to go.

"Ain't the only thing long about me."

His chuckle echoes in the night air as he jogs around to his side. I back out of the parking space, waiting for him to buckle before pulling out onto the main road. It's a good twenty-five minute drive to the small center our parents are hosting the gathering in. I made our parents keep the guest list to twenty people. Maddie had to cancel because Sara came down with an ear infection. Maddie's been MIA since Bentley's return. She hasn't come out and told me, but I know it's too hard seeing him when Coy is still deployed.

"Sure you're good to drive?" Bentley stares out the window.

The pitch-black skies have opened up with pouring rain. Better than snow, but not ideal driving conditions. Heading home and getting our freak on sounds better every second.

"I'm fine, daddy." He can't see the gesture of me rolling my eyes.

"You'll be calling me daddy later."

"Don't ever say that again." I reach over and slap his thigh. He's quick, catching my hand and not letting go.

"You kept me up too late last night. I'm going to check my eyelids for holes for a bit. Gonna need stamina and energy to have you screaming give it to me daddy."

"Get some rest, Bentley." I place extra emphasis on his name.

He squeezes my hand and moments later his breathing grows even. It's the sweetest, calming sound. The best song ever. He stretches his legs out and rolls his head to face the outline of my face.

"Babe."

"Yeah." I'm stopped at a four-way stop.

"You're my greatest love. My Birdie."

Mindlessly, I reach for my necklace. My fingers are memorizing the shape of the pendant.

"You're my greatest love story. Never forget that." His voice trails off. The moon is offering up enough light, making it possible for me to see his eyelids flutter shut.

I've always wanted more in my life. Wanted to date Bentley the moment I realized I was madly in love with him. Yearned to graduate high school and get married to the man of my dreams. Then it was all about getting my real estate license and accelerating my career. From then on it was all about getting pregnant. It consumed me. It's always been the what's next in my life. I enjoyed life and loved it, but was always looking forward to the next big thing.

Until now.

I'm full. Finally able to live in the moment. Exhaling with relief and on top of the world. My husband is home and our baby girl, Hope, will soon be joining us.

My phone dings with a text message, but I ignore it. I know it's Mom wanting our ETA. The back roads would've been faster to take, but the rain detoured me. The highway puts about fifteen more minutes on the trip. It's lonely tonight, leaving me with the beaming headlights and my thoughts.

Hope strikes me with a kick of her heel to my left ribcage. I gasp, wince, and rub away the pain, keeping one hand on the steering wheel. The pain makes me smile. Feeling her move always puts me on a natural high.

The glow of the one stoplight on the highway comes into view, flickering a bright green. Headlights set to high flood the cabin of the truck and I turn my head to see another truck right before it careens into us. My head whips back, hitting the headrest. The sound of metal bending and flexing is deafening. The smell of smoke, blood, and death is all too much. My world goes black.

Part 2
Present
Chapter 18

"Hide your eyes darling people can see your heart through them." –Unknown

The chaos stopped. I have no idea how long I was out for before light filled my vision again. Red and blue flashing colors swarmed my vision. My head was heavy as it took everything inside of me to look to my left. Bentley. I fight to scream for help, but no sound comes out. His body is slumped over, blood covering him, and no movement coming from him.

"Baby." I get a whisper out and reach over to rattle him awake.

My fingers soak in his blood. No movement.

"Call for life flight."

Talking ensues outside of the truck. The door flies open. My eyelids barely a slit. I can't open them all the way no matter how hard I try. A foreign hand goes to Bentley's neck.

"Cancel life flight. Dead on arrival."

A brutal yell echoes around me. It doesn't stop until my door opens and arms move me. I recognize my voice, but can't put all the pieces together.

"She's pregnant and bleeding."

My shoulders rattle.

"How far along are you?"

I stare up into a set of rich brown eyes studying me. The question rolls around in my head. But it doesn't matter because I feel Hope being ripped

away from me.

Thud. Thud. Thud. I shoot straight up out of bed. Sweat coating my body. I clutch Bentley's shirt I sleep in every night and grab for the pink baby blanket. My hand searches the bed for it, never feeling the soft material.

I scream. I leap from the bed, flipping on the lights in a frantic state to find it. I rip away the blanket and sheets from the bed. Nothing. I fall to my hands and knees looking around the floor and under the bed. It's bundled in a heap like their dead bodies next to the edge of the bed. I grasp it, pulling the pink receiving blanket to my chest.

Guy doesn't get up from the couch. He studies me with sad eyes. This occurrence isn't the first time. He's used to it, suffering as bad as I am.

The tears and cries of sorrow begin. My panic attack is still rattling me to the core. I'm unable to calm myself down even though I have the two items I require to survive. I clamber to my feet and with trembling fingers manage to get the top of the vodka bottle off. I fall in the middle of my bed, sitting cross-legged, tossing back the bottle.

The bitter, harsh liquid glides over my tongue. I don't stop at two or three swallows. I lose count, letting the vodka do its job of beginning to numb me. The near empty bottle lands between my crossed legs. I drop my chin to my chest defeated, enduring the lingering pains.

I clutch the blanket to my chest feeling my heart constrict because I've lost track how old Hope would've been. *A year and something or would it be two?* My fingers tremble, and my body quivers with anxiety the harder I fight to remember. Bentley. I picture him and Hope fighting like hell to ground myself. Bentley would no doubt be by her side playing with her while I finished up dinner. I squeeze my eyes shut, struggling to drift off into my fantasy world. Rubbing my cheek with the blanket speeds up the process, taking me to the moment in our home.

The tears rolling down my face sting with bitter reality. They're dead. I'm alive and alone. Inhale. Exhale. The pain is all the same and grows daily by bounds. I open my eyes, glancing over to the butcher knife. It calls me to me every single day even as the year has drifted by. Its voice is growing more determined and higher in decibel each passing day.

Mom. She'd be devastated without my calls home. They're rare in nature. I do my best to call her every so often. I've destroyed her since leaving.

I climb out of bed, drain the vodka left in the bottle, and toss it in the trashcan. I reach into my cupboard and grab the last bottle. My supplies are running low. That thought alone sends off in another panic attack storm.

The rare mountain wind rattles the shell of my camp trailer. The place I'm learning to live again. I left home with no plan. Hitting the road, finding a new place far away wasn't an option. I hate driving, despite being trapped in a vehicle. I took the bus and ended up in a random town where nobody cared who I was. I holed up in a cheap hotel room for little over a year until I mustered up the courage to buy a one-way ticket to Idaho.

The stale room all became too much for me to handle. The nightmares thrived on the musky, moldy air that brewed in the four walls and my fear. They won every single night, driving me closer and closer to the edge of darkness.

One morning, I overheard two men talking in the parking lot. It had become a pastime of mine since the walls were paper-thin. They talked about Idaho and the mountains and some town called Moore.

The thought of fresh, clean air. Open space bordered by mountains consumed me. I had to run again, so I did.

Riding in the back of a car getting to the airport wasn't as bad as I thought. I wasn't in control. I felt the same way when the RV dealership drove me up to the mountains in Idaho.

The responsibility of being behind the wheel didn't weigh heavy on my shoulders. I found myself looking to the right, begging like hell there'd be headlights promising to crash into us to take my life.

It never happened.

And now I'm in the mountains alone with a camp trailer and a periwinkle cruiser style bicycle that has never been pedaled. The salesman who sold me the Airstream trailer had no problem stocking it with groceries, supplies, and vodka. Of course, the request happened thanks to a pretty penny.

I truly only have the bike, camper and what's in it, and nothing else. My savings account shriveled up from the purchases. Money doesn't mean a damn thing to me anymore.

I fall back onto the bed, staring out of the tinted window. The stars are bright enough to shine back at me. Wondering what comes after death brings back pangs of panic. I twist the lid off the new bottle and swallow. I used to believe in heaven and knew Papa Wally was up there staring down at us. But now all of my weak convictions have been obliterated. I don't believe in God.

I sit in silence, staring up at the sky and drinking vodka until my head swims with sleep. I keep the bottle close and lie back down with Bentley's shirt hugging my skin and Hope's blanket cradled to my cheek. I try again to tumble into sleep where my living nightmare stays away.

"Call the OR. Female looks to be in her third term of pregnancy. Loss of blood and thrown into labor."

"Dr. Hilton." I manage to get out between cracked lips.

She appears out of nowhere when I'm wheeled into a room with bright lights.

"I'm here, Marlee." She runs her hand over my hair.

I don't have to ask. I see it in her eyes. I'm too numb and struck with fear to cry. This has to be a nightmare where I can't wake up. A nurse's voice catches Dr. Hilton up to speed. Dead on arrival reverberates around the room. There's pressure on my belly, cool instruments, and dead silence. Dr. Hilton is back in my vision. Her features are no longer holding any glimpses of beauty and confidence. Right now she's the devil.

"I'm so sorry, Marlee. The anesthesiologist will be here any minute."

"Leave her." I squeeze my eyes shut.

"Honey, we can't." I feel her hand grab mine and pull it away.

"Leave her!" I scream.

"We can't. It will kill you."

"Good. I'm dead already."

I feel hands on the side of my neck then a quick prick of a needle. I whirl my head around to see what in the hell. Another doctor with his hands gloved sets down a syringe and then studies a suture kit in front of him. I bring my hand to the side of my neck, feeling an IV rip and pull at the flesh on the top of my hand. My fingertips dip into raw flesh and blood. I fidget in my skin and begin digging at it.

"Marlee." Voices bounce off every surface.

My arms are pressed against a scratchy sheet. More faces come into view, causing me to scream louder and thrash more. My body gives out in a matter of seconds. Everything goes dark once again.

Chapter 19

"You'll forever be my always." -Unknown

It's a vicious cycle doing nothing to heal me. A few swallows of vodka will take away my pounding head, violent, upset stomach, and dry mouth. It's how I wake up every morning and also how I curb the horrible feeling. I take more than a few shots this morning. Last night, God tortured me, forcing me to relive that night in two sets of nightmares.

The nightmares are relentless; so vivid and real. It's my torture. I put down the fifth of vodka that's now almost drained dry. I avoid the topic of having to pedal into town later for the first time. Avoiding is my game, and I rein it. I walk outside to the crisp mountain air, stretching my hands over my head. The red-checkered flannel shirt rises, allowing the chill in the air to tickle my skin.

I never wear Bentley's Army shirt outside the trailer. I keep it cherished and protected, the same with Hope's blanket. It was the first thing I bought when I knew I was pregnant, carrying my baby well into the four-month mark. I purchased a pink and blue one.

I shake the transcending thoughts clear from my head and walk down to the creek with my coffee mug clutched in my palms, keeping the warm heat in. Guy is on my heels. He never leaves my side, still my protector and best friend. We get through each day heartbroken and shattered. vodka swirls around with the black coffee. My creamer of choice. I sit in the camp chair near the river's edge, watching the water ebb and flow over the solid base of smooth river rocks.

A fishing pole lies on the ground next to me. It was part of the supplies the salesman had bought for the camper a little over six months ago. This is as far as it's made it to fishing. I thought I could fish and that it would be therapeutic in a way. I don't have the courage or desire to touch it.

The vodka warms my insides, and the river clears my head. I love the mountains. I'm nestled between two small resort type towns. A handful of locals live here year around where the rest enjoy certain seasons. I peered out the window as the salesman drove me up here and gave me a quick tour. All sorts of varying sizes and styles of cabins are nestled in every crook and cranny.

He also helped me find a spot to park my trailer year around for five hundred dollars. The old woman who owns the place used to have a hopping RV park, small convenient store, bar, and restaurant. Now it's a ghost town. The old run-down buildings and faded Pepsi signs hold so many stories of what once had been.

Lydia, the old woman, put me in the back corner where I wouldn't have to interact with a soul, yet remain near the river with an amazing view and be able to hook up my trailer to electricity, water, and sewage. It's the perfect setup for me and a beautiful place to disappear away in the winds of life. I've never seen her. The salesman dealt with her, but she delivers canned foods and other items once a week. Never knocking or introducing herself. She leaves a bag on the steps. It's the main reason I haven't been forced to go to town so far.

I kick off my foam, cheap flip-flops and dip my toes in the ice-cold river. I don't shiver or shudder. It numbs me. Some days I go waist deep until I can't feel my skin taunting me. It's a short-term release. My skin always prickles back to life once in the mountain air.

I'm located smack dab between the unique mountain towns of Moore and Big Piney. They're exactly ten miles apart, or that's what the salesman rattled on about. I remember him pointing out the grocery, hardware, gas station, liquor store combo in Moore. It's the first town you passed after climbing up then going down the range of mountains. Guess that's where I'll be heading to get more vodka and a few groceries later today after this buzz wears off.

My thoughts morph into morbid ones. The type where blood, guts, and a beating heart pumps for the last time on the winding paved roads of the small mountain towns. I yearn for that feeling. I crave the feeling where my heart beats for one final time. I bring my mug to my lips and swallow down the remaining liquid. With both feet in the mind-numbing water, I let my exhausted eyelids flutter shut, knowing that I've lost everything and have nothing to live for. Yet, I'm the rat in the gutters not brave enough to take my own life.

My eyes open and then flutter shut. I repeat the process over and over until my pupils adjust to the bright, stale lighting of the hospital room. *Mom's face appears in my vision followed by Dad's. No nurses or doctors bringing me right back to the previous events.*

My hands fly to my stomach. It's deflated. The sharp needle in the top of my hand tugs and tears at my skin. I press harder on my stomach, searching for Hope. My body is numb, but the pain is blinding.

"Birdie, careful." Mom's soothing voice drifts in.

I press harder, growing more confused and panicked. My palms slam down on my abdomen. Strong, steady hands catch them. The feel and fingerprints of them familiar. My dad. I turn to him. Tears glaze his loving eyes, and he shakes his head. I know what's happened, yet refuse to believe it until it's spoken. I stare him straight on, taunting him to say the words that will end my life.

"She's gone. The baby didn't make it. Bentley passed on impact, Marlee. They are gone." He delivers the news in the black and white fashion I crave. No bullshitting or promising everything will be okay.

A force takes over my body. I break free from his grip and repeatedly beat on my stomach. One punch, no pain. Two punches, nothing. Three, four, five, six, and nothing. Chaos ensues around me as Mom calls for a nurse, but I don't stop. I'm determined to beat my own life out of the shell of my body. More bodies join my side.

Dad and a few other people fight to hold my arms down long enough until a long, shiny needle meets the plastic part of my IV. It only takes seconds before my world once again goes black.

I startle awake as soon as the same empty pit of blackness takes over. My favorite coffee mug tumbles to the sandy shore in slow motion. I grab for it, but the vodka effects don't allow me to catch it. It bounces off the hard sandy beach and rolls to a stop on the river's edge. One rush of the current and water grabs it, tugging it into the river. It's all in slow motion playing out before me.

Bentley's face printed on the mug beams back at me. The words written above all become a blur as I leap from the chair and stumble down into the hard sand. My knees slap into the fresh water straight from the snow runoff. It pierces my skin. I ignore it. My hands flail for the mug. Bentley.

They sink into the freezing temperatures of the flowing river, dragging me down in the current of that night when I touched his skin, when his heart beat no longer. My trembling finger wraps around the mug, pulling it from the river. Droplets of water run down his face. There's no comfort coming from him or even joyous humming. I clutch the mug to my chest cherishing it. Emotions take over. They're so strong they have the force to pull me under.

Something comes over me. It's a yelling, tugging, dominant force urging me to kick off the sleek, polished rocks, and wither away, floating to my destiny. I do just that. Guy whimpers as I go into the water. The water pierces my back with its sharp needles of freezing. I keep Bentley gripped in my hand. A searing pain from the back of my skull shoots down to my toes, electrifying my entire body. Soon I'm laid out in the water, floating down the river.

The bed of rocks knocks along my spine as the

water takes me away. I have no idea how long I float until I come to a deep pool of water where the current doesn't have the power to sweep me away.

I'm close to the main road. The sound of cars whizzing join the sounds of nature. A gentle, brutal reminder of how my life was taken away. With each passing sound, I grow more and more determined to sink under the water and never come up.

I tense, every muscle in my body shooting out of my relaxed state. My legs dip low in the water, followed by my torso then my face. I keep my eyes closed, waiting for the oxygen in my lungs to disappear.

I take myself to a place where Bentley's hands are on me, his arms holding me, and his lips brushing the shell of my ear, telling me everything is going to be okay. He's there by my side coaching and urging me to fight for life. I grow irritated. More and more enraged. He wants me to live. How can he expect that?

I sink further down, feeling the pressure on my chest. Panic sets in. I open my mouth to let the water seep in and fill my lungs. My toe touches the sandy bottom of the river, and I don't kick up. I bring my hands around the front of my knees, pulling them to my chest, keeping the coffee mug safe in my hand.

I hear Bentley's voice whispering into my ear, "Fight for your life. Live, Birdie."

When my butt hits the sandy bottom, I gulp in a large amount of water then my body is jolted forward. It's as if someone's hands are on me, pulling me up. I battle against the force, kicking away from it. But it's too powerful. My body is sucked back into the current of the river until I'm surfacing, sputtering and gulping for air. I glance down at the mug once the coughing fit is over. His face shines back at me.

I trudge to the shore with the overwhelming urge to slam the coffee mug into the bank of rocks. I can't. Instead, I crumble to the ground in a worthless heap. The rocks form a bed of heat from the sun and I close my eyes. This time, no nightmares come as I sober back into reality.

Chapter 20

"Money can buy you a fine dog, but only love can make him wag his tail." -Kinky Friedman

My legs haven't burned like that in years. A mountain bike or a bike with gears would've been a better choice than my flat land cruiser. From my campsite to Moore, there's a steady incline. No crazy mountain passes like when driving in here with the salesman.

But my thighs felt every single rotation of the pedal. I had to stop three times on the five-mile ride to catch my breath and ground myself. Now sitting in the town I'm more confused than ever before. My body is exhausted and my mind numb from this morning.

I was ready to do it. I was going to join my family. I had the courage built up, and my body was numb. I wasn't worried about Mom or Dad at that moment. I wanted everything to stop hurting so damn bad. I was ready to go. I heard his voice, felt his hands on me nudging me into the current of the water. His face and encouraging words always pulling me out of the darkness, but for what?

I know it was Bentley. It was a sign from him telling me to move on and live. The thought makes me insanely pissed off. How could he? He knows there's no way I can do this.

My fingers run over the webbing of the rusted metal bench I'm sitting on. The locals go about their daily business. The majority of people around here don't drive cars. There are droves of razors, four wheelers, or motorbikes traveling up and down the road. The mountain air breezes through their hair, highlighting their light spirits and glowing happiness. It makes me sick.

As they go about their business, not one of them notices me. They leave me alone. I watch as they wave to other people and share smiles. Maybe I can do this. I want to be left alone. I have the beauty of the mountains and the solitude they promise. It's a glimpse of hope for the rest of my life.

I make sure my bike is leaning against the bench and walk across the road to the main store. It pretty much has everything anyone would need and the only store in this area. It's connected to a bar, and the bar is attached to a restaurant resembling a mini strip mall. Big Piney, ten up the road, only has a bar, a small hotel, and a bunch of cabins from what I recall.

I take a deep breath and reach out, my shaky hands pushing the door open. An old style bell rings out loud and clear, alerting the owners to a new customer. Several heads whip around, making me feel uncomfortable in my skin. I duck my head and dart for the first aisle I spot. Once in the safety of its confines, I smooth out my flannel button up shirt and try again to control my breathing. This is stupid. Seriously ridiculous.

I'm going to have to get over this fear of being around people if I plan to stay here the rest of my life. This would be the place I would shop. I look up to the products in front of me and realize I'm standing in front of the feminine products.

I look at the price of one box of tampons and do a double take. Ten dollars for a pack of 12 tampons. Are they made of gold?

"Holy shit," I mumble to myself.

I guess this one store for all these people has the monopoly on prices. I grab a box, knowing that I have some back at the trailer, but eventually they will run out. And I'm not about to pioneer woman it. It takes a handful of minutes until I'm able to find my footing. I mentally run through the list of stuff I need to get. Vodka is of course at the top of the list.

I go for a shopping cart that's seen better days. Hell, it's so old Mom probably pushed this one around when she was a kid. I spot the vodka and other hard alcohol behind the counter. I'll be getting a few bottles before I go. I have a feeling I'm going to need one tonight to soothe my nerves.

I've been living on processed food that keeps well in the freezer or in a can and is easy to cook in the microwave. I individually bagged and froze fresh meat, which has been long gone. The sight of the produce aisle is heaven. It's not the prettiest or ripest fruit and veggies I've ever seen. It's the fact that I haven't had any fresh fruits or vegetables for months now that makes my mouth water.

My fingers run over the tomatoes, onions, celery, cucumbers, bananas, apples, and strawberries, picking out the ripest of them. A rare smile graces my lips at the small baby steps I'm attempting.

All the prying eyes and curious patrons turned

their attention to me when I walked in, but now they've all left me alone. It's not like back home where everyone was in your business or knew I was the daughter of Sergeant Jones or who my mom was. There'd be seas of pity gazes and worthless conversations about how sorry they were.

It's nothing like that. Nobody in this town knows me or about me. They have no idea I'm a girl who lost her husband and baby in a tragic car wreck. It seems they couldn't care less and that fact is empowering. I float through the next few aisles, grabbing random items and even throw in some junk food.

I'm stopped in the coffee aisle, making sure to buy enough Keurig cups, when somebody taps me on the shoulder. I turn to see a man about my age with olive skin and messy jet-black hair. His gorgeous brown eyes shimmering like a dark Espresso are familiar. I'm forced to blink a few times before my common sense kicks in. It's not Bentley, but Jesus, it's so eerily similar and creepy.

"Ma'am, got these in the other day. Kind of handy little buggers if you like to use the Keurig."

It's impossible to miss the country twang in his voice. Even though he's as big as a shit brick house with broad shoulders, he's not threatening at all. I stare at him confused, trying to take him all in. His red t-shirt looks as if it's about to burst from his torso.

He throws his arms up in the air. "Sorry, I'm not a lurker or anything. I'm Caleb Bryant, the owner of the store."

I nod, digesting the information.

"You're new in town, right?" He extends his hand out to me. "Renting a space from the crotchety, old bitty Lydia."

I nod again. So my presence in the small mountain town hasn't gone unnoticed.

"Don't judge the rest of us from what you know of her. Old age hasn't done anything to brighten her social skills. The rumor is she has major daddy issues."

This makes me choke on nothing, but air. I slap my chest, trying to calm down to be able to talk and nod my head. Hell, he's going to think I'm a mute here before long.

I clear my throat one more time for good measure. "I...uh. I haven't ever met her. The salesman set everything up for me."

"Typical." He shrugs. "Her bark is worse than her bite. She looks like she eats small animals and children for breakfast, but she ain't half bad. Stays to herself."

I remain frozen, unable to string together a simple sentence. This Caleb character has no idea I'm the future Lydia of the mountains who will secretly deliver small bags of groceries to loners.

"Anyway." He plucks a package from the display. "All you have to do is buy some coffee grounds and pack it in this container. That way you don't have to keep buying the one use individual ones."

"Okay," I stutter out the simple word.

"Let me know if you need anything else." He turns to walk away. "Like I said, I'm Caleb. I didn't catch your name."

He plants his hands on his hips, waiting for my answer with a broad smile on his face.

"Marlee." I don't recognize my voice. I haven't heard my name spoken in forever. It feels weird and forced.

"Nice to meet you, Marlee."

And he's off as fast as he appeared. I reach for the contraption he was talking about and read the back. Ingenious idea and with the prices of this store, I will save a shit ton of money in the long run. I throw it in the cart and make my way to the front. There's a short line. I study their selection of whiskey and vodkas while waiting in line, deciding a little Bailey's will go perfect with my coffee in the morning.

"Smart woman." Caleb picks up the Keurig filter from the counter, waving it in front of me.

I smirk. The man is friendly, easy on the eyes, and oozes charm.

"Caleb." An elderly lady pokes her head in the door. "Can you help get that damn bag of dog food in my Razor?"

"Be right there, Gloria." He punches in a few more numbers before jogging out from behind the counter.

"Sorry." She stares at his ass as he jogs past her.

I mean, his jeans do hug the globes of his ass to perfection, but my hell she wasn't even discreet about it. She follows him out of the door that stays propped open. I watch through the small window behind the counter. The bag of dog food is five pounds at most. Caleb was used that's for sure. I shake my head and hear Caleb holler back to her.

"Tell Edwin he owes me a few cold ones." Caleb shuts the door behind him, dragging his hand through his mess of wavy, dark curls. Raven black to be exact. "The women around here."

"You know she just…" I point to the door.

"Used her dog food to check out my ass?"

I nod.

"Feel like a piece of meat around here most days." He smiles at me, staring a bit too long, making me feel uncomfortable.

I glance down, pulling more items out of my cart. An awkward, thick silence fills the air. We're saved from suffering from any more of it when the old-style phone rings, making me jump.

Caleb chuckles before answering the phone. There's no room to judge Gloria as I check out his ass and thick thighs. The man is ripped. In fact, if he bent over he'd probably rip out of his jeans. My intentions differ from Gloria's, or at least I assume that. Mine is out of pure curiosity. Does he have a gym in the back of the store or does he chop the shit out of wood to keep a body like that?

"Banky." A shrieking voice serenades us.

A flash of wild black hair sticking up in every direction peeks from behind the counter. I peer over it to see a little boy dancing back and forth on his toes while holding himself. Where in the hell did he come from?

"Banky, pee now."

Caleb uses his shoulder to hold the phone to his ear and tries to bend down to help him.

"Yes, we ordered two cases."

"I'm gonna pee on you," the little boy declares. "Mergency."

Caleb throws his arms up in the air, growing frustrated.

"Excuse me a second." He covers the end of his phone with his palm. "Marlee, would you mind helping him? My idiot brother has next week's delivery all messed up."

The little boy launches his black boot back and sends it right into Caleb's shin. He may be little, but he's packed a punch with the kick. Caleb winces, bending down, rubbing out the pain.

"My daddy isn't an widiot. You is."

Caleb's carefree, happy go lucky charisma vanishes. The boy continues to hop around worried about peeing his pants. I remain frozen. Fear strikes my core watching the innocent boy. It takes me down a path I don't want to be on. I grow dizzy as sweat begins to trickle down the back of my neck. The edges of my vision blur in and out of focus. Anxiety creeps up my spine.

"Please, Marlee." He points over my shoulder. "The bathroom is in the back. He just needs help with getting in the bathroom and his button and zipper."

Before I have a chance to respond, a little face peers around the counter at me. He's hesitant, studying me up and down. He has Caleb's dark eyes and hair. His cheeks are full and flushed. He has to be his son, but why does he call him Banky?

"Banky, girls can't see my ween."

"Go." Caleb's jaw ticks. "Yes, I'm here. We need that case of produce as well as the meat. I'm not sure how it was screwed up."

The little boy steps around the counter and walks up to me. I don't move. I can't. It's all too real. A brutal reminder of everything I lost. He jerks his head to the side and then begins down an aisle, doing his version of a pee-pee dance.

I clench my hands into fists until my fingernails dig into my palms. My eyes flutter shut, and I fight to pull myself together. Yes, it's tearing open a very fresh wound. The pain is worse than waking up in the hospital because I can't escape it with pills. I eye the vodka on the shelf and pull in air.

"You's coming?" Rich chocolate brown eyes stare back at me.

I nod.

"Here." He holds up a hand to me while the other one is between his legs. "I show you."

I show you. Those three words echo around in my head. His words have more meaning behind them than showing me to the bathroom. It's like he's promising so much more with his curious stare and genuine heart. When my hand connects with his little, warm one, I tense for a second before I'm able to relax. We stop in front of door with a "staff only" sign hanging crooked on it. He drops my hand, pulls up his shirt, tucking it under his chin, his tongue darts out to the side as he fumbles with the brass button on his jeans.

"Here." I kneel down. "I'll get this and help you inside."

"Okay, I hold my shirt." He pulls it nearly over his head with his little hands. "Don't look at my wiener."

I bite down on my bottom lip, keeping in the laughter. "I promise."

"Or my nuts. I got nuts."

"I promise."

Once his zipper is down, I make a show of covering my eyes, only peeking out to open the door and flip on the lights. "I'll wait right out here."

He darts into the bathroom. I hear him peeing before I'm able to shut the door. Once the door clicks, my back slams into the wall. My heart beats out of control. The anxiety attack has backed down to a dull roar. That little boy hurts to look at; he scares me, but above all of that, he makes me laugh.

He resembles everything that's good, honest, and pure in this world. A blank canvas. The world is at his fingertips. It takes me back to the days I once had that. That train of thought slams right into what I had and lost. Would Hope have been so open and trustworthy as she grew up? Would she have had my eyes or Bentley's? The lists of questions are endless and will never be answered.

The door flies open with no warning. A soft humming sound follows it. A blur of wild black hair comes into vision. He has his shirt up around his neck, struggling to zip and button his pants. The harder he concentrates, the louder he hums the tune of "Twinkle Twinkle Little Star."

I kneel before him once again. "Here, let me help you."

"Don't look at..."

"I promise." I zip up his zipper and fasten the button. "There you go."

He tilts his head deep in thought. "Are you a mom?"

I swallow the lump in my throat and shake my head.

"My mom left us. She didn't wike me."

"Oh." His response takes me by shock. I place my hands on top of my knees.

"Maybe you can be my mom." He grins wide, all of his baby teeth on display and then skips off.

It takes me a long beat before I'm able to stand up and gather my thoughts. That little boy just flipped my world upside down. His sweet, innocent heart shattered by his mom. A gentle reminder everyone is battling their demons sent straight from hell to cause havoc.

Caleb hangs up the phone as I reach the counter. I don't miss the ticking of his jaw and the tension racing through the veins of his neck. He runs both hands through his hair before letting out a long breath.

"Thank you, Marlee. That's not typical. My brother is in town, and I'm watching his son. Shit has been crazy since he came back home."

"No worries." I open my wallet. "So, he's your nephew?"

"Yeah." A ghost of a smile appears on his perfectly sculpted lips. "He's quite the kid."

I let out a light laugh. "Yes, and for the record I didn't look at his ween."

Caleb throws his head back, howling in laughter. "He didn't."

"He did," I answer.

"I had no idea a barely four-year-old would be

obsessed with his wiener and poop."

"He is a boy," I offer.

"That's what Mom says, too. Claims my brother and I were just as intrigued."

"His dad?" I cringe, prying for more information. I'm colored intrigued.

"Yeah, my twin brother, Jed. Paternal not identical. I'm the better looking one." Caleb starts bagging my groceries, spilling their life story. "Jed was on top of the world winning CMA's and touring the world until he came back home."

"Jed?" I ask, the name somewhat familiar.

"Jed Bryant, country's hottest singer a year ago."

The light bulb goes off. Holy shit. I used to own every single one of his songs on my old phone.

"Oh." Is my one word stunned response.

"Yeah, like I said I'm the better-looking brother."

I smile at his response. The door bursts wide open and none other than Jed storms in. He and Caleb are so similar in looks I'm not sure how I didn't pick up on it. Jed is not quite as big and defined as Caleb, but everything else is spot on.

"Hey, Sunshine," Caleb chirps.

Jed glares at him, slamming the door shut. "Fuck off."

My jaw drops as I stare at the angry man.

"You gotta problem, princess?"

It takes me long beats before I realize Jed's addressing me. He doesn't give me time to answer before he strides off to the back room. The twins may look similar, but from first impressions are now in no way alike.

"Ignore him. He's going through some shit and is a dick."

I wave off Caleb's apology, trying to act cool. He places two requested vodka bottles and a Bailey's in my bags. I settle up with my debit card.

"Gave you the family discount for being so patient." Caleb helps me stuff the grocery bags into two oversized bags with sturdy handles.

"Thanks."

Caleb grabs for one of the bags, but I'm quicker than him, plucking up both of them. Before the door shuts, Caleb hollers out. "Don't be a stranger."

I smile back at him. Before I turn my head, I catch something out of the corner of my eye. Jed. He's leaning on the side of the building toward the back in the shade. His chest is heaving, face up toward the sky, and then he brings a bottle of Jack to his lips, taking a long pull.

I don't know what he's dealing with, but it's clear it's something is haunting him. I can relate. I feel for someone else for the first time in what seems like eternity.

Chapter 21

"We are born of love; Love is our mother." - Rumi

"Hey, boy." I climb off the bike, keeping the two bags balanced on the handlebars.

Guy comes closer, sniffing at the bags. His curiosity is getting the best of him. I pat his head then scratch the back of his ears and unhook him from the homemade leash tied on the camper.

"Got you some treats. I'll have to make another trip for your dog food though." I tear open the bag of dog jerky and give him a few pieces. I smile, remembering the time Bentley and I gorged ourselves on dog jerky, thinking it was a new brand from Costco. Mom was appalled and couldn't believe we didn't put two and two together since the bag had a picture of a Golden Retriever on it. We were starving twelve-year-old kids.

Guy has them down in one inhale. His eyes light up when I pull out the huge rawhide. It makes me smile. It's rare for both of us to be happy with a smile on our faces. And he's smiling over the fact he's about to get his all-time treat.

He goes to town on the rawhide while I put away all the groceries. He's on his last bag of dog food, and it's a little under half full. That trip to town will require a bit of creativity. He's a big enough dog that a five-pound bag won't last. We started with four fifty-pound bags when we settled here.

I make myself sick on fresh cut fruit and vegetables before settling outside in a plastic chair to watch the sun go down. It's my favorite time of day up here. Once the sun hides behind the mountain ridge, the temperature drops a good ten degrees. A chill so thick you feel it in your bones.

"Come here, boy." I pat my lap. Guy ditches his treat and leaps up in my lap.

He hasn't slept on the bed with me since the accident. He lies near the closest door with a sad face. The guilt eats me when I think about it. I haven't been the best partner or owner to him.

"I've missed you, boy." I run my nose along his soft curly hair. "I'm trying to get better."

He turns, licking my face like he understands what I'm saying. I'm greedy keeping Guy on my lap long after the sun disappears. His large body and thick coat of curly hair keeps me warm. As a small child, the dark used to be my biggest fear to the point of developing a phobia. I'd crawl in my momma's bed even though every single night she tucked me in safe and sound in my own.

Now the dark skies comfort me. I remain in the same position until it's too cold and I'm forced to head into the camper. Guy trucks behind, stopping only to pick up his rawhide. I watch as he enters the trailer ahead of me, making bounding up the steps look easy.

I'm expecting him to run to the couch or settle in by his dog dishes near the door. But he shocks me. He leaps into my bed and burrows around in the blankets like he used to do at our old home. And then grabs the rawhide with his teeth and begins working it over.

It sounds crazy and very well could be since I'm skirting around being certifiably insane. The sight soothes a patch of ache in my heart. An emotion other than grief, sadness, and despair strikes me. It's a foreign feeling that has become a stranger to me. It warms me from head to toe. Offering up a glimpse of promise that one day I may choose to live again.

I reach into the cabinet and pull out a new bottle of vodka and mix it with Diet Mountain Dew. It's a change for me instead of drinking straight from the bottle. I sit on the bed, leaning my back against the wall, thinking about the events of today. I survived going to town, that's a plus. I take a long drink of my cocktail. I guess I could say I met a new friend in town. I take another drink. A little boy warmed and broke my heart in the matter of a handful of minutes. I take another long drink.

Guy grows restless with his rawhide and weasels his way over to me. He cuddles up into a ball as close as he can to me. I don't wait because I know exactly what he wants. My hands begin roaming through his hair, my fingers dancing through his curly locks.

My eyelids grow heavy and soon sleep begs to take over. I place my drink on the counter. I drank three-fourths of it, and I'm so tired I can barely keep my eyes open. I strip quickly out of my clothes and climb into Bentley's t-shirt, I find Hope's blanket and tuck it to my chest. I watch Guy to see what he's going to do.

It dawns on me that I've shut him out since the accident. I haven't neglected him, but I haven't welcomed him either. I plop on the bed next to him and watch as he tilts his head to the side. So I pat the bed again. He moves slow and with caution as he creeps up to my side and lies down. Hope's pink blanket lies between us. In this position, it's as if I've created a barrier or a shield between me and the world to protect myself from everyone and anything.

I fluff the blanket out, so he has a piece to lay on, too. What he does next makes me cry in an instant. He sniffs the blanket over and over and then places his cheek on it. I look into his blue eyes that have always made me happy and smile. We are sharing what we had and are making new memories.

I'm not able to keep my eyes open for much longer. They're thick and heavy, and I guess it's from today's events. From floating in the river to my near drowning accident, and peddling five miles to and from town has left me exhausted.

As my eyes flutter shut, I whisper I love you to Bentley and Hope. And then I do something I haven't done in a very long time. I talk to God. I beg him to allow me one night of a peaceful sleep with no threats of a nightmare. And with that, my eyes flutter shut. Guy's rhythmic breathing soothes me into slumber within a matter of seconds.

***

The morning sun shines through the windows of the camper. The light's blinding force makes me bury my head in the pillow.

"Wait." I sit up on the bed, the light sending an immediate headache shooting through my skull. I grab my cell phone that has no service or data and check the time. Ten a.m. I blink once then twice and wipe the sleep from my eyes, and indeed I slept in.

"No way."

Guy pries open his sleep laden eyes and peers up at me. I smile at him and his grumpy expression. I haven't slept that long in months. And I use the word sleep loosely because it generally never comes and when it does, it's riddled with my living nightmare.

Last night, I remembered not being able to keep my eyes open after not finishing off my cocktail and then falling asleep. I stretch my arms over my head, craning my neck from side-to-side, stretching out my limbs from my fingertips all the way down to my toes. There's no massive throbbing headache, dry cottonmouth, or a queasy stomach. I'm not hungover. Sore legs, aching muscles, but not hungover .

I didn't finish off a bottle last night. It's all too confusing for me at the moment. I get up out of bed and try my new Keurig filter, and it works like Caleb said it would. Quite a handy-dandy little contraption. I'll have to remember to thank him next time I see him. Thoughts of Caleb in the grocery store yesterday makes me grin a shy smile.

I splash some Bailey's in my coffee to help warm me up. I don't need vodka, and it feels good. I throw on my flannel, leggings, and grab Hope's blanket. The crisp mountain air smacks me in the face when I open the door to the trailer. The air is always fresh and crisp in the mornings, waking up every single part of me.

Guy rushes past me, bounding down the steps, barking. It's his defensive bark that makes the hair on the back of my neck stand up. There's a mini cyclone of dust before everything settles. Caleb stands with his hands over his head, backing away in slow motion. There's a truck. There's Caleb. At my trailer. My haven, the place I'm trying to heal.

"Guy!" I leap down from the steps, jogging to him. "Guy, back."

I grab his collar, pulling on him. He growls, and it's a menacing one.

"Easy, boy. This is Caleb." The growling ceases, but Guy stays on high alert, not comfortable with our visitor.

I peer up to Caleb confused and not quite sure what in the hell is going on. Maybe I'm dreaming? Or I drank too much vodka in my sleep? The hell?

"Sorry," Caleb offers. "Wanted to drop this off."

He heaves a fifty-pound bag of dog food off his shoulder onto the ground.

"Wow." My eyes grow wide in shock then a questioning stare takes over my features.

Caleb reads the question printed on my face. "You bought a bunch of dog treats yesterday. Figured you either had a dog or a screwed up diet."

He smirks at me, and I can't help but laugh at his lame joke.

"I'm sorry for yesterday; it was straight-up chaos when you came into the store. I appreciate you helping me out with Fender. And I thought it might be a bitch to haul dog food on your bike. And by the size of the rawhide you bought, I figured you had a pretty big dog."

His gaze goes down to Guy, and he nods his head happy with answering his question.

"Hey!"

I glance over to the truck to see Fender waving out the window. His black hair is as wild as it was yesterday and his cheeks are rosy red. His little hand waves back-and-forth with excitement, as if I can't see him even though he's only fifteen feet away.

I give him a finger wave and smile. And then I see Jed, his dad, in the driver's seat of the truck. He wears the same expression as he did yesterday. The man is angry at the world and miserable. When I make eye contact with them, he pulls his aviators resting on top of his head over his eyes and faces forward.

"Hey, lady." Fender waves both arms at me this time. "Can I pet your dog?"

"No, sit down, son." Fender's face falls into defeat.

Caleb ignores his brother's instructions and pulls Fender from the truck. He sets him on his feet in front of Guy and shows him how to approach a strange dog to make sure he's friendly. It's cute how loving and caring Caleb is with his nephew. Soon Guy is licking Fender's face.

"Leftover syrup from breakfast," Caleb offers.

Fender looks up to the sky, giggling so hard it's contagious.

"Daddy, I made a friend," Fender squeals between licks.

Jed shocks the shit out of me when he gets out of the truck striding toward us. I steady myself prepared for his wrath. He stops next to Fender, and I'm legit scared for the boy. Jed is a mystery. I don't think he'd hurt his kid, but hell, I have no idea who he is or what has him so damn angry.

"Good looking dog." Jed kneels next to Fender, petting Guy's head.

Guy eats up all the attention, leaning into Jed.

"What breed is he?" Jed's deep, gruff voice catches me off guard. It's warm and welcoming, and nothing like I've heard from him before. There are hints of his rich, melodic singing voice as he talks to Guy and Fender. The man has the voice of a God.

"He's uh…an Aussiedoodle." I stumble and trip over each word.

Fender drops to his knees, crawling underneath Guy. "Does he have a wiener?"

The boy is obsessed with wieners. Caleb throws his head back, laughing. The sound is resounding around the mountainsides. Jed joins him, offering up a genuine hint of them being twins. At this moment, they're both carefree.

"Does he, lady?" Fender climbs underneath Guy, peeking out the other side to face me. Dirt and grime now sprinkle over his features.

Before I have a chance to answer him, Jed bends down, picking him up by the hips, and swinging him up and over his head until he's settled on his broad shoulders.

"Her name is Marlee. Use your manners, son."

"Marwee, does he have a wiener?" Fender runs his hands through his dad's thick wavy hair.

I nod. "Yes, he's a boy."

Fender's eyes sparkle. "I haves a big wiener you know, and that's why took me so long to wee."

Jed's the first to laugh, but cuts it short biting down on his bottom lip. "Caleb, this is all your doing, you know. Since we've moved back, it's all you two talk about."

"Wieners?" The one word in the form of a question slips from my lips before I can stop it.

"It's our manhood and pride by damn."

I grab the flannel shirt, wrapping it tight around my body, clutching to Hope's blanket. "Thank you to you and your uncle for bringing my Guy some dog food. I wasn't sure how I was going to get it back on my bike."

"You have a doll?" Fender points to the plush pink blanket.

"No. I...uh."

Jed steers the conversation in an opposite direction, pointing at my bike. "Doesn't look like you'd make it very far anyway."

I turn to see two flat tires on my bike. Well, shit. My shoulders sag defeated. I quite enjoyed the adventure yesterday, especially if working out my body allows me to sleep in peace.

"Well, that sucks." I chew on my thumb.

Jed strides over to the bike, picking it up with one hand while keeping Fender balanced on his shoulders. It's hard not to admire his body. He walks it right to his truck, tossing it in the back of the old-style, sleek black Ford.

"What are you doing?" I ask, fear in my voice.

"Stealing your piece of shit bike. What the hell does it look like?"

Caleb slaps Jed in the back of the head. The men exchange a few heated words. A switch flips with Jed, and it's right back to the dark, broody man who is suffering in his misery.

Fender turns to me. "Banky says Dad is ponstipated all the time."

"Damn right, the grumpy ass is," Caleb murmurs loud enough for all to hear.

Jed ignores the jabs while he buckles Fender in the backseat safely in his booster seat. Fender begins humming a popular country song I can't place. That humming does something to me.

"Enjoy the bike," I whisper to myself.

Caleb and Fender both wave as Jed backs out in his truck. But it's not them who hold my attention. Jed looks over to me for a long time, and even though he's wearing glasses, I can tell he's studying me. He's stripping away all of my exterior.

Chapter 22

"Love is a trap. When it appears, we see only its light, not its shadows." -Paulo Coelho

I've been determined to chase sleep similar to a few nights ago. The following evening, I chalked it up to being saved from the nightmares. It was the biggest lie I've ever told myself, and I'll be the first to admit that. I woke up in a cold sweat and reached for the bottle without thinking. It offered a few hours of uninterrupted sleep with the side effects of a glorious hangover.

The next day I picked the tallest mountain I could find and hiked up as far as I could go. My lungs threatened to collapse, every muscle in my body screamed in protest, but I pushed through it. That night sleep came.

I did the same thing last night, pushing my body to exhaustion damn near to the fine line of its breaking point determined to avoid nightmares. I woke up once again nightmare free before dawn. It's a small victory, one that offers a positive new pattern of life. I stretch out and go about my morning routine. Albeit much slower and with lots of groaning. It hurts to sit on the toilet. It hurts to stand, walk, and breathe. It's the first time my body has been alive in a long time.

The adrenaline and high my body gets from working out are becoming my new addiction. Guy stands at the door whimpering as I stir a splash of Bailey's into my coffee.

"Just a sec, boy." I button up the flannel,

knowing the morning's briskness will be a good one. It's been growing colder and colder in the mornings. As soon as the door is open, he bolts out of it, not letting one of his paws touch a single step. He takes after a bird, barking up a storm the whole way. It's become one of his favorite pastimes. He scares them away, waits for a new one to return, and repeats the process over and over.

A familiar black truck rolls into my campsite in front of the rising sun. I use my hands to shade my eyes, only able to make out a silhouette. As soon as the figure steps out, I know it's Jed from his slightly trimmer build.

I walk up to the truck, cupping my coffee in my palms, blowing on the steaming hot liquid. This man has been hot and cold, to say the least. The last thing I want is small talk when I'm suffering in my misery, so I stand here studying him.

He reaches into the bed of his truck and pulls out my bike. The muscles covered by his black t-shirt strain as he does it. The shirt is pulled taut across his broad chest. I notice how tan he is. Even up in the mountains, he's as handsome as he was on all of his album covers. Possibly even sexier in his rugged state. His jawline is covered in a light scruff. His eyes aren't covered with sunglasses today.

He sets the bike between us. Something jangles, pulling my attention to it. A leash and a brand new dog collar shine brightly. The tires are aired up. We stand for a long time staring at each other. Neither of us saying a word or making a move. I sip from my coffee and Jed reaches for the leash.

It's then I notice the large bruises on the inside of his arms. Track marks? Is he a recovering addict? Would explain his highs and lows that much is certain.

I look back to his eyes and notice he followed my line of sight. He places the bike back where it was when he picked it up the other day without asking and walks right back to his truck. He slams the door and settles in behind the wheel and glances over to me.

I'm not sure why, but I can tell there's so much more he wants to say but doesn't.

"You have time for coffee?" I worry my bottom lip, regretting the question.

Jed drops his hand from the ignition, shoulders relax, and he nods, making me stumble over my own feet. I glance around my campsite to see a broken down picnic table and one chair. It's not much.

"I'll be right back."

Jed gives me a jerk of his head as he climbs back out of his truck. I fumble around with the coffee grounds, making a damn mess. My hands tremble packing the filter. Soon the Keurig fires to life with a hot stream of coffee pouring into a generic mug that came with the Airstream.

I turn to holler at the door and see Jed standing in the doorway.

"Shit." I clutch my chest. "You scared me."

"Sorry." He shrugs. "Love these style of campers, just taking a peek."

I don't like him in here. It makes my skin crawl.

"How do you take your coffee?"

He points to the unopened bottle of vodka on the counter. "And a dash of creamer."

"Okay." I turn back to the coffee mug, battling to control my breathing.

No one has ever been in this camper with me since it's been parked in the mountains. I wouldn't enter it when the salesman was setting stuff up. This is my place painted with my own memories. No one is welcome. Not even a mysterious, famous country singer.

The stairs creak as he walks back down them and my shoulders sag in relief. I can breathe. I stir his coffee and follow him outside. He's perched on top of the rickety picnic table. His bronzed, rugged hand roams over the rough, splintered top of the picnic table. Head bowed deep in thought.

"Here." I hold the mug out in front of me.

He nods and grabs it. "Thanks."

"Least I can do for fixing my bike."

He answers with his stare and no words. I back up, grab my mug off the arm of my chair, and take a seat. We drink in silence not saying a word. The birds sing in the trees, the river racing away, and the refreshing breeze is whirling around us.

My heart still pounds in my chest from the sight of him in the doorway of my camp trailer. My stare goes from Jed's stoic silhouette to the bright clear blue skies. As the minutes drift by, the situation doesn't grow awkward. I find myself relaxed back in the chair with my tanned legs kicked out in front of me; another perk of living in the mountains.

I take the final swallow of my coffee. "Want

another cup of Joe?"

Jed looks over at me and smiles. It's not a full teeth megawatt one just a glimpse of one making his dimples come to life, and his mesmerizing rich dark honey eyes shine for a beat.

"Please." He goes to stand up.

I beat him to it. "I'll get it."

This time I shut the screen door and main door behind, leaving no room for question. I feel like a bitch. I trust him and maybe I shouldn't. I'm not ready. I put another splash of Bailey's in my cup and doctor up Jed's coffee. I use my elbows and balancing skills to get the door open. Jed's focused on the river not noticing me.

"Here you go," I whisper, not wanting to spook him.

"Thanks, Marlee."

My name rolling off his lips does something to me, making my stomach roll in excitement, and then it goes sick. I shouldn't be feeling. This is wrong.

Jed reaches out, placing his large hand on my arm holding my mug of coffee. I flinch. Jed runs his fingers over my prickled skin. He soothes it out with his words. "I needed this. I need a friend, Marlee. Thank you."

I roll my lips between my teeth digesting his words. He has no idea how bad I need a friend as well.

"Ditto," I whisper.

He drops his hand from my arm, and I shiver, trying to hide by briskly walking over to my chair. My skin burns, coming to life where his hand once was. We sit in silence finishing our second cup of coffee.

"Much appreciated, Marlee." He stands up, stretching, and then putting his hands in his pockets. His low rise, well-worn jeans dip a bit with the action.

"You good to drive?" I ask, picking up his mug from the picnic table.

He smirks. "Yes, takes a hell of a lot more than that to even get me buzzed."

"Thank you, Jed."

He raises his eyebrows. "Back to reality."

His long strides carry him easily to his truck. The roar of the engine rattles my insides, and he's gone. I walk over to the bike and notice he didn't air up the tires. He replaced them with brand new ones and the tread looks to be thicker and sturdier. The dog leash dangles off the handlebars. I grab the manly leash and collar, running my fingers over the smooth leather.

Guy has always worn the collar Bentley and I picked out for him. It's worn and fading. Maybe it's time? I shake the thought away as quickly as it entered my train of thought.

He brought a leash and a collar so Guy could go with me on bike rides. To say I'm confused and dumbfounded is an understatement. I think about those marks on his arms and feel guilty for my first thought of it being track marks. It could be anything; he could be sick, or I guess have a drug problem.

I haven't been connected to the Internet since living out here; it's been a breath of fresh air being disconnected from society. But right now, I would do anything for a quick Google search on country's biggest singer, Jed Bryant. The news would have to be plastered all over the World Wide Web because someone of his stature doesn't quit singing without heads turning.

Chapter 23

"To love oneself is the beginning of a lifelong romance."
-Oscar Wilde

Jed has been by the last week for morning coffee. We sit in silence and drink. I look forward to it. He comes earlier, right before the sun peeks over the mountains and only drinks two cups to be home when Fender shows up. There's been minimal conversation between us. I know his parents are on a trip and will be home shortly. He hates helping run the grocery store and despises vegetables.

The early afternoon drags on with me sitting in my chair toes in the river, going over the entire situation. Guy is on repeat bringing me a stick, waiting for me to toss it, galloping after it, and then repeats the action over and over.

I don't beat myself up over the night my life ended, as I know it. I bring my fingertips up to the side of my face where a scar lives. It's narrow and a few inches long. The rest I'm able to hide underneath my clothes and in my soul. I miss Bentley every second of every day, but right now it's dulled a bit. My heart is finding a new rhythm, allowing me to survive. I glance over to the bike, biting down on my bottom lip.

After making a quick peanut butter and jelly sandwich for lunch, an idea strikes me. Caleb didn't have to bring the dog food. Jed didn't have to fix my bike. But they did. They're good men. Not to mention Jed is the best coffee companion.

I rummage around in my cupboards not seeing much. It's not like I can whip up an apple pie or cake. So I grab the closest thing to a dessert. A box of frosted strawberry Pop-Tarts. I shrug my shoulders and then shake my head. It's mountain life, you do the best with what you have. And it's the idea that counts and more important with me it's all about the effort. I'm stepping out of my comfort zone.

Guy and I used to go on walks all the time. He would always be waiting at the door when I got home with his leash dangling from his slobbery mouth. He'd nudge the side of my thigh until I was so tired of him pestering me that I'd give in and take him on a walk out to the pond or to Mom's house.

His ears perk up when he hears the rattle of the leash. The new collar clutched in my hand burns my skin. He's at my side in a beat. His tail waggles and his body wiggles in untamed excitement. Guy's joy urges me to go on.

"Here goes nothing." My fingers tremble unhooking his old one. Tears fall. Memories flood me. All of it wrapped up in the old collar. Once the new one is fastened around his neck, I clutch his old one to my chest. Memories. A new chapter. It hurts to try, but I want to. Guy nudges my leg with his nose, showing off his new pretty.

"Darn handsome, mister." I lean down, kiss his head, and wipe away the tears.

His excitement is uncontainable, making me a bit nervous to be riding a bike with him on the other end of this leash. I've never ridden a bicycle and walk a dog or would that be called riding the dog? I slap my forehead, giggling. It would not be called riding the dog.

Laughter escapes me with my thoughts. It feels foreign and odd, but no guilt hits me from enjoying a good chuckle. I keep Guy on my right side as I begin to truck down the paved road. I keep the leash short to avoid any oncoming traffic. Just like I thought, he starts out strong, giving me no time to warm up my legs. I'm pedaling as fast as I can, keeping an eye on the tail end of Guy who is running with all his might.

His ears flap with his movement. I get peeks and glimpses of his tongue hanging out of his mouth as his legs fly down the road. He learns my speed, and I grow accustomed to his speed, and soon we settle into a comfortable pace.

The basket Jed put on the bike comes in handy, especially when having Guy on the end of the leash. I missed the basket and rack he installed on my bike at first glance.

Nestled between the front handlebar is a white wicker basket. I don't have to worry about balancing any grocery bags on my handlebars and pay attention to Guy. The metal rack installed on the back is perfect for hauling several bags of groceries back home.

As I peddle, my lungs work overtime. Adrenaline courses through my body, creating a natural high. My daily mountain climbs have shaped up my legs, but it's still a push on my body. I feel alive again, living.

My mind drifts to Jed. I'm more determined to figure out the puzzle of the man he is. I pedal into the store to find the parking lot empty. Nothing like the other day when there were several customers. I grow frantic, wondering if they're closed on certain days of the week or maybe shut down for a few hours of the day. Reality slaps me upside the head...I know little to nothing about the dynamics of this town or family. I'm walking in the dark with no light. Jumping into the deep end with no life preserver.

I get off the bike and tug Guy to me and pat him then kiss the top of his head. When I stand back up, I notice the open sign and also the no pets allowed printed underneath it.

"Well, shit," I whisper to myself.

I didn't think that one through very well now, did I? I swivel around to walk down to the river to get Guy a drink of water since he's panting up a storm. As I do, the door to the store flies open, slamming into the center brick wall.

Fender's hand waves frantically as he runs toward me shouting my name. Even though he's shouting my name, it's not me he wants to see. He skids on his knees across the gravel and dirt, not making eye contact and I'm thankful for the jeans he's wearing.

Guy is as excited to see him. His tongue darts out, lapping up Fender's face with doggy kisses. The two roll around on the ground, Fender giggling and Guy enjoying all of the attention. Before long, the two are both dirtballs.

"Fender!"

I look up to see Jed storming out of the store. As soon as he sees his son, his whole body relaxes, the tension leaving. He runs his hands through his dark hair, making it stand up on end. There are dark lines underneath his eyes. He looks stressed and like shit. I've noticed his skin color change over the days.

I muster up the confidence to wave. "Hey, stopping by to bring you Bryant guys a thank you gift."

I peer over at the basket where the stupid box of Pop-Tarts rests. This might be one of the dumbest decisions I've ever made. Like these three men need a box of Pop-Tarts! They own a whole goddamn grocery store, and more than likely have a cabin with an oven, fridge, and stove where they could make a lot more things than a toasted freaking Pop-Tart.

Jed walks over to Fender, kneeling down next to him. He ruffles Guy and Fender's hair, glances over at me, gifting me with one of his sexy head jerks, and sighs, the tension building right back up. Then he cups his son's cheek, making him look at him.

"Fender, what have I told you about running off and not telling me where you are going?" Jed's voice is stern but not mean or menacing.

Fender drops his face into the top of Guy's head and mumbles. "I sorry, Dad. I got so sited when I saw my best fwiend."

Jed grabs his son, pulling him to his chest, hugging him tightly. "Fender, that's a good thing to be sorry and admit it. Thank you. I know sometimes things get a bit exciting and you forget to tell me where you are going. You need to try hard to tell me where you're going next time. Even though Moore is a small town and everybody knows you, it's no different than when we were on the tour bus going from city to city. Do you understand me?"

Fender doesn't respond with words, but his little head bobs up-and-down against his dad's firm and steady chest. Jed kisses the top of his head and rubs circles on his back with his loving hand.

His arms are covered in a flannel shirt. It's then I notice Jed looks like he's been out chopping wood or working on something with his hands. He's covered in dust, smears of dirt on his face and arms.

"Well, what do we have here?"

I look up to see Caleb striding out with a big smile on his face. He doesn't hesitate, making his way to wrap me in a hug. His thick arms go around me, pulling me to his chest. My body slams into his, and I remain stiff as a board. Caleb doesn't seem to catch onto it because he doesn't stop hugging me for seconds. It's all a friendly gesture and what I've come to expect from this man from the couple of times that I've met him.

He steps back and plants both hands on his hips. "Just in time for the family fishing trip, Marlee."

My eyes go wide. The single phrase family fishing trip sends trepidation through my body.

"No." I shake my head and fidget with the hem of my old t-shirt. "I wanted to bring you guys something for being so kind to me."

I hold up the box of Pop-Tarts with a weak smile. "I know this looks cheesy and is stupid. You can tell me it's stupid. But I'm thankful for how kind you guys have been to me from bringing dog food and Jed for fixing my bike.

"It took a lot for me to venture into town and you guys made it easy on me. I would've baked an apple pie or something more spectacular, but the old Airstream makes it kind of hard to do that."

Caleb grabs the box of Pop-Tarts from my hands, letting out a victory cry. Fender bolts into action, taking after Caleb, leaping up his body trying to grab the Pop-Tarts from him. Jed shakes his head and stands up, brushing off his tattered jeans. They're worn and well broke in with tears along the front of his legs. It does something to me.

He walks over to his brother and son who are fighting over a box of sixteen count strawberry frosted Pop-Tarts. The whole scene is confusing. I'd guess Jed is about to slap Caleb in the head and roar out a warning, but there's a sly smile on his face. His bow-tie, angel lips frame his pearly whites.

Caleb doesn't notice Jed sneaking up on him from behind as he continues to taunt Fender with the box of Pop-Tarts. Jed's long arm reaches over and grabs the box. It takes Caleb and Fender a few seconds to realize they've both been played. Jed tears the top of the box open then rips into a package. His large, strong hands I've admired strumming a guitar on his music videos sandwiches two Pop-Tarts together and takes a huge bite. Damn near, downing half of them in one bite.

"Thank you, Marlee. Something you need to know about us Bryant boys is that we take our Pop-Tart game very seriously.

"We couldn't figure out who bought the last box of the strawberry ones and it put us all in a shitty mood. You're more than welcome for me fixing your bike. Hope it's working well for you."

He barely gets the last word out before Caleb has him wrapped in a headlock and bent over. Fender reacts without a second thought, grabbing both the box and the pastries his dad was chowing on. There wasn't much left of his little sandwich.

"Got 'em, Banky." Fender jumps up and down in victory, holding them above his head. "Dad, you is a sucker."

Fender is up and over Jed's arm in a flash. Caleb saves the damn Pop-Tarts before Jed begins spinning in circles and tickling Fender's sides. The joy streaming from Fender is contagious until Fender declares his big wiener needs to go pee. Jed jolts inside for the bathroom. His long legs eat up the parking lot until he disappears into the store.

"Where is his mom?" I shake my head. "Never mind, I shouldn't have asked that."

Caleb shrugs, getting to enjoy a Pop-Tart. "Naw, it's okay. She's a bitch. Left when Fender was a week old. Jed never really loved her. He knocked her up, and she wanted to continue her career in being a groupie in the country music scene and not a mom. Jed's raised him ever since even while touring the world. That little boy has seen more of the world than I ever will."

I open my mouth, but there are no words even to begin to respond to what he shared. Caleb waits for a few beats before continuing to spill their life history.

"Mom and Dad moved here six years ago after our family went through hell. They bought the store, bar, and restaurant and have been running it ever since. Having their only two children home has been good for their spirits and well around here since old age isn't being nice to them, it makes them feel more at peace. Jed was busy on tour and still made the time to make short visits, but now he's back home."

My curiosity is overwhelming, dying to know more about the hell his family endured. Call it misery loves company or some shit like that. Caleb's shoulders fall, and that simple gesture tells me it has more to do with him than Jed.

The phone inside the store begins ringing with a shrill. The door is left wide open from when Jed and Fender busted in. Caleb gets a devilish grin, and he winks at me.

"Hey, mind going and grabbing that for me? And I'll go grab you a fishing pole."

I take a step back, shaking my head, refusing to step foot into that store. I have the man all figured out. Somehow, he sensed I was going to bolt and not go fishing with them. But if he has me answer the phone and he goes and grabs a fishing pole, there's no way I can escape.

"Come on, Marlee, you'd make Fender's day. We have a pretty cool spot where there's a fishing hole and also a low stream Guy and Fender could play in."

With each word, Caleb takes a step back until he's almost to a little shed off to the side of the store.

"Dammit," I whisper.

He has my back pressed up against the wall, leaving me with no choice. The phone rings another time, and I dart inside the store, round the counter, and answer the phone. I stumble, opening my mouth not recalling the name of the store. How in the hell am I answering the phone in a store that I don't even know the name of? This is ridiculous.

I open my mouth again and answer with a simple hello.

"Is this the Bryant's Store?" The voice is confused on the other end.

I clear my throat. "Yes, it is."

"Oh, okay. Is Jed Bryant available?"

I shake my head nervous for some reason and then realize the person on the other end cannot see me.

"He's busy right now. Can I take a message for him?"

"Yes, please. This is Sandra with the Intermountain Cancer Institute, and we need to talk to him as soon as he has a free minute."

My hand begins to tremble around the phone. "Okay. Does he have your phone number?"

The lady lets out a sigh on the other end. "Mr. Bryant surely does have our number and knows the extension to my direct line."

I pause dumbfounded not able to understand

any of this. "Okay, I will be sure to relay the message. Thank you."

I hang up the phone, the sound of the receiver hitting the base echoes around the empty store. Cancer. The Intermountain Cancer Institute. None of it makes sense. It can't be true. My first thought goes to Fender, but he's a healthy little boy. One of the most active kids I've seen in my life. He's always running on the tip of his toes excited about life.

The sound of Fender running down an aisle pulls me from my thoughts. Maybe it's a fundraiser or donation that Jed Bryant donates to regularly? He is, after all, a country star. Maybe they want him to perform for a fundraiser? That has to be it.

My gut's telling me it's none of those things. It's much, much bigger than anything I can process. So massive that it may make a person hate life. A problem that erases a career from a man who was on top of the world in the country music scene. A problem so horrific it has turned a man into a skeleton of despair and anger.

I look up to see Fender sprinting out of the door, hollering over his shoulder, telling his dad he's going to find Banky. I don't know the whole story or even the reason behind it, but I'm assuming it's because Fender wasn't able to pronounce Caleb's name and Banky stuck. Ironically, it's a good fit for the goof.

Jed stops on the other side of the counter, placing his palms down, staring at me. I feel like my face says it all, yet I don't know where to begin.

"Was the phone ringing?" he asks, leaning on

the counter.

I nod, and he waits for me to go on. He scared me from the first time I met him with his pissy attitude, but the rest of the time he's been respectful, gentle, and quiet.

It all makes sense now. He's sick.

I clear my throat and steady my voice before speaking. "It was Sandra calling for you."

I'm too big of a chicken shit and coward to give any more details. He nods. A simple reassurance letting me know he doesn't need any other details on who was calling. I want to say something else to him, offer up some comfort, or even just be a friend with a listening ear. I know more than anyone how infuriating it is to have people wanting to help you when there's not a damn thing they can do.

Words are useless when you're so fucking hurt you barely manage to put one foot in front of the other. A scab torn from a wound that's been infected time and time again when someone asks how you're doing or offers help. All it does is pump poison through your veins, making your wound seep.

Caleb leans his head in, letting out a little whistle. I look over to him to see his hands on each side of the door jamb, leaning in as if he was going in for a push-up. He has a grin plastered on his face, but that's typical for him. I've only seen him flustered when the orders were messed up, and I had to help Fender to the restroom.

And it all comes together making sense in a crystal clear picture. He's the glue, the backbone, the foundation keeping this family held together. Everybody handles stress, anxiety, and worries in a different way. Some of us show up and run away, some of us grow fearful and frightened and quit living, while others are able to joke and laugh remaining resolute for the best outcome. There's no doubt in my mind that's what Caleb is doing for his twin brother right now.

"Damn, girl, you look good behind the counter." Caleb lets out another little whistle. "How much for that milkshake you rocking back there?"

Jed pushes off the counter, shaking his head. "Jesus, Caleb, do you ever give up?"

Caleb mirrors his twin brother's action, pushing off the door jamb. "Can't keep a good guy down or that's what I've heard in one of your cheesy-ass country songs."

"Get me to the goddamn river to fish. I need a beer in my hand and some distance from you, dip shit." Jed walks right past Caleb and outside.

I turn and look through the window to see Jed scooping up Fender in his arms, tossing him up in the air and bringing him right back down to his chest. Fender cups the cheeks of his dad, bringing their noses together. And then grows restless in his dad's arms, but Jed doesn't let him down.

He grabs the back of his head and brings his lips to Fender's forehead. I watch as he squeezes his eyes shut, his body full of tension and anxiety as he takes a minute to soak in his perfect son.

Caleb clears his throat. I didn't realize he was now standing next to me watching the same scene.

"It ain't good, Marlee."

Tears well up in my eyes, threatening to spill over. But they're not for me. They don't represent my loss and everything I endured. No, it's for the little, sweet, innocent boy clutched to his dad's strong chest who has no idea his dad is sick.

The tears fall for the man holding a little boy who knows he's sick and more than likely dying. I have no idea how I would've felt if I knew my days were numbered before the accident. What would I have done knowing day in and day out I was going to lose it all?

Would I have grown bitter and angry? Yes, I would've because how else do you manage to survive and embrace life when you know your days are numbered?

We stand shoulder to shoulder, looking out the window. Jed's lips are still pressed to Fender's forehead. Caleb's fingers lace in mine and we stand here watching the beautiful moment hand-in-hand.

Caleb is the first to talk and it comes out as a whisper. "So do you want to go fishing with us?"

I go back to the question I was running through my mind earlier, how would I have lived knowing Bentley and Hope's days were numbered, and I only had a handful of them left to live and experience the wonder and enjoyment of being pregnant? I don't know what the answer would've been back then. But I sure do know what it is now.

Fender loves Guy and Guy loves Fender. I enjoy Caleb's company, and if I'm honest, he keeps my mind off the past. I'm intrigued by Jed. I have been since the day he came into the store growling like a rabid beast. There's something there, and if I can be of any help or assistance to him, I will be. I know with a shattered and tattered heart like mine, I'm not the best person to offer comfort or a solid foundation for somebody, but the entire situation tugs at my heartstrings. It's the same sensation I had the day I tried to drown. A higher power is nudging me in the back.

"Sure." I shrug.

Caleb claps his hands together. "Good. Company is always good. Thank you, Marlee."

Caleb kisses the side of my head. There's nothing sexual about it. I feel the relief flow from his body. He's exhausted.

Chapter 24

"a sky full of stars and he was staring at her"
Atticus

"What's your story?" Caleb nods his chin my direction.

I can't take my gaze away from Jed and Fender downstream. Fender is loving his dad tossing him in the water. Jed pretends to get sucked into the water when Fender tugs on his leg. Ain't no fish going to be caught with this damn ruckus around us. I'm used to it by now. All three of the Bryant men were shocked I was able to out fish them. It always starts out serious then Jed and Fender end up in the water.

It's still all the same. I'm out fishing with friends.

"What?" I ask Caleb.

"What's your story?" he repeats.

I look over at him and then back upstream. Fender splashes out of the water to Guy who is sunning on a set of rocks while Jed strides over to us. He pops the lid on the cooler, reaching in for a cold beer.

Over the last several fishing trips, we've seem to grow more comfortable with each other. They've never pried or asked any questions until now. Caleb was an open book from day one or at least appeared to be. Jed, on the other hand, has kept his distance, but has warmed up to me in his own time. I catch him staring at me. We both find every excuse to brush past each other for no reason.

"Your story, Marlee?" Caleb takes a step closer, keeping an eye on his line. "Ain't no one like you come out here without a story. We all got one that haunts us, bringing us to the mountains."

Jed stares me down. Even though Caleb's question is directed at me. It's been two weeks since I answered the phone. Days of wondering, wanting to know more, but haven't asked. I've noticed Jed's absence recently. I miss our coffee dates. I stare right back at Jed, answering Caleb's question.

"I was driving. My husband just returned home from deployment. I was in my last trimester of pregnancy with our little girl, Hope. A truck ran a red light, killing both of them."

It's a black and white answer covering all the bases. The flat tone of my voice showcasing how hollow I am. Jed swallows, the Adam's apple in his throat flexing. His knuckles grow white around the beer bottle. Caleb clears his throat but doesn't attempt to say a word.

"I ran from our home and our family. I call my mom every once in a while, checking in with her. I couldn't stand to stay there any longer." The more I talk, the better it makes me feel. "Picked Moore, Idaho, bought a trailer, my dog, fishing pole, and few other items. Drink myself drunk most nights to keep the nightmares away, but those nights are becoming fewer and fewer."

Fender streaks through our conversation, singing a song at the top of his lungs. He shoves his dad out of the way to get to the cooler. Jed moves with ease, still processing my words. He doesn't send me a pitying stare.

"I'm sorry, Marlee." Is all he says before he bends over to help Fender make a turkey sandwich layered with barbecue potato chips.

I brought my own pole today. Haven't cast it in over a year. The material burns the tender skin of my palm as I cast it out. Guy is at my side, laying his head on my leg. He's my person, knowing the feat I'm overcoming right now. The water remains calm since Fender is sitting on a blanket eating a sandwich. Jed relaxes down next to him, tipping back his beer.

He never offered up the information, but Caleb did. Jed's going to town tomorrow to begin the process of beating cancer. Caleb asked if I could help out at the store since their parents will be taking Jed. They've been home for three days. It all boiled down to me helping out with Fender. I didn't even have to think twice about it.

The silence that has fallen over us isn't awkward or thick with tension. We're all going through dark times, fighting to find a glimpse of light to bask in. We're on the same team.

"You got a bite."

I turn back to see Fender's head propped on Jed's thigh with half of his sandwich left in one hand while he sleeps. Jed has his arms behind him, hands planted on the blanket, and legs spread wide.

I turn back to the fishing pole and sure as shit, I have a fish on the other end. I freeze.

"Marlee." My name comes out in a soft, caring tone from Jed's lips. "You can do it."

I nibble on my bottom lip, focusing on his words. My hands begin to reel in the pole in slow and precise movements. I give the pole a jerk like Papa Wally taught me and continue to reel. Soon a large rainbow trout pops up from the water.

"Nice one," Caleb cheers.

Once the fish is in, I grab it and go about unhooking it. The sharp point of the hook piercing my skin, causing blood to drain from my body. I gasp from the jolt of pain and then smile. I have blood in my body; my heart beats stable and steady, I'm living. I bring my scarred finger to my lips and kiss it.

Happy tears form in my eyes. I keep them at bay. Once the fish is off the hook, I place it in the cooler filled with ice. Once the cooler lid closes, it's as if I'm closing a door on a part of my life. Not forgetting, but closing the memories and regrets that haunt me. They'll always be a part of me. But it's time.

I wash my hands off in the river and dry them on my pants before sitting on the blanket.

"Hungry?" Jed asks in a low voice.

I nod.

"You can have the rest of mine if you want?" He holds out the sandwich wrapped in a paper towel.

"Not hungry?" I ask.

"No." He grabs his beer, being careful to not rustle Fender and takes a long pull. "Gotta get all these in now."

I smirk at him and take a bite of the fully loaded turkey sandwich. The Bryant boys not only take their Pop-Tarts serious but food in general. I've learned that much over the last few weeks.

"Hey." I wipe the corner of my mouth with a piece of the paper towel. "You wouldn't happen to know about anything funny going on around my campsite?"

"Funny?" He raises an eyebrow.

"You could also consider it fishy or someone having too much free time on his hands." I take another bite and damn, the man knows how to make a good sandwich. Mine always turn out dry. I either don't use enough slices of lunch meat or my bread is super dry.

"Like?" He pries.

"Where should I start? Seems a little elf has been making nightly visits. I now have four matching chairs to lounge in. They appear to be made by hand. Gorgeous, I might add. The rickety picnic table that was out front is now sturdy with a coat of red paint. Also, a new clothes line is pulled tight between trees, and it's the perfect height for me to reach."

He leans back on one elbow, twisting his torso to face me, yet keeping his thigh still. Fender sleeps through all of it.

"Don't forget about the fire pit." He winks.

I uncross my legs, kick off my shoes, and bring my knees to my chest, taking the last bite of the sandwich. "Why?"

I lean over and brush the crumbs from my fingers over the rocks instead of on the blanket and toss the paper towel over to the fish cooler. I clutch my knees, waiting on his answer. He holds out his hand to me. I stare at it for a long time before tentatively reaching out for him.

He tugs me to him until we are face-to-face, our positions mirroring one another. I rest my cheek in my palm and wait for his answer.

"Because we all need someone."

"How did you know?"

"Know what?" he asks.

"I needed someone."

"You've changed since the first day I met you. You're starting to smile more. You ride your bike to town on a daily basis." He pauses, studying my lips, and there's no mistaking that both of us want this. "And mostly because I like to see you smile."

"You do?" I whisper, a flush of heat covering my face.

He nods.

"You don't like to stand in the woods and wait for my reaction in the mornings, do you?"

He chuckles softly. "No, you have a good imagination, Marlee."

I throw my head back. "Ahhhh. Well, thank you. You haven't stopped in for coffee for a while."

"Don't like missing when Fender wakes up. He's starting to wake up earlier and earlier. Don't know how, but he is. The coffee was damn good though. I've been missing it."

"And the company?" I ask, glancing down river to see Caleb with his pole in the water. The man loves to fish.

"Nice. Really nice."

He leans in. I lean in. Our lips brush against each other's. It's surreal. Jed's the first to move, deepening the kiss. I find myself matching each of his actions. It's over too soon and before I can blink, we are both pulling back. It was a perfect, tender, sweet kiss.

"Will you sing to me?" I have no idea where that request came from.

Jed Bryant smiles. I've seen a genuine smile on his face a few times. His dimples frame his lips, and he slowly nods his head.

"Might be a bit rusty." He tucks his chin to his chest. "Got any requests?"

"You? Rusty?" I shake my head back and forth. "No way and don't tell me you're going to get shy on me now."

"Haven't sung other than in the shower, while working, or to Fender in a long damn time."

"How long?" I ask. A barrier between us has been torn down, letting the unanswered questions free.

"Six months."

"Do you miss it?"

He nods. "Have a benefit concert coming up in Boise. Just hope I'm well enough to follow through on the commitment."

"Tell me about it." I should regret the request, but I don't.

Caleb and him pushed me to get my past out, and now it's his turn to share.

"Stage two appendix cancer." He keeps his voice low and stares at me. "Was feeling like shit. Had severe lower abdominal pain. My manager made me go to the doctor for a complete physical. That's when they found the cancer and took a hundred different tests. Came home as soon as I got the news. Tomorrow is the big day where my treatment plan will be laid out."

He barely gets his last word out before my lips are back on his. I kiss him this time, pouring all of my heartache and his into it. We're both shattered remnants, clinging on for survival.

Fender begins to rustle around on Jed's thigh.

"Thank you, Marlee."

Jed leans back and without warning begins singing one of his most popular songs, "Lost." It's a raw song about being lost in the world with a shattered heart and no home. It's beautiful when accompanied with instruments and his band. With him singing, it's downright bone-chilling. I can't help the shiver that races through my body. He doesn't break eye contact until the last verse. His eyes slam shut, and he puts everything he has into it.

Fender wakes from his nap, enjoying the last bit of his daddy's singing. He climbs up into his lap with sleepy eyes, wiping at them until he has his arms wrapped around Jed's neck. Fender's tiny voice joins his dad for the final part.

"More, Daddy. More, pwease."

Jed kisses his forehead. "You pick this time."

Fender jumps to his feet, strums his arm in the air, and gives the air a good pelvis thrust. "Ain't nuffin but a hound dog."

"I knew it," Jed muttered and then joined his son.

He picks up singing along with Fender keeping the pace of the song. Jed's deep, gravelly voice booms out; he taps the rhythm of the song out on his leg. He's one of those singers that you'd immediately recognize his voice like Brantley Gilbert or Jason Aldean.

Before the final words of the song are finished, Fender throws his hand out, stopping Jed. "Johnny Trash!"

"Cash," Jed corrects him.

"Trash, that's what I said."

Caleb joins us on the blanket, holding up his phone. "Here you go, little man."

The opening of the song begins to play. Fender strums his air guitar and instructs his dad to do the same. I'm mesmerized by Jed's fingers as he plays his air guitar with his son. Precise movements and I guarantee he's playing the right chords. I could watch and listen to this all night. And that's exactly what we do until the sun goes to sleep behind the mountains.

Chapter 25

"Always be brave." –HJ Bellus

Caleb insisted on leaving his truck at my place, so I didn't have to ride to the store at the crack of dawn. He pushed and pushed, but in the end, I won out. Driving may be one thing I never do. It's a trigger even when I think about it.

The upside of riding into town this early is the chilly temperatures and vacant roads. Guy stays out in front of the bike, acting as if he's the pace car. He knows where we're going. He always bounds right into the store, ignoring the no pets allowed warning.

I used to pull him out only to have Fender wrap his little fingers around his collar and drag him right back into the store. He parades him down the aisles, back into the storage room, and then out back past his playground set.

This morning the store is quiet. The clouds portraying the brooding mood stirring inside of me. The familiar bell above the door sings out. Caleb turns to me. There's no smile, crack of a joke, or carefree attitude. It's all gone. He's worried for his twin.

"Hey," I squeak out.

He sends me a quick jerk of his head and goes back to counting the money in the cash register. "Fender is still out. Mom, Dad, and Jed just pulled out. You missed them by a few seconds."

"Is he okay?" I whisper.

"Best he can be."

"What do you need me to do?"

"Mind walking through the storage room, past the playground, and to the cabin out back? He's in the third room on the left. You can take Guy." Caleb offers nothing else, going back to tending to business behind the register.

It's gutting me to see him so damn distraught and worried about his twin brother. I've witnessed glimpses of their connection during the time spent with them. They're each other's right hand and always in sync. If Fender's cup begins to tumble off a counter, Caleb reaches for it if Jed isn't looking and vice versa. That little boy is the center of their bond.

I walk through the familiar storage room that Fender has coaxed me in to play hide and go seek a handful of times. It reeks of overripe produce and stale cardboard. I could do without the smell. I push through the swinging doors out into the fresh mountain air filling my lungs with it.

The sun well on its way to settling high in the sky for the day. The playground is deserted with an eerie feel lingering over it. It's almost like a promise of bad news to come. Jed and Caleb's parents returned home from a short vacation. I haven't met them yet. I overheard a few heated conversations between Jed and his mom via a phone call. He didn't want them to come home for this.

The Bryant cabin is one in the area I'd consider a mansion. It's insanely intricate from the rich wood to the immaculate detail and very private, hidden well by the large pine trees. Gigantic, sturdy steps lead up to the door carved with their last name in it. There's a swing on one side of the porch and several other lounge chairs on the other side covered in various colorful cushions.

A handful of Fender's toys litter the porch, making it look like it's been lived in. My hand trembles on the doorknob because I'm not used to going into somebody else's house, especially a house where I don't know the owners because I've never met Jed and Caleb's parents. When I step in, it's quiet with Guy on my heels, following me. I know what he's doing. He's looking for his best friend.

I remember which room Caleb told me, but I'm struck in awe looking around the beautiful home. It's one of those cabins out of a magazine with an A-frame ceiling, rugged logs, and river rock.

It's the pictures adorning the walls that take my breath away. Each one strategically is placed and hung with care, preserving years worth of memories. There's a dozen of Fender throughout the years from when he was a newborn up until now. And if I thought he looked like his dad and uncle, I'm for sure certain he's a carbon copy of them now.

Then I see them. Just the same as Fender's pictures from birth throughout the years. In every single picture, Jed and Caleb stand beside each other with an arm wrapped around the other's shoulder. There are several of them from when they were young and played sports. When they were younger, I have a tough time deciphering who was who.

As they grow older in the frames, it was Jed with the guitar in his hand, and Caleb with a football tucked under his arm. I walk around the expansive, open living room soaking in Jed, the king of country and one sexy man in his element. His eyes are alive in each shot as he sings for hundreds and thousands. His frame strong and hot as hell, screaming for attention. His signature black t-shirt is stretched across his chest.

Then Caleb who is in a Clemson football jersey, beaming at the camera with pride coating all of his features. I've seen the man happy and carefree, but there's a fire in his eyes in the football pictures. A simple snapshot showcasing the man's passion.

I spin around and take the room in one last time before going down the entrance of the hallway. The fireplace catches my attention; it's huge. Scratch that, it's enormous, framed in river rock varying in muted colors and sizes. On top of the mantel is all of Jed's music awards. I walk closer to them to inspect each and every one. Entertainer of the year, single of the year, and the list goes on and on and on. Unlike most awards that collect dust, these do not have a single speck on them.

When I glance over, I see more pictures of Caleb and his winning smile, and there's one of him winning the national college championships. It seems his football story ceased after that picture next to Jed's awards. There's not any evidence of his football career. Something doesn't add up.

I shake all the thoughts free and feel at home even though this is not my home. It's a painstakingly beautiful cabin filled with love and admiration for a family. I walk down the hall, the hardwood floor creaking underneath my feet. I enter the room to find a bundle of blankets in the middle of the bed. When I walk closer, I see Fender's black crazy hair poking out in every direction.

I sit on the edge of the bed, and that's when I see it. A yellow piece of paper folded in half with Fender's name on the front in a crisp, block handwriting. Next to it is Jed's cell phone and a single strawberry frosted Pop-Tart.

Fender shows no signs of waking up. His chest keeps a sturdy rhythm, and his breathing is deep. I kick my shoes off and lie down next to him on the bed. And I smell him, Jed. His scent is lingering on the pillows and sheets. This is Jed's room. His masculine, rich woodsy scent mingled with hints of sweet mandarins strikes me in the gut.

The smell of Jed is more than overwhelming; I would wrap up in it, allowing it to hug me so damn tight I'd feel like I would never lose my footing again in life. My head is spinning in confusion, and it's a feeling I don't like. All the grieving counselors and my family told me life would go on, things would happen, and I would learn to live again. I believed it to be complete bullshit. I would grow angry every time somebody would say it to the point of wanting to die myself.

But now, here I lie in the bed of a dying man next to his innocent, sweet son and I'm wondering if God is determined to prove me a liar, showing me that life does go on as will my story.

Fender wrestles around next to me in the bed

until he's clinging to the front of me. His crazy black hair is tickling the tip of my nose. I use my hand to smooth it down and then kiss the top of his head, close my eyes, and say a prayer.

Dear God,

I know what you're doing. You're proving to me that life does go on. You're showing me love, where I least expected to find it. Be careful with my already shattered heart, hold it in your hands, and be tender with me. Also be by Jed's side today as he gets the news that will steer his direction. I hope I can do this, God. Amen.

I look around the room as I begin to drift off to sleep right along Fender's side. I'm not sure if Jed's mom decorated his room with the pictures hanging on the wall. But there's not one ounce of evidence on these four walls that Jed Bryant is the king of the country world.

All of the pictures are of Fender and Jed. Every single last one of them. One of them catches my attention, and I find myself suddenly awake so I study it for a long time. It's of Jed. His arms were much bigger than they are now. He was ripped with chords of muscles bulging from his signature black t-shirt. He has a baseball cap on backward, peering down into the eyes of a newborn baby. The tears aren't rolling, no they're sitting on the edge of his eyes waiting to roll down. Genuine joy and happiness fill every single picture.

Not a glimpse of the man I'm coming to know. Not the man battling for his life. And it's at this moment that I make a decision. It's the biggest decision I've ever made in a blink of an eye. It may end up being one of my biggest regrets, but I'm going to jump in headfirst. I want that look back on Jed's face. For him. For Fender. And for his family.

My eyelids finally flutter shut with the thought of it and the day it happens. Soon sleep takes over, and even though my body isn't physically exhausted, I don't have a nightmare. Not a single one. I dream of fishing down at the river, Jed throwing in Fender, Guy right in the middle of the action, and Caleb cursing them for scaring away the fish. It's one of the best dreams I've had in a long time.

I have no idea how long I'm out until the sound of the sweet giggles and a wet dog tongue glides up my face. I blink open one eye and then the next and come face-to-face with a wet dog nose and two gorgeous rich brown eyes staring at me.

"He's kissing you," Fender sings out. Followed by another sweet chorus of amazing little giggles.

"Ew doggy kisses." I wipe the slobber off my face. "How long have you been up?"

Fender shrugs his little shoulders and gives me an I have no idea face.

"Are you hungry?"

Fender rolls over me and grabs the note and phone. He holds up the corner of the Pop-Tart and smiles while sitting on my belly.

"Daddy left these for me. He told me he had to go to the big city with Nanna and Poppa this morning."

My heart breaks for the innocent brown-eyed boy so full of wonder. He has no idea what his dad is going through.

"Did you read your daddy's note?"

"Are you crazy, woman? I don't know how to read."

He just sounded so much like his uncle Caleb it's creepy.

"I can read it for you if you want."

"Sure, but are you ponstipated in the mornings like Dad?"

This time I'm giggling at his silly question. "Well, Fender, I'm not quite sure what ponstipated means."

He doesn't need any further urging to burst out with pride, telling me exactly what ponstipated means. "Banky told me Daddy's been ponstipated because he's so full of poop that he gets mean and grumpy. But I don't get it." Fender nibbles on his breakfast and shrugs his shoulders. "All he has to do is sit down and sing the alphabets and poop, and he'd be all better."

I clutch my stomach, laughing my ass off, and the pain of laughter shooting through my stomach. "Well, I'm not ponstipated, and I think what you're trying to say is constipated. How about that note?"

Fender throws the note in my face peering down at me waiting for me to read it. The boy is so loving and caring and has no boundaries at all. I unfold the yellow piece of paper and freeze. I've never been so taken by the art of somebody's handwriting. It's as if Jed's handwriting is as soul-searching as the songs he sings. It's a script, yet bold and masculine at the same time.

"What's the wrong, Marwee? Do you not know how to read?"

I reach up and ruffle his hair.

"Calm down, Mister. I know how to read." I clear my throat and squint, keeping Fender on edge. "Okay, this is what your daddy's letter says."

I glance up at Fender to see that he's still bright eyed and bushy tailed, eagerly waiting for the words.

"Fender boy,

I hope you found your Pop-Tart and didn't leave too many crumbs in the bed for me. I've gone to town with Nanna and Poppa for the day, but I'll be home this evening. Have I ever told you my favorite guitar is a Fender and now my favorite boy is Fender? Hey, now I can see you rolling your eyes at me because I tell you that story all the time.

Be good for Banky and Marlee while I'm gone today. If I get a good report back that you're a gem of a young man, we will go down to the fishing hole in the next few days.

Always remember your daddy loves you no matter what, Fender. I'm your biggest fan and I'll always be here for you, don't you ever forget that.

Love, Dad

PS – I left my phone behind for you and have your favorite playlist up in the music app. Lots of Elvis and Johnny Cash on there for you, son. Love you to the moon and back."

Fender sighs, grabbing the paper from me. He clutches it to his chest. "Daddy's been whiting a lot of these to me. I love them."

I smile a sad one. "You should, Fender. He loves you."

"I know." He lets the sheet of paper flutter to

the bed and goes about punching in the passcode for the phone.

"You know your dad's code?"

He nods. His tongue is peeking out of the corner of his mouth. "It's zero, three, one, zero."

"Wow. That's a long number for a little guy like you to memorize."

Fender throws both of his hands on his hips, keeping the phone clutched in one palm. Disgust covers his features. "Marwee, it's my birfday, duh."

I remember the numbers he said and repeat them in my head. Zero, three, one, zero. Nothing registers, so I repeat them over and over in my head until the date appears. March tenth. Shock grips my heart. I find it hard to breathe. It can't be.

"March tenth?" I ask.

"Yep, my birfday. The best day ever."

Chills race up my spine, sweat beads form on my forehead, and I'm going to be sick. Hope's due date. My sight clouds and a sudden surge of body heat rises. This has to be a cruel joke. I take one step forward just to be slammed back into my reality by a bulldozer.

"Marwee." Little hands cup my cheeks. "Did you hear me?"

I shake my head.

"Is you okay? You look sick."

"I'm just uh…" I bite down on my bottom lip and decide to go with the truth. "I'm sad, Fender."

His face lights up with a grin. His little teeth are shining back at me. He leans forward and kisses my forehead then flutters his jet-black eyelashes along my face. I peer down at him to see his face scrunched up in concentration as he gets his lashes to cooperate.

"Butterfly kisses. Daddy does this when I'm sad until I'm happy again."

I wrap my arms around Fender, hugging him tight and wait for the magic of the butterfly kisses. My breathing steadies out as the seconds tick by. A tingling warmth creeping throughout my limbs replaces the searing hot pain burning my insides. I close my eyes, letting each brush of Fender's eyelashes ground me. This isn't a cruel and sick joke. No, it's another gentle nudge from Bentley to move on.

"You happy yet? My eyes hurt."

My heart damn near radiates out of my chest. I grab him by the waist, lifting him up in the air. His hands fly out, and his giggles fill the air. Fender settles back down on my midsection entranced by the phone. Soon music fills the air. It isn't Elvis or Johnny Cash, but the growling, sexy voice of Jed.

"It's my favorite song ever." Fender places the phone on the bed and begins bobbing his head to the beat of the music.

Soon he's jamming on his air guitar to his dad's upbeat song about late nights and a wild love story. It's all about falling in love and ignoring the fact you may end up with a broken heart. Living in the moment and embracing each day.

Okay, okay, Bentley. I get it.

Chapter 26

"And in the middle of the chaos, was you." - Unknown

"He's exhausting." I smile at Caleb.

"He never slows down." Caleb brushes his hand through his thick hair. "Thanks for today. I couldn't have run the store and kept a good enough eye on him."

"I had more fun than I have had in a long time." I drag the toe of my sandal through the dirt. "There's something about the pure joy and innocence of Fender that makes any situation a happy and enjoyable one."

"Yeah." Caleb steps closer, pulling me in a hug. "He's the only bright spot in all our lives right now."

I let Caleb hug me, and I hug him right back, burying my face in his chest. One tear followed by several more run down my face and he catches every single one.

"Have you heard anything?"

I feel his chin run back and forth over the top of my head. "Yeah, Mom called, and it's not good."

"How?"

"That's all she said." Caleb grips me tighter. "Our family went through hell and back. Right when we rose from the ashes of it, then this. They told him his best odds were to have the surgery. He did. Went through the treatments two years ago and kept up with recording his music and now it's back. Why?"

I lean back, still holding Caleb. "I don't know why. I've asked that same question over and over until I drove myself crazy. All I know is this place is healing me, Caleb, and that includes you and your family. I didn't think it was ever possible, but it is. I'm not going to tell you to find faith or pray because honestly, I don't know if it works."

"I hear you, Marlee." He kisses the top of my head and steps back as Fender flies out the door. "You're good for Jed. He'll never admit it, but you are. He likes you a lot, Marlee, and he never lets anyone in."

"He's good for me, too," I whisper as Fender takes his uncle's hand and they walk to the cabin.

I clutch my chest with both hands. My heart is hammering like a drum. I can't believe the words I spoke. I don't recognize them or my voice as I spoke them, but feel them resting in my heart. I'm a shattered woman who has found a broken man and am facing a second chance. Love heals.

I brush away the tears with the back of my hands and decide dinner at the Bryant restaurant sounds perfect. I've grown tired of peanut butter and jelly sandwiches and am not in the mood to cook. My Airstream doesn't quite offer up the perfect cooking environment.

I place Guy in the large dog run near the playground. It's new. I don't have to wonder who put it there or why. It seems building new things is Jed's way of keeping his mind off things.

The restaurant is deserted. I've had food from here before, but in Styrofoam takeout boxes. It's always been delicious on the greasy side of food.

The elderly waitress is friendly, giving me a menu and taking my drink order.

"Crown and Coke."

"Be right back. I'll have to grab it from the bar."

"Thanks." I smile at her.

I roam the menu, not needing to look since my stomach is already set on a bacon cheeseburger with a dinner salad. Headlights shine in the front window, but don't pull into the parking lot. They slow down and round the building. My heart sinks down into my stomach, knowing it's Jed and his parents.

"Ma'am, would you mind sitting in the bar to eat?" The waitress sets down the tumbler filled with dark liquid. "I need to wax the floors and thought I'd get an early start."

"Sure, no problem." I rise and grab my drink. "I'll take a bacon cheeseburger with a dinner salad."

"Dressing?"

"Thousand Island."

"It will be right out."

I push through the swinging doors that lead into the bar. It's dim, speckled with only a few patrons, and music is coming from the jukebox. The sound the jukebox emits is nostalgic with a George Jones's song "He Stopped Loving Her Today." Of course, the saddest song of all times would be playing.

I devour my cheeseburger once it arrives and order another drink. The whiskey is doing its job relaxing my entire body. It makes me sick to think of how many nights I muted the pain with vodka.

The cold reality is I still have nights like those where I can't fight the demons.

The bar's walls are lined with Jed from pictures to album covers. It makes me smile. It's as if my thoughts willed him to me. The back door of the bar bursts open. I glance over to see Jed storming in. His snapback cap is shading his eyes. There's no need to see his eyes to figure out his mood because his body language says it all. His shoulders are thrown back and tense. The muscles in his arms are flexing with pent-up anger. I watch from the corner of the bar as he helps himself to a bottle of Jameson and glass of ice.

He doesn't notice me or anyone for that fact as he sits at the end of the bar. He twists off the lid, not even bothering to pour his first drink over ice. The bottle grazes his lips, and he throws it back. I watch him repeat this over and over until he drops his face in the palms of his hands.

I'm on my feet before I realize what in the hell I'm doing. A Keith Whitley song begins to play. The other patrons are now long gone.

"You gonna lock up, Jed?" The bartender tosses down a white rag on the bar top.

Jed nods, not looking up. And now it's just us left in the bar with a lonely jukebox. I don't speak when I walk up to him, instead, I grab his hand and wait for him to raise his head. When he does, it's a sight I'll never forget. His eyes are wet, his fingers twitch, forearms strained, and his neck goes stiff.

"Dance with me." I tug on his hand.

He doesn't move, so I move closer and whisper in his ear. "Dance with me, Jed."

I tug again, and he stands to his feet. I don't wait until we are in the middle of the dance floor before wrapping my arms around his neck. I feel his hands clutch onto my hips. I press my forehead into his chest.

Our bodies sway to "When You Say Nothing At All." His muscular body is rigid and wound with tension. It doesn't take long until his body begins to relax into mine. His back slumps, his face is nestled in the crook of my neck, and his arms are wrapping low and tight around my waist. I turn my head to find my lips brushing against the shell of his ear.

I whisper to him, "Sing to me."

He doesn't lift his head or say a word. I run my hand up through his thick black hair, gripping it.

"Sing to me. I love the look in your eyes when you sing. The way your lips curve, making love to the words. Just sing."

Jed moves us around the dance floor with no effort. After long beats of time, he raises his head, tears streaming down his face, and begins singing the words. His voice cracks at first, but then he finds his deep voice. It starts out slow, but within a matter of seconds, he's out singing Keith Whitley in every way.

We dance through timeless country songs, and Jed sings the entire time. The tears dry up, the tension eases, but our bodies never pull apart.

"Do you want to talk about it?" I cup his cheeks.

Jed's eyes snap shut as he pushes into my touch. "Scheduled for surgery in four days to remove my appendix then chemo treatment."

I press my lips to his, determined to take the pain away from him. My fingers push into the apples of his cheeks. A hiss of pain leaves his lips, and I drink it in. His hands go up into my hair, fisting handfuls, tugging on it as he begins to kiss me. I let my eyes flutter shut, seeing the bright starbursts explode behind them.

I run my tongue along the seam of his lips, and he opens for me. I lead the kiss, exploring his mouth with my tongue, absorbing his taste. It fuels me. It's everything and more than I thought it could ever be. Jed sinks his teeth into my lower lip, clamping down until a spike of pain shoots through my body. An echoing popping sound surrounds as he lets go.

He drops his forehead to mine. "Make it go away, Marlee, please. I'm a selfish bastard, but I need you."

I take a step back, reach for the hem of my shirt, and pull it up to my torso. Jed's searing gaze soaks it all in. I lick my bottom lip, tossing my shirt to the floor. Jed loops an arm low around my waist, dipping his head to my collarbone.

He blazes a trail with his tongue along my skin, setting me on fire. He begins backing us up until my back hits the unforgiving edge of the bar.

"Wait here." He nips the skin right above my breast.

Jed steps back, leaving me quivering with anticipation. I feel everything storming and brewing inside of me. The strongest of all…want. The desire for this man is off the charts. I want him to hold me and wrap me up in his strong arms as we careen into a new future. The end is unknown, but I'll make the best of every day.

I glance down my exposed torso. A raised scar rises up the side of my abdomen. I run the pad of my finger along it. It will always be a part of me. The accident left so many scars and marks upon my skin. It's my story, but not my ending any longer.

I glide my fingers along my stomach, feeling the indents and rises of the stretch marks left behind. The jangling of metal makes me look up. Jed's twirling a set of keys around his finger as he reaches for a light. I glance around, seeing he pulled all the blinds and I'm assuming locked the doors. He reaches for the light switch.

"No." I shake my head.

"Marlee, we don't have to..."

I close the distance between us, placing my finger over his lips. "This is me. The imperfections will remain. Time with you has helped me understand this is my armor and it tells a story. I'm ready, Jed."

He drops the keys on the bar top, raises his hand to my cheek slowly, making his way up into my hairline. He grips a fistful again, pulling me to him. When our lips crash we both take from each other, not apologizing for it. Our tongues tango in a heated dance, and Jed grabs me by the hip, grinding into me. His hard length is pushing through his jeans.

I'm off my feet before I realize what's happened. My ass hits the solid top of the bar. Jed's hands wrap around my back, splaying out. The heat from them cause me to grind into his chest. I need friction. He unsnaps my bra with one hand. I reach up for the straps, letting them fall off my shoulders.

"You're gorgeous," he whispers, never taking his stare off of me. "I'm a selfish bastard."

I lift his chin with my finger, making him look up at me. "Why?"

"I'm a dying man, and all I want is you."

I smile. "In my book that makes you a human. A man with a huge heart that wants to be loved. I understand what you're going through. I get it. I'm not fragile. I want you."

"Marlee..."

He stops talking the second I reach down and pull up his shirt. My hands roam over his bronzed skin, relishing in the sensation. His muscles wound are taut with anticipation. I place my palm flat and run it down his chest to his abdomen.

He throws his head back, moaning. It empowers me to go on. I flick the button of his jeans open and pull the zipper down. Jed leans forward, sinking his mouth around my nipple and reaches over, rolling the other one between his fingers. I freeze, nearly falling into an orgasm.

My free hand goes to the back of his head, pulling on his hair, begging him for more. Jed moves from side-to-side, devouring me like he's a starving man. I hear one of his boots drop to the floor and he kicks out of the other one. My hands are frantic, reaching to push down his pants.

He lays me back on the bar before I have the chance to get them all the way down. His strong hands make quick work, pulling down my jeans and panties. My back arches off the bar when he runs his fingers through my folds.

"Jed!" I scream.

His rugged palm glides up my stomach as he dips his head. He rests his hand between my breasts. I grab onto it, clutching it as my anchor. My fingers dig into his hand as he licks between my folds. His tongue circles around my clit, making my head spin. When he bites down on it, I scream so loud my throat's left raw.

He cups my ass with his other hand, pulling me closer to his face, letting me ride out my ecstasy. It goes on and on, making me dizzy and hungry for more all at the same time.

"I need you," I beg and plead once my body is drained.

I prop up on my elbow then use my hands to sit up. Jed places me back down on my feet. The world spins for a tick. I press both of my hands into his chest, back him up until the back of his legs hit a chair, and then push him down. I'm hungry, thirsty, and impatient as hell, not wanting to wait any longer.

My hands dip into his boxers, wrapping around his rock hard thick length. Jed hisses, digging his fingers into my flesh. I can't help myself and indulge in a few strokes of his cock before pulling him from his boxers.

"I can't wait," I whisper, straddling his powerful thighs. "Help me."

Jed clutches the base of his cock, guiding me down on him. A sharp pinching pain zings throughout my body. I wince while continuing to rock on him.

"Take it slow, baby." Jed runs his palms up and down my spine, soothing away the ache.

I bite down on my bottom lip, working my hips until the friction becomes delicious. He holds me tight to his chest as I move. Our bodies fit perfectly together, making me cry out his name over and over.

Jed drops his head to my chest, digging his fingers into the flesh on my back. He holds me with a force that promises he'll never let go. I mirror the same action, wrapping my arms around his neck, clutching on with everything I have. I'm offering up what's left of me. It's all his forever. And may that include an endless count of days.

"Marlee," he growls.

I feel his dick pulse inside of me. It's my final undoing. We roll, tumble, and somersault into our own orgasms. My fist full of his hair tightens, my knuckles turning white, and my promise deepening, never to let go. Now it's time to smile.

Chapter 27

"What's meant to be will always find a way." - Unknown

"There's a little cabin behind the restaurant tucked away in the pine trees..."

I cut him off. "Take me there."

Jed stands with me in his arms. We ignore the mess we made as he dresses. His hands are roaming every inch of my skin as he does his best to put my clothes back in place. I relish each touch and lingering graze of his knuckles. We walk hand in hand back to the cabin with the glow of his cell phone.

Jed gave up looking for his shirt. His tanned skin glows under the full moon. I gaze up at the brilliant, perfect round object in the sky, staring at another sign, urging me on. I'm already a goner. The moon's light reflects off the bottle of Jameson clutched in Jed's hand. He needs it tonight. I'll give him that, but refuse to let him fall victim to the bottom of the bottle.

He was spot on about the little cabin hidden by the tall trees. A door creaks open, Jed flips the light on, and a quaint interior comes into view. It's simple with all the essentials. I run my hand along the back of the charcoal gray couch with hints of navy blue mixed in while Jed flips on lights and a shower.

"Where is the bed?" I ask, peeking into the bathroom.

My jaw drops, coming into view with Jed in the

middle of dropping his boxers. The light is showcasing his perfect ass.

"The couch has a hideaway bed."

I nod.

He holds out a hand to me. I place mine in his. He tugs me to him. I go easy and free like an elastic rubber band snapping, giving into the force behind it. He guides me into the stone-walled shower. There's barely enough room for the both of us. His towering body damn near swallows up the space on its own. He keeps me cradled to his chest. His hands roam all over my body in a sensual and romantic fashion, easing my tense muscles. It's natural, not forced in the least.

Jed cleans me while the shower does its best to erase away the memory of tonight. Thing is, it's etched on my heart in permanent ink. He towels me off, then himself, and leads me to the couch. I watch his naked figure strip away the cushions and pull out the bed.

I study the one-room cabin, recognizing his handiwork. Jed built this place. The Fender leaning up against the wall seals the deal. This is his haven, and he invited me in. When I glance back to the bed of soft sheets, piles of pillows, and a thick sleeping bag comes into view. Jed guides me down to the bed and shuts off all the lights.

The mattress dips as he climbs toward me. His encompassing body wraps around mine, pulling my back to his chest. The silence wraps us up in an everlasting hug.

"I'm scared, Marlee."

I lace my fingers in his draped over my hip. "I

am, too."

"I was a dick when I first saw you. Seeing Fender with you in our family store did something to me." He kisses the inside of my neck. "I flipped. The tug and pull you brought out of me couldn't be ignored. I like to build things, and that's what I did to pass the time."

"You built this." It comes out as a statement instead of a question.

I feel him nod against my over-sensitized skin. "When I can't be on the stage, my hands have to be busy. When I'd visit my parents over the last six years, I'd work on it. They were always short visits."

"You'll be on the stage again. I do not doubt that."

"I want to believe that."

"You will. I'll make certain of that."

"Tonight was..." He pushes his body closer to mine.

"Perfect."

Jed's lips graze my skin, soothing me to sleep. The force overwhelms me, making my eyelids heavy. So heavy they shut in the arms of the man who brought me back to life. Dreams of happily ever after with Jed and Fender highjack my dreams. It's the sweetest of sweet.

***

"Baby, I got you."

A husky, rich voice sings out. The words continue to serenade me with the sweet harmony. I pry open my eyes, the dull light taking a few beats to adjust to. And the view is sweeter than the man's voice. His perfect, sculpted ass clad in black boxers comes into view.

Good morning to me.

Jed sways his hips as he sings. I don't miss his carefree nature as he belts out the song. It's his passion. He turns around with two buttered Pop-Tarts in his hand and smiles. Those damn dimples. Broad chest. And that man.

"Perv," he taunts me.

I cover my mouth, keeping my giggle in.

"Breakfast in bed." He places a knee on the mattress, tossing one leg over me until he's straddling my midsection. His rich cocoa eyes are staring down at me with a mischievous twinkle in them and his hair standing on end reminding me of yesterday.

"You know Fender was in this same position yesterday morning."

"Trained him well." He winks, juggling the pastries in his hands as he tumbles over to his side.

"So, you do have a bit of Caleb in you." I roll to face him.

"Yeah." He takes a bite out of the Pop-Tart. "Used to be a bigger smartass, carefree, and loved life until the..."

"Cancer," I finish for him. "I may be the one person who understands how life changes you, morphing you into a new person. One that you don't even recognize."

He nods, brushing his cheek against the pillow. "This fucking sucks. I'm scared, but can't crumble. I have to stay strong for Fender."

"You do. But fall into me." I reach forward and take a bite out of his Pop-Tart he hasn't offered to share. "You intrigued me the first time I saw you. Warmed up my heart and opened my mind to more with our silent coffee dates. But yesterday when I saw those pictures in your room and that smile you used to have, it sent me over the edge. I want you to smile like that again."

"Me, too. Me, too," he murmurs.

I lean in for a soft kiss, but snatch the Pop-Tart at the last minute and bolt out of bed. It's three long lunges before I'm safely behind the bathroom doors.

"You little shit," he bellows out, followed by laughter.

"Learned from the best."

I glance around the bathroom, finding a roll of paper towels then wrap up my Pop-Tart, placing it on top of the water heater. I pull open the door enough to peek out of it. Jed is stretched out on the bed, legs spread wide and arms propped behind his head.

"How do you feel about sharing your toothbrush?" I raise an eyebrow.

He shrugs and winks. "Not usually, but considering my mouth was in your..."

"I'll take that as a yes." I shut the door before he finishes.

The chorus of laughter floating into the bathroom warms me from head to toe. This place is stocked with all the essentials. Jed's an organized man and has everything lined up in neat rows in the medicine cabinet. After brushing my teeth and tying my hair up, I open the door with my Pop-Tart in hand. Jed's in the same position.

"You know what's weird?"

"What's that?" He pats the pile of blankets next to him.

"I know little to nothing about you. Shit, I can count it off on one hand." I jump into the bundle of blankets, snuggling close to Jed's side. I take a bite out of the pastry and hold up one other hand, starting to tick them off. "You're a famous, drop dead, gorgeous country star, you make phenomenal turkey sandwiches, you have a huge heart even though it's hidden behind your fear, you're raising the most lovable boy I've ever met, and Caleb is cuter than you."

"No, you didn't." Jed leaps from his relaxed state where he was soaking up each of my words and has me pressed into the mattress. His body covers mine. "Take it back."

"Fine, your turkey sandwiches are so-so."

"Marlee." He dips his head, nipping at the tender skin on my neck. I roll into a fit of laughter, struggling to push him away. The Pop-Tart crumbles between us, creating a mess.

"Fine. Fine." I push up on his shoulders. "You're way more handsome than Caleb, but don't tell him that. And that wasn't my fifth one."

"Go on." He rubs his nose against mine.

"I'm falling for you."

"Much better." He rolls us over until I'm sitting on top of him, my palms planted on his chest.

"Your turn," I urge him on.

He raises his hands, running them through his

hair. That familiar intoxicating sensation courses through my veins, making me drunk on him.

"Wait. I forgot one. When you run your hands through your hair, it's the sexiest thing I've ever seen." A fiery flush floods my cheeks admitting it out loud.

"Good to know." His hands come down to my waist, gripping tight.

"Your turn." I tap his chin.

He groans. "You're right. I have no idea of the basics. Don't know your favorite color, foods, or anything, but what I do know is you're a survivor, curious, and have a big heart."

I worry my bottom lip, not sure about the last one. It's felt like my heart has shriveled up and drifted away over the last two years. Jed brings his hand up to my chest, splaying it over my heart.

"It's in there, baby. I can feel it beat. The rhythm sweet."

"I'm in awe, Jed. I never thought this was going to happen."

"That's the thing about life, you never see it coming."

"It's brutal and unforgiving."

"It is."

"I'm ready for my second chance."

Jed tenses and his expression falls.

"Don't. I'm in, by your side."

"Fuck." He throws his arm over his forehead. "I feel like shit for putting you through this."

"Stop." I reach down and kiss his lips, twisting my head, maneuvering around his arm. "I'm here. Done. End of. It may not be the perfect circumstance, but you're helping me live again, Jed. I want this. It feels liberating, and for the first time in what has felt like forever I'm not drowning anymore."

"Color?"

"Uh?"

"Favorite color?"

"Peach," I reply. "You?"

"Black."

I pull his arm away from his eyes, lace my fingers in both his hands, keeping them held out to the sides.

"Food?" He raises an eyebrow.

"Dessert. Anything chocolate."

"And you?" I wrinkle my nose, waiting on his answer.

"Prime Rib. Rare."

The question-answer goes on and on, covering everything from allergies to favorite hobbies. Jed has an appetite for all sorts of food, but this is something I already knew, loves the outdoors, which I could've guessed, and his biggest fear is falling in love. Life hasn't been kind to him.

"I hit the music scene right out of high school. We grew up in a small town in Oklahoma. The day after graduation I drove to Nashville, and it started from there. Seems since then everyone has used me, besides my family that is. The women wanted my body and access to my bank account, and so-called friends wanted to use me as a stepping stone." He brushes the loose bangs dancing in my face to the side. "I became hard and protected my heart especially after Fender was born, knowing true love and friendship would never come as long as I was seen as Jed Bryant."

"I recognized you when I first saw you, but then could've kicked myself for not placing Caleb."

"Yeah?" he growls.

"You two are twins after all. I see the differences, but still, you're Jed Freaking Bryant," I squeal and wiggle around on his midsection.

"Shit, turned you into a groupie. Gonna ask me to sign your titties next?"

My mouth falls open. "They really ask that?"

"Oh, yeah, among other things."

"What's the strangest thing you ever signed?" I shake my head. "Never mind, I don't want to know."

"Last question and I think we have all of our bases covered." Jed rolls us over again with him hovering above. "Favorite sexual position?"

A heated flush creeps up my spine; I duck my head. "Doggy."

"Dirty girl." Jed throws his head back, roaring in laughter.

"What?" I slap his chest.

"It's adorable how easily you embarrass."

"I should be used to it. Bentley was a dirty talker." I slap my hand over my mouth.

He pries my hand away, shaking his head side-to-side with a gentle smile. "It's okay. I want to know about him and your life before. You share as much as you feel comfortable with."

I nod and whisper. "Thank you."

"Mine is reverse cowgirl." He shrugs a muscular shoulder. "I'm an ass man."

"Last night was amazing," I whisper, brushing the pad of my finger down his breathtaking jawline.

"It was." He kisses my forehead and then stands. "Want more than anything to go back to the bar and not for a drink either, but gotta go check on my boy. I'm sure Mom and Pops are smothering him by now."

"What time is it?" I throw my legs over the bed.

"Almost seven a.m."

Jed reaches out his hand, helping me up. He pulls me in for a long, strong hug, kissing the top of my head. We dress in silence and walk hand in hand out of the cabin after Jed puts away the bed and locks it up. When we near the back of the store I tug my hand away from his, ready to go for Guy and then my bike.

"What are you doing?" Jed asks with a prying stare.

"My bike."

After the events of last night and now it gets awkward. I flick my fingers on my free hand, waiting for his response. We did share an amazing night, and I'm devoted to being in his life, but not about to become a stage one clinger at this point. Hell, we didn't exactly take things all that slow.

"Gonna break Fender's heart if you and Guy skip out of here without paying him a visit." Jed tugs me toward his parents' cabin.

"You don't play fair, Mr. Bryant." I squeeze his hand. "Won't your parents be...I don't know pissed, confused with a random woman waltzing in their home?"

"You do know Caleb has a big mouth, right?" He peers down to me. "They pried and pried, trying to get details about you. Asshat took it upon himself to tell them all about the new pretty woman in town and his suspicion about me being fond of her."

"Oh my God." I slap my palm over my face. "Oh, he did."

"Told them about the kiss, too."

"This is embarrassing as hell."

Guy's eager bark cuts into our conversation. Our gaze cuts to the sound to see Fender on the back of Guy, clutching at his collar. His knuckles are white and a grin is plastered on his face. Guy gallops toward us with his tongue hanging out, and I swear a matching grin.

"He is riding him." I pull my hand from Jed's. "Holy shit, he could get hurt."

Jed snags me by the waist, pulling me back into his chest. "He's fine. Look at that smile. I live for it."

Jed leans around and kisses the side of my head.

"Me, too. Makes the world seem right," I whisper.

Guy nears us, slowing down, being cautious of his best friend on his back. Fender remains safe by the time Guy reaches us. He hops off, wiping his brow with a determined little hand.

"Daddy." He collides into Jed's legs. "We were chilling on the porch, and when Guys sawed Marwee, he took off. I held on. Tolds you I'm gonna be a cowboy riding them wild horses."

"I saw, buddy." Jed's hand drops from my waist. He bends over, picking Fender up. He tosses him up in the air a few times, garnering squeals from him before pulling him to his chest.

"I missed you yesterday, Daddy." Fender's little arms go around his neck. "I tried keeping my eyes open until you gots back."

"I know, buddy." He ruffles his hair. "You have no idea how much I missed you yesterday."

"Nana and Papa are back for a while now!"

"Nana have her famous French toast ready yet?"

"Piles and piles told me I had to wait for you." Jed places Fender back on his feet. He darts away with Guy close on his heels.

Jed pulls my back into his chest, wrapping his arms low around my waist, nuzzling his nose in my neck, and begins walking. I clutch his locked hands.

"When are you going to tell him?"

"Tonight," he sighs, his breath tickling my sensitive skin. "Mom bought a child's book that she thinks will help him. I don't think anything is going to. He won't understand any of it."

"He won't, but your mom is smart. Kids can relate to things they don't understand when it's written out in picture books."

"The lovebirds have risen." Caleb stands on the porch with his arms above his head.

"He's going to be relentless," Jed whispers in my ear.

"Get your asses in here. Mom won't let any of us eat until she meets Marlee."

My stomach knots in nerves. This is new for me. Meeting the parents and impressing them and all.

Chapter 28

"Love yourself first and everything else falls into line. You really have to love yourself to get anything done in this world." -Lucille Ball

Mr. and Mrs. Bryant are the perfect combination of Jed and Caleb. The men sure did get their welcoming, friendly vibe from them. I didn't feel uncomfortable for one second in their presence. We were ushered straight to the table and ate for a good hour. The French toast was the best I ever had.

"Will you stay?" Jed grabs for my hand, whispering.

Fender lies between us deep in his afternoon nap. He's been extra clingy to his dad today. He knows something is going on. He refused to lie down without Jed then demanded Guy, and I joined them. Jed's frustration was apparent. I kissed him on the cheek and crawled in bed.

"If you want me to. I'll be here."

"Please."

I smile, running a finger down his jawline. "No need for manners now."

"The cancer institute called, and I need to be in Boise the night before the surgery. They took a bunch of blood yesterday for tests."

"Okay."

"The day before that, I'm going through with the charity concert."

"You think your mind will be clear enough?"

He nods against the pillow. "Want to do that

more than anything else. Always love playing for the veterans."

I lick my lips, not knowing what to say. There are so many unanswered questions swirling around in my thoughts. Who will watch Fender? How long will he be in the hospital? What will I do when he's gone?

"I want you there."

Those simple four words that tumble from Jed's lips answers every single one of my internal questions. I nod, ignoring the anxiety rising in the back of my spine. I'll have to be in a car, in a hospital, and surrounded by dying people. It's a crippling thought. Before the attack wins out, I rise from the bed and round the bottom of it. Jed lifts his head, watching me. That unruly black hair...wiping away a bit of the ache.

I crawl into bed behind Jed. He tries to roll on his back, but I keep him in place with my palms then body as I wrap my arms around his chest. My head is above his, so I'm able to kiss his face. When my lips graze across his bronzed skin, the attack begins to dissipate. I lose myself in Jed.

"Smile."

I look up to a cell phone hovering above us. I bring my arms up to underneath his jawline, so they're in the picture. Half of my face is hidden with all of Jed's gorgeous one filling the frame. He counts down and when he gets to one, his dimples go on full display.

"Let me see it." My voice is full of excitement. Taking selfies hasn't been in my life for a while. The picture is perfect.

"Want me to send it to you?" He angles himself enough to get his lips on mine.

"My cell phone doesn't have service," I murmur into his lips.

"You can connect to Wi-Fi here," he offers.

"No, like it's not connected to a provider at all."

He rolls the rest of the way over, wrapping me in his safe, loving arms. "We can fix that, and you can still hook up to Wi-Fi."

"Don't remember any email passwords or anything."

"We can fix that."

I shake my head, rubbing the tip of my nose along his.

"You're a determined man."

"Isn't that what we are doing, Marlee? Fixing each other, breathing life back into our hope for the future."

"Yes." I smile against his lips.

He moves first, creating our connection into a deep kiss. I open up to him. It feels like we've been kissing for days and days because of how perfectly our mouths move against each other. His hand goes to my ass, palming it tight. I do the same. His length pushes into my center. Our bodies begin to move, both craving connection and friction.

I bite down on his bottom lip, breaking the kiss, knowing this is as far as it will go with our current predicament. "We can't."

"I know," he pants. "But I want to."

I reach down between us, palming his evidence. "Later. Your mom told me I could make a peach pie with the fresh peaches. She left out all the ingredients for me before she left for the store."

"You've been dead set on making that pie for us, eh?"

"It's how my mom raised me. She loves cooking." My smile falls. That came out of nowhere. My heart feels the grief at the core.

"Go." He squeezes my ass. "I'll snooze with Fender and wake to the smell of a warm, homemade peach pie. And, Marlee, there's a phone in the living room. Use it."

Tears pool and only spill over when I step out of the room. It's time to call Mom. It's way overdue. My fingers tremble as I near the black, cordless phone. The ten-digit phone number tumbles around in my head. I'll never forget those ten numbers that represent my home.

My fingers quake and tremble as I punch them. The tears fall faster and heavier. The first and second rings go unanswered. The easy thing to do would be to hang up, wipe away the tears, and shove it all back in. Avoiding it all.

I don't.

Two more rings and I know the answering machine will pick. I squeeze my eyes shut, wanting nothing more than hearing a piece of my home.

"Hello."

I slap my palm over my mouth to cage in the gasp.

"Hello." Mom's voice rings out again.

I'm unable to speak, move, hell, even think.

"Marlee," she whispers into the phone with faith and trepidation. "Are you there?"

My voice cracks and walls shatter. "Mom."

"Sweet baby girl. It is you."

The line fills with sobs from each end for long beats of time. I hear Dad in the background, soothing Mom's cries. I can picture him holding her, rocking her back and forth until she calms down.

"Are...are you okay?" she finally asks.

"I am." I pause and speak the truth. "I'm better than I have been in a long time. I'm happy and learning how to live again."

"Where are you?"

She's always asked since I ran and I've avoided it. Not anymore.

"In Idaho, up in the mountains in a small town."

A new voice joins the other end of the line. I recognize it right away. It's Maddie coupled with Sara's voice.

"Maddie's there?" My hand shakes violently.

"Yes, Marlee."

"Tell her," Dad says in the background.

"Tell me what?" I ask.

"Coy never returned from his last deployment. Happened two months after you ran."

"No!" I shriek.

"Yes, baby, Maddie spends a lot of time here. I've never told you because you were so broken, but it's time. It's time for you to let all of us back in."

I nod. "I miss you guys. I'm sorry for what I put you through. I couldn't stay there, Mom."

"We know. The past is the past. We want our daughter back."

I freeze at those words. "I'm not coming home. I

can't. I have a new home."

Mom remains silent.

"And I want you and my family to see my new home in town."

"Okay," she stutters. "We'd love to come."

"I promise I'll call more, Mom. I love you and Dad more than you'll ever know."

Her sniffles slow down on her end. "Okay, Marlee. We love you."

"Bye, Mom."

I force myself to hang up the phone. The overwhelming urge to vomit rocks my world. I race from the phone, busting out the front door, the clean air smacking me in the face. When I'm at the bottom of the steps, I hunch over, retching. Tears are non-stop, cascading off my face.

Coy is dead.

My last memory of Maddie was when I scowled at her at Bentley's funeral. I couldn't stand the cries of Sara. I had her sent away. She was always there for me, and I sent her away, turned my back on her. Shut her out of my life. My body begins to go into shock, facing the devastation I created and left behind.

"Marlee." The sound of racing footsteps near me. "Marlee, is Jed okay?"

Caleb wraps me in his arms, pulling me to him. I fight him with all I have. Caleb doesn't give up until he has me in his arms.

"What is it?"

I shake my head from side-to-side, my loose hair whipping me in the face. "Not Jed. He's okay."

"Breathe, calm down, and breathe, Marlee." He

repeats over and over until I'm able to talk. I tell him everything. The pain is tearing right through me all over again.

"Marlee." He brushes my hair out of my face. "We all do what we have to, to survive. And that's what you did. The important part is taking steps to mend relationships. They'll understand. Trust me."

"No." I shake my head. "No, they won't."

"Yes, they will," he argues. "I've been in the same spot you are. Different circumstances, but the same feelings."

His eyes are raw and full of honesty. He's speaking from experience. I do not doubt that.

"Please don't tell Jed about this. He has enough on his mind."

"Agreed. Speaking of your boy toy, where is he?"

"Napping with Fender. I'm supposed to be baking a peach pie."

"No damn excuses. Get your ass in the kitchen, woman." He puts his hands on my shoulders, guiding me into the house until we are in the center of the kitchen.

Caleb plops his ass on the counter. "Get to it."

He chats with me about random shit as I do the prep work. Each off the wall fact he shares begins to ground me.

"Did you know a pregnant goldfish is called a twit?" he asks, popping a slice of fresh peach in his mouth.

I swat his hand. "No. And stop eating the peaches, or there won't be any left for the pie."

He doesn't listen, grabbing for another fresh

peach slice. This time I catch the top of his hand with a sticky spatula, yet he still manages to get the peach. "How about this one. Human birth control pills work on gorillas."

"Good lord, Caleb. You do need your head checked."

It goes on like this until the top layer of the peach piecrust has brown sugar sprinkled on it and an intricate pattern carved into it. Mom always did that. I loved watching her hands work when I was younger.

The pie has been in the oven for a little over ten minutes before Martha and Luke Bryant walk in the front door.

"Smells amazing," Martha sings, cuddled in next to her husband's side.

"Get a room, you two." Caleb rolls his eyes.

Martha darts for her son. "You may be the oldest son, but I'll still whip you." She snatches a wooden spoon from the counter, taking after Caleb.

"Get your ass off my counter before I beat it."

A full-out WWF wrestling match ensues between mother and son. Luke snags a beer from the fridge and offers me one. I nod. He's a gentleman like the men he raised. He pops off the top with a quick flick of his hand. It takes me a few beats to realize how he did. He used his wedding ring.

"Thank you." I manage to get out over the roar of the ruckus in the living room.

Caleb has his mom pinned down on the floor, tickling her ribs.

"Doggy pile." A bright-eyed and bushy-tailed Fender comes sprinting down the hallway with both arms raised over his head.

He leaps in the air, landing dead center on Caleb's back.

"Get him, baby boy. Help Nana." Martha urges him on.

Fender soaks up the words of encouragement, wrapping his arms around Caleb's face, bending his neck backward, giving his nana the perfect opportunity to gift her son with a serious titty twister.

"This will go on forever." Jed comes up behind me, rubbing his nose along the length of my scar that runs from my ear up to my hairline.

Luke chuckles. "And they will get vicious. They've mellowed out since Fender started to join them, but back in the day I swear one of them would end up crying or bleeding."

"Seriously?" I ask, turning to Luke.

"All in fun and games, but those two." He points his beer bottle to the wrestling match. "But those two are the most competitive people I know."

"I'll agree to that." Jed grabs the beer bottle from my hand, taking a long pull. "Smells delicious in here."

The three of us sit back and wait for the wrestling match to dwindle. Luke was right. It goes on for a good twenty minutes before everyone has been tickled out.

"Ready?" Jed steps forward with me in his hands.

I'm confused for a bit of time before it dawns on

me. Martha nods and relaxes back on the couch with her elbow propped up on her knee. Caleb scoots over on the floor until he's next to her. He puts an arm around her. Tears fill her eyes.

"Hey, buddy. Dad needs to talk to you." Jed scoops Fender up off the floor and takes a seat on the couch with him in his lap. I sit on the edge of the couch while Luke takes a seat on the other end.

"It's family time." He claps his hands together, peering around at everyone. "Wait."

He jumps from Jed's lap, runs out the front door, and returns with Guy.

"Now, it's family time." He climbs back up to his spot on his dad's lap.

Guy sits obediently at his feet, placing his nose on the top of Fender's leg. Tears are now rolling down Martha's face, but Fender doesn't notice.

"Daddy needs to tell you something, and I need you to pay real close attention, okay?"

He nods, still smiling his signature toothy grin.

"Nana bought you this book to help me explain it. It's about a little boy your age."

Jed opens the book and begins reading it. My throat constricts, and my eyes blur as he nears the end of it. The pages have held Fender captive the entire time. When Jed shuts the book, Fender looks up to Jed.

"You're sick with cancer?" He blinks slow.

Jed ruffles his hair and tucks him to his chest. "Yeah, bud, I am. I'm going to be in and out of the hospital for a bit. And this is going to be our home."

Fender whirls around in Jed's lap, clutches the

side of his face, tears filling his eyes. “I don’t want my daddy to be sick.”

“I know, buddy. I don’t like being sick.”

The tears spill over, falling fast and with force. “I can’t sweep without you. No, Daddy, no.”

The final thread of strength that was holding me together snaps. I lose it, crying as hard as Fender when I see Jed’s shoulders fall with his tears. “Nana and Marlee will bring you to see me. We’ll get you a hotel room so you can stay near the hospital while I’m there. I’m not leaving you, Fender. I’m going to fight with all I have to beat cancer.”

Fender’s shoulders shudder as his dad holds him tight. The rest of the family joins in hugging the duo. I watch from the outside, my conviction growing by leaps and bounds to be by Jed’s side. The thought of his touch and how it sets me alive makes me shiver.

He reads my thoughts because at that moment his hand covers mine. I can’t see his face, but his touch is all I need.

Chapter 29

"Life is a game and true love is a trophy." -Rufus Wainwright

Fender shovels a heaping forkful of peach pie in his mouth. Martha sliced him the first piece and is dishing out everyone else's. This woman may cherish her kitchen and feeding her family more than my mother. The two of them together would be dangerous. I know they'd click right away. It's what has made today so easy and natural.

Fender wrinkles his nose and shakes his head, grabbing Jed's attention.

"What's wrong, buddy?"

"It's weird. Doesn't taste like Nana pie."

"Son, that's not polite." Jed leans his elbows on the table.

Fender mimics his father's stance. "I'm not lying."

"I understand that, but..."

I join the stance, placing my elbows on the table. "Want to know something, Fender?"

He shakes his head, his bottom lip beginning to tremble, so I begin fast.

"I used to be married to a man named Bentley. He loved my momma's cooking. Didn't matter if I followed the recipe exactly or even had my mom cook it. He'd say the same thing you did. Want to know what that's called?"

He shrugs. "Sure."

I'm drilled from every angle with Bryant stares. I can't stop long enough to think about the fact I'm talking about Bentley.

"A damn good cook and a loyal lover of food or that's what Bentley used to say."

"You hab a husband?" His head tilts in confusion.

"I had a husband." I place extra emphasis on the word had. "Things happened, and we are no longer together."

There's no way in hell I'm going to go into detail with Fender about where Bentley is. His fragile mind is already on overdrive.

"So, you baswaclly saying my Nana is the bestest cook."

"That's exactly what I'm saying."

Fender rolls his eyes. "See, Dad."

I don't know about the rest of the adults, but I exhale and can relax back in my seat. Fender continues to pick at his pie. I don't mention it, but he ends up finishing the piece minus the thick ridge of crust. I chalk it up to a kids and crust thing. Mom was still peeling the crust off my bread when I was home.

"Time for a bath. You're all sticky, and Nana needs some time with her boy." Martha leans down, kissing the top of Fender's head.

His eyes are heavy. The poor boy has had his world turned upside down today.

"Daddy, can you help Nana get the water started please?"

Jed rises from his seat. "Of course, buddy. Man, you're talking like a big boy."

Fender shakes his head. "I know, I have nuts."

Martha shakes her head, holding in a giggle.

Fender's statement doesn't take her by surprise. It's clear this is nothing new around here. Jed throws Fender up on his shoulders.

"Oh, one day your Uncle Caleb will have kids of his own, and it will be on."

Fender leans over, struggling to see his dad's face, his petite palms covering Jed's forehead. "What dat mean, Dad?"

"Paybacks are a..."

Martha cuts off her son, placing her hand on his back, ushering him down the hall. "Paybacks are dandy. That's what your dad was going to say."

"But why?" Fender's voice trails off down the hall.

Their voices grow muted. I run my palm over the enormous log table, enjoying the melody of a family within a loving home. My head spins, making me sick from the dizziness...how did I find myself here? I'm a broken record on repeat, unable to believe what is happening.

"I can do this. I will do this," I whisper to myself. "Thank you, Bentley, for teaching me how to be brave."

I busy myself with putting away the dried dishes. It's a jigsaw puzzle of sorts, pulling open and closing the cabinet doors over and over until I find the correct spot. I leave a few items on the embroidered terry cloth, not having the slightest clue where they belong.

With the dining room clear, I take a seat back at the well-loved dining room table. It's evident this table has grown with the Bryant boys. Shallow lines cover the surface, and I imagine it's been from over the years of hours of homework and family dinners.

I glance over to see Jed walking toward me. He has his head down but a big grin plastered on his face. His stride is powerful as he nears me and settles next to me. His hand in mine. It seems it's our solace of comfort. So much can be told in a simple touch versus talking in circles. God knows I do enough of that in my head.

Caleb and Luke have been settled in the living room with longnecks, watching an old tape of a football game, arguing over the plays. It's funny to listen to the two men go over and over the same play, arguing their tactics.

Jed shakes his head and glances over to me. "Those two will talk football until they're blue in the face."

"Caleb gets his love of football from your dad?" I ask.

"Yeah."

"Noticed from the pictures Caleb seems to love the sport."

Jed nods. "He does."

"And you got your singing from your mom?" I ask, on a wild guess.

"Sure did. How'd you know?"

"She hummed and sang songs the whole time while serving dinner."

A reminiscent smile ghosts Jed's face. "Has always been that way. When we were little, she'd pull out her old vinyls. Patsy Cline being her all-time favorite."

"It was fishing in my house all because of my

Papa Wally. Well, fishing and Army. That's how I was raised."

"Look at us learning more and more about each other in a few seconds." He leans over and kisses my forehead.

The man has been through hell and back today, facing one of his biggest fears. "Look at us go." I climb in his lap and kiss his cheek, rubbing the back of his neck, trying to ease the tension out.

"How do you feel about everything that went down tonight?"

"It was horrible. I'll be honest, Marlee, it was the hardest thing I've ever had to do. When he started crying and wrapped his arms around my neck, my whole world shattered."

"I'm sorry, Jed. I can't imagine what that was like."

He opens up, pouring out every single detail about his future and his battle with cancer. Jed's rock hard exterior of armor shatters right before my eyes with me wrapped up in his muscular arms.

He's gifted glimpses of it before, but now listening to him talk it's as if I'm the cancer patient and he's the doctor telling me exactly what to expect. He hasn't talked much about it, but it's obvious it's been on his mind twenty-four seven.

I learned that Jed is going to have his appendix removed and then will endure chemotherapy. I try to keep focused as he rattles on about the treatment. I do my best to absorb each piece of information even though I have no background information to ground to.

"Going to be hard, Marlee." He chuckles, it's a nervous one. "Yeah, hard is an understatement; it's going to be fucking hell. My own personal lot in hell."

"Yes, it will be." I cling to him, wrapping my arms tight around his neck.

I still have no idea how this love story happened overnight, but it did. A higher force brought two broken and shattered souls together at a time where we needed it the most. Me on the end of a bottle and Jed fighting for his life and yet we discovered one another.

Hell, I don't know if I'm in love. But I do know this man needs to be in my life, and I will be there rain or shine…anxiety be damned.

"You will get through it. Look at this support you have around you. Your parents remind me so much of mine it makes me homesick. My life before the accident happened, I could do anything with the love and encouragement of my family. Man, I could attack anything and get through whatever I wanted because of the love from them, Jed. And you have that here in spades. And now me."

I squeeze my eyes tight, knowing this isn't going to be the easiest of topics to bring up. I haven't spoken about them to anyone, about the demons that lie in my body, until now.

"I haven't been behind the wheel of a car since that night. I've only ridden in cars when it was the last resort. And that's been barely a handful of times. But listening to you tell Fender that I will be by his side in Boise, made me believe. Didn't take me two seconds to think about it. I will climb into a car and be there for you and your family and especially for Fender. You have no idea how much you're forcing me to live. I use the word forcing loosely because I haven't had to think about it. It's natural." I take a long pull of oxygen in. "You always hear about those stories where during the first kiss someone's skin tingles and zaps with electricity. A current so strong it's undeniable. I don't believe in that. From the first time I saw you, my body buzzed with intrigue and excitement. It was meant to be. I will be at your treatments if you want me there, by your hospital bed, or taking care of Fender if that's what you want, I am there, no questions asked."

Jed's lips connect in a quick kiss, only to be separated from the cheering and hollering from the living room. We both laugh, our lips vibrating at the crazy antics of his father and brother.

"Jed." I cup his cheeks, my favorite place to be. "I'm going to go before the sun goes down."

His hands snake around my waist, pulling me closer to him. The grip he has on me is damn near painful. "Stay here tonight. Stay with me. I need you."

It would be easy to drown in those words, swimming in their ecstasy, but I can't.

I shake my head. "Jed…"

I stop mid-sentence to study his beautiful, handsome, rugged face unable to keep my fingers from trailing down his prominent jawline. The light whiskers on his face tickle the pads of my fingers.

"I can't, Jed. I love it here, and I love your family, and I obviously love spending time with you. But tonight, Fender needs you. Your parents will be here, and you need to love on that little boy with all you have. I don't want to interrupt that. I'll be back here bright and early in the morning."

His face falls in defeat. "With your peach pie? It was delicious."

I manage a feeble smile. I see the moment he understands what I'm trying to say. And he nods his head.

"I'll walk you out to your bike. I don't like that you're riding so close to sunset."

Jed leads me outside the house. I understand his worry, and I probably should've left ten minutes earlier if I'm honest with myself. I was lost in the moment. It's going to take everything inside me to pry myself away from this man, who I crave and hunger. He consumes me.

Once we reach the porch, he grabs my hips, pulling me to him, guiding my hands up around his neck. And whispers in my ear. "Dance with me, Marlee."

I turn my head to the side and grin like a fool. "Are you using my lines on me?"

He gives me a jerk of his chin. "Yes, I am. I'd still be hungover as hell or who knows, cracking open another bottle of Jamison if you hadn't saved me last night. You made me move and use my voice to let some of the pain and anger seep out. God gave you."

I can't help it. A bubble of laughter escapes me. Jed scrunches his eyebrows in confusion.

"Did you just use a country song on me?"

His cheeks deepen with a light pink hue. "Blake's always been a pain in my ass. He's a good guy, but the bastard is always on my tail. And now I just used his line on the woman I'm falling fast and hard in love with."

"Must know what he's doing." I smirk.

Before I know it, a song is playing on his phone. And it isn't Blake. It seems Jed has some jokes in him after a day from hell. Miranda Lambert's "Pushin' Time" begins to play. The song right away strikes me in the gut with soulful words and the ache in her voice. Miranda is packing a punch with each word she sings.

Our bodies meld together easy as we sway. There couldn't be a better song that fits us to perfection. Jed's hand goes up to the back of my hair. I squeeze my eyes, knowing our love happened overnight.

"I think we found our song, baby." Jed's lips graze across mine.

"Yes," I whisper.

We get lost in the lyrics of the song, swaying back and forth. Our lips are a breath away, but never touch. Our eye contact never breaks either. It's a constant. I know beyond a shadow of doubt that I'm staring into my future.

The last chords of the song fade out. Silence wraps around us. "Hound Dog" by Elvis starts up, and we both erupt into laughter.

Chapter 30

"What I love most about this crazy life is the adventure of it."
-Juliette Binoche

Every day is a new beginning. I've heard it used often, but now understand the magic of it. The Keurig hums to life, the sweet aroma of coffee is filling the air. I lick my lips, wishing like hell I had my favorite coffee date here. It all started out with a simple cup of hot coffee, sitting in silence.

I pull on my flannel button up shirt and pick up Hope's pink blanket, bringing it to my face. I kiss it and then tuck it away up in the cupboard safe on Bentley's faded Army shirt. They'll always be a part of me.

Guy's whining at the door ready to get out and chase birds. I throw it open, greeted by the chilly, fresh morning air and gasp. Not from the cold breeze, but the man perched on my picnic table. Black long sleeve Henley, backward ball cap, aviators, and those dimples that would light up anyone's world.

"Jed," I whisper.

He smiles. He inches off the table and strides to me. "I had to come."

"I see that." I bring the mug to my lips, blowing on it. "Fender?"

"Mom declared it Nana day. She has crafts and all kinds of crap for him."

"You smell like syrup." I lean forward and brush my lips over his.

He's standing on the first step. I like this advantage.

"French toast."

"You're a momma's boy, aren't you?"

"Through and through." His arms wrap around my thighs until he's palming both of my ass cheeks.

There are no more barriers between us. All of my walls have crumbled down, leaving just us. I want him, not only in my life but involved in every aspect of it.

"Want to come in?" I run my free hand over his shoulder.

"You sure?" He pulls me closer, squeezing my ass. "You don't have to."

"Shut up and kiss me."

I don't give him the chance to answer me. My lips are on his. I juggle the cup of coffee in one hand while tugging on his shirt, doing my best to walk backward. The small of my back hits the counter. Jed takes the coffee mug from my hand and places it down. Our hands go wild, tugging and tearing at each other's clothes. We trip over our own feet as Jed backs me up to the bed. We fall together tangled up, breathing heavy and urgent for so much more.

Jed has me stripped naked then kneels up and unzips his jeans. He's a breathtaking sight I'll never grow old of drinking in. His arms flex as he plants his elbows down on the bed. He holds me as if I'm fragile and delicate as he sinks in.

"Kiss me," I whisper. "Make love to me."

I continue rambling on until he covers my

mouth with his. Chills coupled with pleasure prickle and nip at my skin. He moves slow and steady, building up the pleasure with each movement. My hands tug on his hair, pulling him closer and deeper. I lock my ankles right above his ass, wanting more. Demanding more and Jed gives it. Our gentle lovemaking spins out of control. Something snaps inside of Jed. He rises above me. My lips immediately miss the feel of his on mine. I don't have long to grieve because my breath is taken away. Jed slams into me over and over. I close my eyes and scream out his name as it all becomes too much. I'm blinded by the orgasm that strikes me hard.

His large palms go to the back of my thighs, gripping them tightly and then pulling them up. Jed hitches both of my legs flat against his chest, resting both of my feet on one of his shoulders. One of his hands wraps around my ankles, holding them in place.

The change in position makes my head spin. His other hand drifts down along my stomach and up to my breast. He rolls my aching nipple between his fingers and I'm right on the edge of a steep cliff, ready to fall with him.

Each grueling thrust is loyal and grows frantic. Jed bites down on his bottom lip, snaps his eyes shut, and throws back his head. Even though I'm falling into a deep pool of ecstasy, we both reach our height at the same time. Jed growls low and husky, milking out each ounce of pleasure.

Silent seconds tick by before my body cushions him falling forward. His body weight is only on me for a quick beat before he rolls us to our sides. I brush away the hair from his face.

"Best coffee date yet." I let my fingers trail down his jawline.

"It ain't over." Jed squeezes my ass.

"I like the sound of that."

"Before I get too carried away, I need to ask you something."

"What's that?"

"Want to head to Boise with me and the family tomorrow? I have that concert and then staying until the surgery."

I nod without thinking. "Yes, but what about the store and stuff?"

"Mom has it under control with some of her employees."

The trailer door slams shut, startling me then Guy howls, scratching at the door.

"What about him?"

I grow disappointed, knowing it won't work out.

"Pet-friendly hotel." He rolls over me, strides to the door, and lets Guy in.

His ass and broad back have me hypnotized.

"You're naked," I remind him when he climbs back over me.

"I'm in the mountains. The only person around for miles is Lydia. Probably would make her day if she got a little show."

"Or give her a damn heart attack."

We both begin laughing uncontrollably about the vision. I kiss his face all over and tell him yes. Yes, I'll go. I have a sinking suspicion I'll be telling this man yes the rest of my days.

Jed makes good on his promise of extending our morning way into the late afternoon.

***

"This is like the real deal." I stare around one more time in complete awe.

"Sure is and this is small scale for Jed." Caleb stuffs a handful of popcorn in his mouth and chases it with a long pull from his beer.

"Wow, I can't begin to imagine." I take seat in the front row.

The outdoor arena is an intimate setting, allowing fans to get up close and personal with the performer. I've only been to a handful of concerts throughout my life, so everything looks huge to me.

"It gets old after a while," Caleb mumbles around another mouthful of popcorn. "Not my cup of tea."

I see the opening and take it. "Football."

His head jerks to attention with that one word.

"Was my cup of tea." He drains the rest of his beer.

"So, what's your story?" I toss his question back in his face.

He shrugs. "Life happened. The end."

"Are you serious?" I shake my head. "You don't get off that easy."

We are interrupted by a security guard. "Caleb, Jed wants you to bring Marlee backstage."

"Will do."

The security guard strides back to the edge of the stage.

"Let's go." Caleb holds out his hand to me.

I take it, snag his popcorn, and dart for backstage. The lanyard granting me access whips around my head.

"You little shit." Caleb pounds the ground behind me.

Popcorn flies out of the butter soaked bucket as I pick up my pace. I dash through the gate, the two security guards already know me. I've been backstage hanging out with Jed and Fender. I didn't leave until Caleb begged me to get junk food with him from the concession stands. Two chilidogs, a handful of beers, nachos, and a bucket of buttery popcorn was all demolished by Caleb, and it seems now it has slowed him down.

I reach the inside of the enormous, open-sided, hospitality tent before Caleb reaches me. I spot Fender and rush to him, winding and weaving through tables and band members and their families. Once I reach him, I gently shove the popcorn in his chest.

"Fank you." His eyes light up, shining with glee.

"Anytime." I sit down in the chair he's standing by.

Fender fills his palm with as much popcorn as he possibly can and shoves it in his mouth. These boys and their food are something to watch. He wipes his palm off on the front of his jeans then wipes his eyes using the back of his hands.

"What's wrong, buddy?"

"I'm tired, Marwee."

It warms my heart how he sometimes nails the r sound in his speech.

I pat my thighs. "Want me to hold you?"

He nods, sending me a yes. I place the bucket of popcorn on the table and pick him up. Speaking of the popcorn, I notice Caleb across the tent, chatting it up with a blonde, popcorn long forgotten.

"Are you excited to see your dad sing?" I cradle him in my arms like a newborn baby.

Fender snuggles right into my chest. His eyes flutter shut when I run my fingers through his hair.

"I slept like poop last night."

I crane my neck to see his face. "You did? Why?"

"I don't want my daddy to get sick."

"I know, baby, I know." I kiss his forehead, holding back my worries.

"He can't get too sick because I don't have a mom."

"Oh, Fender." I kiss him again. "You'll never be alone. Your daddy is sick, but he has you, Nana, Papa, Caleb, Me, and Guy. We are all going to be his sidekicks getting him through this."

"'Cause he's our superhero," Fender replies.

"Yes, he is."

His eyes flutter shut and his breathing evens out. I trace a line with my finger down his face. Glancing up, I see Jed watching me from the other side of the tent. He's casually leaning back on a table, ice-cold bottle of water gripped in his hand and that damn black t-shirt. His eyes are watery with tears threatening to spill over.

I can't imagine how we look from his viewpoint. I do know how damn amazing it feels from my position. Home. Forever. Movement out of the corner of my vision catches my attention. Luke swiped the bucket of popcorn from the table and waltzed off. I let Fender sleep through the two opening acts, tapping my foot to the beat of every song.

He doesn't flinch or stir with the loud music. You can definitely tell he's been raised in this environment. The damn near deafening country music is his lullaby.

"Here, let me take my sleeping prince charming." Martha holds her arms out. "He can be a bear when waking up."

I smile gently and pass him over then shake out my numb arm. Tingles pinch up as it comes back to life. Jed and I meet halfway in the middle of the tent. Everyone disappears, and all sounds mute as he clutches my hip. He doesn't have to move me forward this time because I'm already there.

"Don't know how I'm supposed to sing with you wearing those damn sexy cowboy boots and short dress," Jed growls, then runs his lips over my neck.

I tilt my head to the side, wanting him never to stop. "It's not that short."

His rough palm runs the bottom of my dress, reminding me how short it is.

"Fine, but it's your fault. You sent me out with your mom and credit card."

"Heard you refused to buy an outfit, so Mom had to finally pick one."

"Told you I didn't need one."

He shrugs. "I know. Heard you say it about fifty times. I'm damn proud of you for going out."

"I love your mom. She made it easy."

"Next time shopping trip will be to Victoria's

Secret, and you will be swiping that card."

"Victoria's Secret?" I quirk an eyebrow up in question.

"You know for the rough days I'm going to have. Gonna need some brightening up and stuff." Jed runs his nose along my jawline.

Our deep and serious conversation is broken up, and Jed is led away. I follow his family out to our seats. Andrew James, the final opening act, is finishing up. Jed told me he's the next big star. It doesn't take a country legend to make you believe it. He has the whole package from his looks, to downhome country nice guy vibe, and those pipes. I'm already a believer.

"Alright, Boise, Idaho, are you ready for the reason we are all here?" Andrew booms into the microphone. "The one. The only. Jed Bryant."

Andrew draws out Jed's name in the microphone. The audience goes wild, screaming and jumping up and down. I'm in awe of the magic happening. They're screaming for the man I've grown to know. He's simple. Has a heart of gold and loves his Pop-Tarts, but to these fans, he's a God.

"Boise, Idaho, let me hear you." Jed comes jetting out down a long runway, guitar in hand and immediately begins strumming a high pace song. His band members follow him. Andrew is right by his side, singing one of Jed's chart-topping songs. It's fast and upbeat and I can't help but move to the rhythm of the song.

I feel a tug on my hand and look down to see Fender. I bend down, placing my ear to near his mouth. He cups his hands over his mouth and shouts. "Dance with me."

I nod. Fender wastes no time pulling me out of my chair. He's already full-out rocking by the time I stand. He grabs my hands and does his best to swing me around. We sing, laugh, and wiggle until the song is over.

Jed catches my attention when he strides with power and confidence over to our side of the stage. I'm struck dumb. Jed and I formed an unbreakable bond and have explored each other's bodies a handful of times now, but it's like I'm seeing him in a whole new light. A sense of pride, intrigue, and love coat me in his presence.

Caleb grabs Fender, pulling him onto his shoulders. Jed smiles and then flicks his guitar pick to his son. Fender's arm shoots up in the air in pride and victory. Martha leans in and whispers in my ear.

"He's done that since Fender was born. He always gives him the first guitar pick of a concert. It's their thing."

The deal is sealed on my tender heart. Jed Bryant officially owns it. Jed plays song after song once Andrew left the stage. We watch as he pours everything he has left of him into his work. This crowd in Boise, Idaho, will never know how fortunate they are because Jed is singing like it's going to be the last concert.

"Gonna slow it down for a bit." Jed shotguns a cold bottle of water. The women go nuts. "This song has been around for a while and might be a favorite of my songs. I wrote it during a time in my life that was flipped upside down. And now I find myself coming back to it. Just going to be me and my guitar for this one."

He settles onto a barstool, adjusts his guitar around for a bit, and steadies his fingers on the chords. "Ever wonder why we find our most prized possessions in the darkest times of our lives? That question has plagued me a time or two over the years. Took me going home and grounding myself before I found the answer. Destiny. It's all about those stars lining up and bringing the right people into your life."

I will not cry. I will not cry. Jed strums the chords of his song "Lost." The crowd is silent in awe. The sound of his melodic voice and guitar fills the air. He's exposing himself up there in the rawest form. And there's not one dry eye left in the house. Well, except for Fender who is smiling with pride at his daddy.

It takes several minutes when Jed finishes for the crowd to quiet down.

"Thank you." Jed drops his head. "Thank you, Boise, Idaho."

He receives a standing ovation. The crowd doesn't quit for several minutes. Jed rises and begins talking. I had no idea he was going to do this.

"Boise, I have some news, and you're the first to hear it."

Andrew James saunters out on stage, standing next to Jed, shoulder to shoulder, with a microphone in hand.

"Oh my God." a chorus of women squeal.

"They're going to Magic Mike us."

The comment loud enough to reach the stage causes both men to smile like teenage boys.

"Darlin', this boy ain't got enough moves to keep up with me." Jed hitches his thumb in the direction of Andrew. "He's still a bit green on the edges. A young pup of sorts."

"Hey, now," Andrew warns.

The crowd enjoys a good laugh.

"Time to get serious." Jed grips the microphone in his hand. "I have some news and no better place to announce it than in the fabulous state of Idaho."

He waits for another wave of cheering to die down before speaking.

"You all might have noticed that my band members were playing for Andrew. If you didn't, you can blame it on the beers." Jed holds up his water bottle, saluting the members of the drinking crowd. "Got a good reason for that, too."

Andrew wraps an arm around Jed's shoulders, encouraging him to go on.

"No easy way to say it. I've been diagnosed with Stage 2 Appendix Cancer. Starting my fight against it the day after tomorrow. That means I'm handing my crown over to Mr. Andrew James here. This is his gig now and I know he won't disappoint you."

Jed's voice cracks on the last part. Martha squeezes my hand as Jed's words clamp around my beating heart. The crowd grows hushed with a somber tone settling over the venue.

"Now onto the important stuff." Jed winks over at us. "Gotta play my boy's favorite song."

Andrew brings the microphone to his mouth.

"What's that? Let me guess, it's a Tim McGraw song."

"No!" Fender hops to his feet, yelling with all his might.

Jed can't hear his words but sees Fender's reaction, making him laugh.

"Get up here, son, and let's show Mr. James how you rock out with the King."

A security guard has Fender wrapped up in his arms and hauling him to the stage. Once his little boots touch down, Jed and his band tear into their rendition of "Hound Dog" swinging hips and all. Fender does his best copying each of his dad's actions. The smile on his face will be one that will always be burned into my memory.

Chapter 31

"There is more pleasure in loving than in being beloved." -Thomas Fuller

I stir awake in the soft sheets. Fender insisted I slept in the same room with him and his dad. He built pillow lines down the bed, so we each had our section with him smack dab in the middle.

My vision focuses in on the sleeping angel next to me. Fender's curled up in a tight ball, snoring away. Moonlight shines in through a sliver of the curtain, and a silhouette appears.

I lift up my head, everything becoming clearer. "Jed?"

"I'm here, baby," he whispers.

He's in the oversized lounge chair. Elbow leaning down on the arm, a glass in his hands, and legs spread wide, highlighted by enough moonlight to make his form out.

"Are you okay?" I do my best to creep out of bed to not disturb Fender.

"No." He brings the tumbler to his mouth, taking a long drink.

The closer I get, I make out the bottle of Jameson on the table next to him. My heart sinks. He was holding everything together after the concert for his family and me.

I straddle his lap, my knees sinking into the plush cushions of the chair, wrap my arms around his neck, and tilt my head. "Talk to me."

"Nothing to talk about. Just gave away what I've worked my whole life for. Thank you, fucking cancer." The venom in his voice is thick.

"You didn't give it away, baby." I cup his cheek. "That wasn't your last performance. It may have felt like it, but it wasn't."

"The future tells me otherwise."

"It did to me once upon a time as well. My life was over. Everything was gone. Until you."

Jed throws back the last of the Jameson, sets the tumbler down on the table with a clink, and pulls me to him. I let him cry, be pissed for what he's going through until he gets it all out. We remain in the same position for what feels like hours and only a matter minutes at the same time.

Jed stands, keeping me tight to his chest. I wrap my legs around his waist, hooking my ankles right above his ass. He walks out into the main living area of the suite. This isn't your typical hotel room; no, Jed rented the biggest suite they had. I teased him that it must be nice to be able to rent the entire floor of a hotel.

Jed lays me down on the couch. The crisp, white leather is going straight through the thin material of my shirt. I watch hypnotized as Jed strips away each piece of clothing until he's naked in front of me. There's no question in my mind what he wants.

I reach down to pull off my pajama shorts, but his hand stops me. He kneels down next to me, stripping away each piece of my clothing. He lets his knuckles linger on my skin as he does it. Then his mouth is everywhere, licking, tasting, and devouring me. It all becomes too much, and his name slips from my tongue in a cry.

Jed covers my body, trapping my pleas and screams. My fingernails pierce into the top of his shoulders when he drives into me. He replicates each motion with precision over and over. My legs wrapped around his middle quiver with excitement and anticipation as the torrid storm builds up in both of us. I clamor out incoherent words as I feel his length pulse once then twice before he spills into me. It's his final thrusts coated in his release that sends me over the edge.

We spend the next day sneaking off, repeating the above over and over.

Chapter 32

"I have found the paradox, that if you love until it hurts, there can be no more hurt, only more love." -Mother Teresa

Jed's surgery was pushed back a day. It was torture and sweet hell at the same time. We shared plenty of lovemaking sessions on borrowed time and took Fender to the Boise Zoo.

The doctors have been amazing with Fender since arriving at the hospital. He's been a constant by his dad's side. One of the OR nurses gave him a scrub top that fits him like a dress, but he's wearing it, pretending to check his dad's pulse every so often.

I know the hardest moment of his life is about to happen. I asked around and finally got an answer.

"Hey, sexy." I kiss Jed's forehead in the pre-op room. "I'm going to go get Guy for Fender."

"They said yes?"

"Yeah, they did, but I was waiting until the last minute in case you stood up, and I got a glimpse of that fine ass of yours."

Jed chuckles. "Thank you, Marlee."

I refuse to cry right now even though it's the only thing I want to do. I will not. I will remain strong and steadfast. Jed's overbearing frame in the hospital bed hooked up to all sorts of IVs is devastating. A sight I never want to see again, and I know this is only the beginning of his battle.

I steal a final kiss before walking two blocks to

get Guy.

"I love you, Jed Bryant. You've taught me love finds you when you least expect it and you have to love fierce and passionate like there's no such thing as a broken heart."

He grabs the back of my neck, pulling me down for another kiss. "You saved me, Marlee. I love you, too."

The threat of tears spilling over becomes too much to handle. I kiss him one more time before leaving to fetch Guy. Once outside the hospital's carousel doors, I break down. My feet never quit moving. With each step, the tears of fear drain from me.

On the walk back to the hospital, the tears keep falling. Some say tears dry up over time. I call bullshit. I manage to sweep them off my face before entering the hospital and checking in at the front desk to get a visitor badge for Guy. I know my eyes are swollen and red, yet can't find a reason to hide my pain.

I check the family waiting area first and find all of the Bryants minus Jed huddled around a weeping Fender. I waste no time rushing over to them.

"Fender, someone wants to see you." I grip on the end of Guy's leash.

It doesn't matter how tight my grips is because Guy bolts from me. His two front paws land on the chair next to Fender's legs. He laps up all of his tears.

"My best friend." Fender's arms wrap around Guy's neck. He buries his face in the safety of his best friend.

There's a huge television nestled in the corner. I have Jed's patient identification number memorized by heart. I study the monitor, waiting for any updates. I've never felt seconds that seem like hours until now. Fender has long fallen asleep cuddled next to Guy.

"Damn good idea, Marlee." Luke points at the sleeping pair.

"That dog has offered so much comfort to me over the years, and he loves Fender."

"I can see that," Luke replies.

I don't know what forces me to do so, but I open up to Martha, Luke, and Caleb, telling them all about my family and Bentley. I start from the beginning and don't leave a single part out until the ending.

"We'd love to meet your parents, Marlee. You know our house is always open." Martha clutches my hand. "I've never seen my Jeddy in love, until you."

"Jeddy, really, Mom?" Caleb leans forward, resting his elbows on the top of his thighs.

"Jed will always be my Jeddy Teddy Bear."

Caleb shakes his head in disgust at the nickname.

"You'll understand one day, boy," Luke adds.

"Yes, you will, Poopy."

"Jesus, Mom." Caleb blushes to the point of turning red.

"I get why you call Jed, Jeddy the Teddy, but I have to hear the story behind Caleb's nickname, please," I demand.

"Mom," Caleb warns.

It does nothing to stop Martha, a momma determined. "When Caleb was about ten months."

"Mom! I swear." He buries his face in his palms.

"My Poopy loved his bath time. I couldn't pry him out of the tub. Well, once his little bum would hit the warm water, he'd poop. Every single time. The first time it happened I flipped, screaming for Luke. We ended up fishing the turd out with a strainer. Well, then I became a seasoned pro and dealt with it on my own."

My abs have never been worked out so hard. Half from the story Martha is telling me and from the sheer embarrassment cascading off of Caleb. I didn't think the man could be embarrassed.

Clutching my stomach, I manage to get out. "Oh, Poopy, you didn't shit the bed, you are a tub shitter."

"Thanks, Mom, thanks a lot."

The childhood stories fold out. Martha holds nothing back. A wave of reassurance ghosts across her face as she continues to toss her boys under the bus. I'll be chatting with Jed about the time he was busted with his first porno magazine and sock by his mom.

The time is spent divulging funny stories until a doctor walks into the small waiting room. Fender is still fast asleep on Guy, and neither of them stirs when he begins talking.

The droplets of blood on the doctor's white Dansko clogs transfix me. I'm unable to pull my stare from them. Jed's blood. I freeze, unable to hear the first few words.

"He's out of surgery and doing great. His appendix is no longer there. We're going to continue with treatment to ensure the cancer is completely gone. It's never a guarantee, but Jed is a poster child for this treatment."

"When can we see him?" Martha asks.

"He's in recovery for now. The nurses will come and get you once he's awake. He'll be transported to a room on floor three for his after surgery care until he's able to go home."

"Then the treatments come."

Everyone glances to Luke who has tears leaking from the corners of his eyes. None of us know if it was a question or statement.

The doctor nods.

"Yes, everything will be proactive. Not an easy journey, but one worth fighting." The doctor stands. "Oh, Jed kept asking for a Marlee toward the end of the surgery. Claimed he needed her and wanted to make her scream."

My eyes bulge, heat chases over my cheeks, and I want to crawl underneath the chair I'm sitting in.

"Patients say some of the funniest stuff when waking up."

Yeah, really funny. Caleb gets the biggest kick out of the comment. Karma at its finest.

Chapter 33

"Intense love does not measure, it just gives." - Mother Teresa

Jed's palms grip my ass. Even in his weak state, he's never lost his appetite to touch me.

"Hold still." I bend over, grabbing the clippers.

"Don't want to." Jed runs his hands through his hair. Clumps remain in his grip. "I'd rather be doing something else."

It's a rare day where Jed has some energy and isn't throwing up. Out of all the pain and suffering he's in; his hair bugs him the most. It's nearly gone with only a few sparse spots left. He's covered it up with his favorite beanie from one of his tours from years ago. Today he'll no longer be covering it up because the Bryant men have risen to the occasion.

He's lost his love for eating, is covered in bruises, and can barely get out of bed most days and even through it all, he hasn't lost his will to live and express his love. The days he has the extra energy he spends it living big. It doesn't mean there haven't been dark nasty times where his deepest fears come out to play. We share those days as well.

Today we are shaving the bits of hair he has left. Three other chairs are lined up next to his side. Fender, Caleb, and Luke are taking the dive as well. Martha is in the house, rounding them up. Fender wants to look just like his daddy.

"Feeling sick?" I ask, planting my hands on the

top of his shoulders.

Jed pulls me into his lap. The weight loss Jed has experienced is heart-wrenching. He's a shell of the man he once was, but it never stops him. Fatigue and vomiting have been the worse side effects so far. Some nights the retching of bile he pukes is uncontrollable. Caleb is always by his side, passing him a joint once the puking stops and the muscle aches settle in. Those two have been higher than kites. It always dulls the pain for the time being.

Martha marches the troops out, setting them in their seats. We each have clippers in hand. I told Martha she could start with Jed, but she refused, telling me he has a new woman in his life. I love her. She's the perfect mother not being intimidated by anyone.

"I want Nana to make me bald," Fender declares.

Luke takes a seat by his son while Caleb and Fender sit on Nana's end. God bless her she has a much bigger job with those two than I do. It only takes a few passes over Jed's head until he has no hair left. His face is swollen, dark lines under his eyes, and is pale as a blank white sheet. I hate seeing him in this state.

"Dad, you don't have to do this."

"Sure, I do, Jed. Don't need Caleb marching his ass round here claiming to be sexy and bald. Boy needs some competition."

I don't wait for any further instruction before running the clippers in long lines over Luke's head. The slamming of a truck door causes us all to turn our attention to the driveway. I've seen the man around town, but have no idea who he is, yet know I should.

"Pastor Williams, so nice to see you." Martha places her clippers on a table and brushes at her apron.

"My wife made you all dinner. Just wanted to drop it by."

Martha and Luke are faithful in their devotion, attending church every Sunday since they've been home. Jed told me it's always been like that. It's the way the boys were raised, but their parents don't judge them for not going or force them to attend because they know their boys are God-fearing men.

"Tell Willa Jean we sure appreciate it." Martha grabs the dishes.

"Yes, thank you, Pastor. You're more than welcome to help yourself to some ice tea and visit a bit." Luke points to the glass container of tea brewing in the sun. Not the least bit concerned he is currently sporting the worst haircut known to mankind.

"Thanks, but I got to get going. Delanie calls every Tuesday afternoon, and I don't want to miss it. Take care, and God bless."

He's back in his truck and gone.

"Who's Delanie?" Jed asks.

"Pastor's daughter. Lives in Texas. Heard she's a fox," Caleb offers.

"What's dat mean?" Fender peers up to him.

"A chick with massive t..."

Martha whacks Caleb upside the head with the clippers, halting him mid-sentence.

"Son of a bitch, Mom." He rubs the spot.

She whacks him again. "Language."

"Son of a biscuit." He rubs the new spot. "Control your woman, Dad."

"You're a big boy, Caleb." Luke chuckles.

I finish before Martha does. I knew her job was going to be a rough one. Jed shivers, growing a light shade of green.

"Need to go lay down for a bit?" I ask him.

He shakes his head. "No, don't want to miss any of this. Can you grab the blanket off the couch?"

"Yep." I kiss his cheek and run my fingers over the sores on the corner of his lips. They're finally drying out. "Martha, want me to toss that casserole in the oven the Pastor brought?"

She tilts her head and bites her bottom lip. "This doesn't leave this porch. Willa Jean is a horrible cook. Let's freeze it and forget about it for now."

"I'm telling," Caleb sings. "Gonna share that piece of gossip with all the old ladies in town."

Another whop to the side of the head. I laugh, walking inside to grab the blanket. The cabin that was once one straight from a magazine has now become a home to me. We moved my Airstream down here eight weeks ago after it became too much of a toll going back and forth. Jed's treatment intensified once the doctors realized it wasn't as effective as they once thought it would be. It was never a doubt in my mind that I wanted to be there for every single second of the day for Jed.

I never sleep in it anymore. It's become Fender's playhouse. Martha bought Fender a bed and let him help decorate a room of his own. It's rare that he ever asks to sleep between Jed and me and when he does, we welcome him with open arms. No questions asked.

Jed has never followed any parenting magazines. He's ignored all of it, allowing his heart to be the only guidance when it comes to Fender.

The porch is eerily silent when I walk back outside. I'm in the middle of a yawn. The kind that takes over your entire face, causing you to only focus on it. Mouth wide open, eyes shut, and head thrown back. Caleb's hair is half gone and Fender's rustling around with Guy in the dirt. His bald head is shining through it all.

I wrap the thick Aztec pattern blanket around Jed's shoulders. I kiss the top of his head, sensing he has a slight temperature.

"Come here." He pulls me into his lap.

I cringe internally every single time he does this. The man is so frail I hate sitting in his lap, so I always keep most of my weight centered on the balls of my feet. I've gained a good ten to fifteen pounds since moving in and being spoiled by Martha's cooking.

"Need me to warm you up?" I ask, running my palm over his now smooth head. I can't believe we've waited this long to shave off the few patches of hair.

"Something like that."

God, I crave to be in this man's arms or holding him. It's my favorite thing to do when he sleeps. I run my hands all over his body, committing the feel of his skin to memory.

He grabs my hand under the blanket, and I feel

a cold piece of metal slip around my finger. I gasp, but Jed holds my hand in his and whispers. "Marry me, Marlee. Marry me after my hair grows back, and I'm strong. Let's build our cabin and start a life."

The words are lodged in my throat. I try and try to get them up, only to have them get stuck. I begin to nod my head slow at first then faster.

"Yes. Yes. Yes, Jed."

I grab the sides of his face and kiss his lips. "Yes, I will marry you anywhere and anytime."

"Hit it, Fender."

I turn to see Caleb with his hands cupped around his mouth. Everyone was watching us, and I had no clue, that's how immersed I was in Jed Bryant. Fender pulls his dad's phone out of his back pocket and pushes the buttons. Loud guitar strums begin to play, startling me.

Jed points out the large Bluetooth speakers on the porch.

"Give Me Love" by Ed Sheeran surrounds us, swallowing us whole.

"Dance with me," Jed whispers in my ear.

I rise from his lap, giving him time to get up on his own. It's a fine line where I never want Jed to feel like he has to rely on anyone stripping his pride away from him and I also don't like to see him struggle. Once he's standing, I grab the blanket on his shoulders and wrap up in it with him.

We move back and forth cocooned in the warmth of the blanket and highlighted in the glow of our love. A rare kind of love that I once already lived and now get a second chance at. I rest my face in the crook of Jed's neck, soaking him in.

"I've got a Mommy." Fender races up the porch, wiggling his way between us.

I don't flinch or feel pain strike at his comment. It's all the complete opposite. I melt and become a Mommy.

"Pictures," Martha declares, waving her phone around.

I pick up Fender, nestling him between us.

"Smile, you ugly, bald bastard," Caleb chides with a huge grin on his face.

Jed may be sick, but nobody treats him any different. Caleb kisses the top of my head, Fender sticks his tongue out at the camera, Guy puts his two paws on my side, and I smile.

"Let me see." Fender races off.

Jed pulls me back into the blanket. "I want to take you down to the little cabin, strip you naked, and make love to you all night. I've imagined it over and over in my head. It's all I want."

"In time it will happen, but for now you'll have to settle for cuddling."

Jed winces, and I know it's not from what I said. He's going to vomit. The gut-wrenching and relentless vomiting is about to ensue. Nasty bile that never gives up.

I grab his arm and guide him in the house.

"Almost to your room." I turn back, checking on him.

Jed is barely on the edge of the bed, reaching for the bucket, bending over and heaving into it. The happy moment is obliterated by the harsh truth of reality. I rub his back, waiting for the spell to get over.

After long moments, he slowly sits back up. "One step forward, five hundred back."

"No, baby. It was a good day. The best day. Cling to that. This will pass." I lay my head on his shoulder and hold my hand up in front of us. "We have forever."

"I'm tired of being sick. I feel worthless all the damn time."

"Baby, you're halfway through."

"And when it comes back? I'll never be cancer free. It will always be a threat."

Jed's mind and body are always on a constant roller coaster of ups and downs. I promised at the beginning of his treatment his sidekicks would get him through it.

"It might come back, or this treatment may fail, but you're not a quitter no matter how brutal this is. You are going to get healthy for a night in the cabin and many more after."

He turns his head, kissing my forehead. "I'm down. You know how it goes."

"I'm going to go help your mom with dinner. Want to come out in the recliner?"

"Fuck football. I'm sick of watching old tapes and listening to those two asses."

"Me, too." I stand up. "Let's go wash you up a bit."

I follow Jed into the bathroom and stand back as he splashes water on his face and brushes his teeth.

"Daddy!"

I turn in time to see Fender run face first into

the wall.

"Dammit. Son of a..."

"Fender." Both Jed and I call out at the same time.

"Biscuit eater," he finishes.

"I swear, if Caleb ever has kids it's going to be on," Jed mutters under his breath.

"Daddy." Fender rubs his head that collided into the wall. "Nana bought this new book about dinosaurs. Will you read it to me?"

That makes Jed beam with pride. He does it every single time Fender nails all of his r sounds. "Yes, climb in bed."

I rush over to the bed, grabbing the bucket and pulling back the blankets before the boys make it. After rinsing out the bucket in the bathroom, I lean on the door jamb, arms folded, and watch Jed read about dinosaurs. I don't know what it is. I can't put my finger on it. But in moments like these I know everything will work out.

It's hard day in and day out seeing a person you love suffer so much. But when you hear Jed's rich voice reading each word on the pages about dinosaurs and see Fender immersed in each syllable with a big grin on his face, you have to believe in the good of the world.

I sneak out of the bedroom, not either one of my boys noticing me. Like Jed predicted Luke and Caleb are settled in front of the TV watching football, arguing like always. I find Martha in the kitchen cooking up a storm.

"What can I help you with?" I ask.

Martha used to tell me nothing and to go away,

but I think she's learned I'm not going to give up and always ask if she needs help. She points to a pile of potatoes and asks me to dice them and put them in a boiling pot of water.

"Is he okay?" Martha asks.

I shrug, not really knowing how to answer the question.

"Do you think he'll feel like eating tonight?"

"We can always try."

The other night Jed wanted a chocolate milkshake so bad that he didn't give up until his mom walked over to the store after hours and bought the ingredients to make one. It's the first thing I've seen the man slurp down without taking hours to eat. However, it was only ten minutes before he was relentlessly throwing up. He still claims it was worth every single swallow.

"Are you feeling okay, Marlee?"

I glance over to Martha with a quizzical look on my face. "Bit more tired than usual, but I haven't been sleeping all too well at night. When Jed has a coughing fit it takes me hours to fall back to sleep, but nothing other than that."

She shakes her head, nibbles on her bottom lip, and goes back to stirring whatever is in her mixing bowl.

"What?"

Martha shakes her head one more time before speaking. "It's really not my position to say."

I set the knife down, more intrigued than ever. "Martha, say what you're thinking. You're really confusing me."

Martha sets her cooking utensils down and

begins talking. "Well, like I said it's none of my business but, Marlee, is there any chance you could be pregnant?"

My head snaps back, and I have no idea how to respond to that. Pregnant. What in the hell? This came out of the blue. Out of left field and I'm left speechless.

Martha takes a step toward me and clutches my hands in hers. "Call it a mother's intuition or a woman's intuition whatever, but, Marlee, you have been more tired than usual, I noticed the other morning when you raced to the bathroom after breakfast and heard you throwing up, and pregnant women always have a glow and I can spot it a mile away. You have the glow."

It all slaps me in the face. Rushes at me like a pissed off bull chasing a matador with the red cloth.

"I did race to the bathroom the other morning after breakfast. The scrambled eggs didn't settle well on my stomach. I've always been finicky about eggs."

My voice shakes with each word, trying to find some sense in whatever in the hell is happening.

"Marlee, you've been tired, but I know you're going to come back with me that you've not been sleeping very well because of Jed which is true. But that glow never lies."

I slap my palms over my mouth in shock, utter shock. I'm pregnant. I know beyond a shadow of a doubt that Martha is right. I am pregnant.

"How in the hell did I not pick up on any of the signs?" The words fall from my lips in a whisper.

"Because you've had a lot on your mind, sweetie."

My period. My period. When was the last time? I had light bleeding. But how many months ago was that?

My whole body begins to quiver with excitement, fear, and trepidation all mixed in until it leaves me confused. Gobsmacked straight in the face.

"Okay, one thing at a time. You finish up those potatoes and get them in the boiling water. Dip the steaks in the egg mixture then the breading over there. I'll be right back with a pregnancy test from the store." Martha turns her back on me, almost to the door before I can stop her.

"Martha." She whips around to face me. "Martha...uh." I fumble with my words and the utensils in my hands.

She nods her head and smiles. "I got you, Marlee."

With those simple words, she's out of the door faster than I can blink. She knows exactly what I was referring to. After spilling all of my darkest fears to her in the waiting room at the hospital, we've had several conversations about my past. Martha has been the biggest advocate in my corner. She pushes and nudges me to call my parents on a weekly basis. It doesn't take much. The desire is there; it's just facing what I did to them.

With each slice of the russet potato, I struggle to face the truth. I am pregnant. I fought so damn hard in the past to get pregnant and lost it all in the blink of an eye. That one wound that's been buried for a long time, and I never ever thought I'd feel its wrath again. Yet, here I stand peeling potatoes and knowing it's happening all over again.

I have everything up to speed on dinner before Martha returns. She ushers me to the bathroom before I can protest. Hell, I don't want to make a scene with Caleb near then it would all turn into a spectacle, and that's the last thing I want.

Martha pushes me into the bathroom before she has the chance to shut the door as Maddie did so many years ago. I try to talk, but it only comes out in a whisper. "Don't be mad at me, but I'd like to tell Jed the results first either way."

"That's okay with me, because I already know you're knocked up with my grandchild." She winks at me and turns on her heels. Confident with each step as she strides away.

I swear her and Caleb are too much alike. It's eerie how perfect of a combination the Bryant brothers are. They are a subtle mix of both their mom and dad. I shake my head and go about my business. I know the routine all too well. After checking the instructions to determine two lines mean pregnant, I piss away on the stick, not feeling the pressure to be with child like I was before. Washing my hands after laying the stick flat on the counter it dawns on me…I knew my days were numbered all along with Bentley and that's what the rush was for.

It's a bittersweet realization. I no longer yearn for the what-ifs, yet finding myself cherishing the memories. Jed has always encouraged me to talk about Bentley, and I have over the last four weeks. The two men would've gotten along great. No doubt.

I think about Maddie and my parents as I wait. I know it's time to make the call, inviting them out here. There have been weekly calls to them since the first one made in this very cabin. Martha and Jed with their gentle nudges wouldn't have it any other way.

There's been an open line of communication with Maddie. Nothing profound, only skimming the surface of topics, but it's the point that I'm talking to them. Sara and Fender have shared a few FaceTime sessions. To say my parents were dumbfounded and quieted when I introduced them to Jed would be an understatement. But it only took them a few minutes to adjust and warm up to him. They not only demand weekly calls from me but daily updates via email about Jed and his process. The bond between my mother and I has grown by leaps and bounds. It's as if a day hasn't passed that we've been separated.

Full circle. I ventured a full circle in my short span as I stare down at the test. I snatch it off the counter and go to our room. Fender's long gone and sitting at the dining room table eating dinner. Jed is on his side in the bed. His eyes flicker open when I walk in. There's no smile playing out on his lips, but a dim light flickers in his whiskey-colored eyes that I love with no bounds.

"You hungry?" I ask, rounding the bottom of the bed and crawling in behind him.

He's the little spoon, and I'm the big one. It's my favorite position because I get to hold him.

"No." His voice still down and glum.

"Guess what?"

"What?"

"I found another reason."

When he gets in his dark moods, I count off the reasons why he'll beat cancer. We are up to two hundred seventy-five.

"What's that?" He turns his head enough so I can peck him on the cheek.

"Reason two hundred seventy-six." I pass over the pregnancy test until his trembling hand takes it.

I grab his hand to steady it, knowing his body is fighting him right now.

"Is this..."

"A pregnancy test," I answer.

"And."

"There are two lines."

"And?"

I don't miss the hope painting his one-worded question.

"I'm pregnant."

Jed rolls over, his body protesting every move. It's not smooth like it used to be, but he manages.

"Reason two hundred seventy-six." He clutches the pregnancy test, studying the clear window indicator. "But we haven't...since before my surgery."

"I know." I trail my finger down his nose. "Making it a big and very serious reason."

"Are you okay? Is this uh...freaking you out?"

Of course, he'd be scared and worried for me. It's who Jed Bryant is.

"Nope. I'm a girl who got diamonds, a son, learned I'm going to have a baby with the man I'm spending the rest of my life with all in one day. What's to worry about?"

"You amaze me." Jed snaps his eyes shut with a huge grin plastered across his face.

It's a perfect ending to a day in the middle of a never-ending storm.

Chapter 34

"I have found that if you love life, life will love you back."
-Arthur Rubinstein

Light kisses trail up my spine. A large palm glides onto my baby bump until it's soothing circles. It hypnotizes and coaxes me to go back to sleep.

"Sleep," I mutter.

Those sweet kisses make their way all the up to the nape of my neck. Even through sleep I crane my neck loving the feel of his lips on my skin.

"Time to wake up," Jed murmurs, flexing his hips into my backside.

"Sleep," I argue right back.

"We have exactly nine minutes before Fender comes busting in." One more hip thrust. His hard, aching length is pushing into me.

I roll over, wiping the sleep from my eyes. My hands go to my seven-month pregnant belly. Our little one rolls, kicks, and sends elbow jabs non-stop.

"There's my gorgeous woman." Jed kisses my cheek.

I roll my eyes, earning myself a slap to my thigh. It does the trick. I want Jed and know we are on a strict time window. He hasn't kept his hands off my belly since the night I told him I was pregnant. With each touch and caress, my excitement builds to a boiling point.

I rake my hands through his thick, glossy black

hair. Once treatments stopped, Jed's hair grew in with a vengeance. Each day that passed, the strong, healthy man made an appearance. He's devoured each minute back at his healthy state. You can't keep the man down. Jed sings every single day to us and has the foundation finished to our cabin. It's nestled on the edge of the river in a grove of pine trees.

"Seven minutes," I whisper into his lips. "You better hustle up, Mr. Bryant."

He follows my command, grabbing my hips, and rolling me up on him. My thighs straddle his waist. I stare down at him. His healthy glow is lighting up the room accompanied by the rising sun. I stare at him all the damn time never able to soak up enough of his gorgeous as hell features.

Jed reaches down between us, pulling his hard length from his boxers and quirks an eyebrow up, encouraging me to get to it. There's no sexy ripping of the panties from my body. Pregnancy doesn't indulge any of that.

Jed reaches down, wrapping his rugged hands around each ankle, pulling them forward. He's gentle and precise as he drags down my panties. I may be on top in the dominant position, but I'm in no way in control of any of it. Jed always is. He takes care of me with gentle, loving hands that are always encouraging me to be brave and live. He doesn't let one second of the day go by without that subtle nudge. He's stared death straight in the eyes and never backed down.

His fingertips dig into my flesh, pulling me up enough only to guide me down on him. I throw my head back, snapping my eyes shut. It never gets old and takes over every single one of my sensations. Jed drives into me, pushing his hips up from underneath me. It's been on since day one of him feeling well. We make jokes about not worrying about protection since he already got the job done.

"Jed." I dig my nails into his chest.

He answers with a deep growl and faster thrusting of his hips from underneath me. He moves one hand from my hips to my core. It takes only a few slow circles in the right spot before I'm falling hard.

"I'm close. So damn close," I moan.

Jed catches his bottom lip with his teeth. The tender skin is glowing white from the pressure, letting me know he's right with me. My nails dig in his chest and I do my best to stifle my cries of pleasure. Jed growls low and deep, letting go inside of me.

"That was the best ever," I say between panting breaths.

Jed sits up, guiding my legs around his waist and pulls our chests together. I collapse in his hold. All of my muscles are deliciously sated. I could stay here all day letting him hold me.

"Shower," he murmurs into my neck.

"Fender," I mumble.

"Two minutes." He clutches my ass in his large palms.

Then I'm up in the air, moving toward the bathroom, I lock my ankles together right above the globes of his ass.

"How many times have I told you I'm too big for you to pack around?"

"Doesn't matter."

I feel him shrug. Jed reaches into the shower, firing it to life. He never lets me go until steam billows from the top of the glass shower stall. Once under the hot, refreshing water, he presses my back against the chilled tiled wall. He begins to move against me.

"Again?" I quirk an eyebrow, staring into his deep chocolate eyes.

"And again and again."

Jed makes good on his promise, making love to me one more time and then washing every inch of my skin. He runs his fingers over my scalp, massaging the shampoo and conditioner in.

"The perfect morning." I push up on my toes and kiss Jed on his full, sexy bowtie lips.

I see his desires painted on each of his features. He wants more. We have no self-control and always on a strict time window when it comes to adult alone time.

"Every minute with you, Marlee, is perfect." He repeats the tender kiss. "I'm forcing myself to step away right now and dry off even though I want nothing more than to toss your naked, beautiful ass back in our bed."

I stay under the hot spray, not taking my gaze off of Jed as he dries off with a plush, navy blue towel. Tears prick at the corners of my eyes with each flex of his new, defined muscles. He's been diligent in his recovery spiritually, mentally, and physically, dedicating every second to coming back stronger for his family. I groan when he slips into a loose pair of sleek black workout pants. They hang low on his hips, taunting the hell out of me.

I've heard about the amped up sex drive while being pregnant. But that's only a part of our problem. When Jed was sick, there was no sex. And now we are worse than two teenage kids.

Jed sends me a quick wink before opening the bathroom door and stepping into our bedroom. It seems he has perfect timing.

"Daddy!" Fender's sleepy yet excited voice floats into the bathroom.

I hear the sounds of Jed flopping back on the bed and know Fender is climbing right up to cuddle with his dad. Their morning cuddles always turn into wrestling matches. Some mornings Martha and Caleb join in and that's when it gets wild. On those mornings, I sneak out with Luke on the porch and enjoy coffee. There's something about sitting in silence and drinking coffee with the Bryant men. It's the best kind of therapy out there.

I grunt, bending over to smooth out coconut oil over my legs. This belly. I smile like a fool every single time it gets in the way, which is more and more often. Jed treated this pregnancy like precious glass in the beginning until I told him he was making it worse. My nerves were close to fraying between his constant worrying and shitty chemo days. I'm suspecting Martha sat down and talked with him because now I'm just the exhausted, hungry pregnant woman.

I toe open the door while pulling my wet locks

up into a messy bun on the top of my head. Fender is sprawled out on Jed's chest, running the pad of his fingers over Jed's stubble.

"Daddy's beard is coming nice, eh?" I lean over and kiss the top of Fender's head.

Jed gets a quick ass grab in before I sit on the edge of the bed.

"I want one." Fender beams at his dad.

"In time, son." Jed pats Fender's back.

"No, now. Banky told me I need to drink black coffee and shave my face."

"No!" we both holler in unison.

Jed gains his bearings before I do and begins reasoning with Fender, explaining to him you have to be a certain age to grow a beard. I take it upon myself to waltz right back into the bathroom and put Jed's shaving kit up on the top shelf of our vanity. Fender is doing a bang up job of breaking me in for motherhood.

"Banky said you aren't growing a beard because you lost the bet with Marwee, but because women like bouncing on beards." Fender tilts his head, tapping his chin. "That still confuses me."

I bite down on the side of my cheek, holding back my laughter. Only Caleb. I swear he lives to put Jed through hell and put him through hell he does.

"Caleb is an idiot." Jed flips Fender on his back and begins tickling him.

Fender squeals but does his best to get out of Jed's hold. And it's one of those mornings where Martha and Caleb join the mini-wrestling match. A painful yip from Caleb wraps around me as I pour my decaffeinated coffee into my mug. The same mug I've drank out of every single day since I left my shattered world behind. Jed had a new one made since Bentley's picture is beginning to fade on this one. I left it in the box until the day comes I need to bust it out.

"Wrestling match?" Luke rocks back and forth in his chair.

Before I have the chance to answer, roaring and squealing comes from inside the cabin. I consider it answer enough for his question. I settle in the chair and cup the mug, bringing it close to my lips. Luke places his palm on my belly, splaying his fingers wide. Popper begins kicking and fluttering about, making her or his soon to be Grandpa chuckle. Popper does it every single time.

"Popper says good morning." I smile over at Luke.

"Your Papa is excited to meet you, little one," Luke replies.

He keeps his hand on my belly while continuing to rock and drink his coffee. Popper settles down, only giving her grandpa a few kicks. Fender somehow connected popcorn chicken to his sibling growing in my stomach, hence the nickname Popper. I fear the little one may never kick the nickname.

The sun is high above the mountains before the front door swings open. My sexy lumberjack fiancé waltzes out in a red flannel button up, cargo jeans, and a magnificent beard growing in. Jed Bryant is the ideal poster child for lumbersexual.

"Off to work, baby." He leans down and kisses

my forehead, handing me a plate of bacon, eggs, and toast.

The eggs are perfect sunny side up, the bacon is crispy but not burned, and the toast is buttered with ample amounts. I'm one lucky lady.

"Jed, you are going to make someone a one fine piece of ass someday."

He shakes his head. He's heard this compliment a few dozen times from me. He leans down one more time aware of the plate balanced on my belly, catching my lower lip with his teeth. I don't miss the silent growl vibrating against my teeth.

"One day," he whispers before kissing the hell out of me.

"Ready, Daddy." The front door slams followed by a mini version of Jed walking out.

Fender in his red flannel and cargo pants. He has a mini hammer dangling on the side of his leg. "Time to get our lumbersexual on, Dad."

"I swear between you and Caleb razzing me about this damn bet I'm going to have to sink some serious money into Fender's future counseling."

"Get on with it." I squeeze his bulging bicep. "You sexy lumber beast."

He stands, shaking his head. "Only for you, my queen. Your future castle is awaiting."

He grabs Fender's hand and trails off in the direction of our future home. Jed is adamant about building everything he can with his own two hands. It doesn't take a rocket scientist to know it's his own kind of therapy.

I roll my head to peer over at Luke who is also studying the pair retreating.

"Thank you, Luke," I whisper.
He glances over at me.
"Thank you for giving me him."

Chapter 35

"If you have only one smile in you give it to the people you love." -Maya Angelou

"'Cuse me, my mom has an appointment with doctor at one fordy."

The receptionist behind the desk winks at Fender. "What is her name?"

"Marwee Foster."

"Let's see here." She taps her neon green mechanical pencil against the counter, looking down at a stack of papers, which is in no way shape or form a calendar. "Yep, got her. I'll check her in if you want to take a seat."

"I got you, Mommy." Fender grabs my hand, leading me to a seat.

There hasn't been one day go by where he's had a difficult time digesting the fact he's going to be a big brother. Jed and I keep waiting for the fallout, but it's never come. Nana and my mom, now known as Grams, have supplied him with endless picture books on being a big brother.

"Sissy, hang in there. A few more minutes," Fender whispers into my belly after settling down.

A few other expectant couples stare at us. I smile and look back at Fender who is now petting my belly which is the size of Texas. He's convinced that all I need to do is hop up and down on one leg, wink, and clap to get his sister out. We don't know the sex of the baby. Jed and I both chose to wait, but Fender is for sure it's a little girl.

I wince in pain. The Braxton Hicks are becoming

stronger every day. I've already nested or at least that's what Martha and Mom thought. Her and Dad have visited two times since I told them I was expecting and like I predicted, they fell in love with the Bryants.

"Farts?" Fender asks, peering up at me with concern.

I nod, easing his tension. Although he's on board with having a sibling, health is always front and center on his mind. His tiny palm sneaks up the front of my black maternity top. He traces circles, triangles, and then begins writing his alphabet. It always relaxes me no matter how uncomfortable the situation is. I see him before Fender does. His eyebrows are growing back in. The swelling in his face has vanished. His head is still covered in his favorite beanie, but that damn tight as hell black t-shirt is hugging his chest.

He kisses the top of Fender's head before taking a seat on my other side. Fender only stops for a second, sending his dad a toothy grin.

"How'd it go?" I ask.

"All is good. Real good, baby." He laces his fingers in mine.

We've coordinated our trips to Boise since it's almost a two-hour drive. Jed hates it because he doesn't want to miss an appointment. His cancer is in remission, and we are at the stage of check-ins and check-ups. It will never be gone or too far from our thoughts. We aren't fools and know at any time it can make its presence known.

"I knew it." I kiss his cheek, and when he turns his head, I take full advantage of his lips.

I wince again. The cramp seizing my lower back is intense. It's like a period cramp, but on damn steroids. I only have a brief moment to realize they've never been that close before the door to the waiting room flies open.

"Marlee Foster."

"Here." Fender shoots up his hand.

Hell, you'd think the kid won a raffle or a door prize. He's a part of every step. The nurse weighs me in then Fender. I get my blood pressure taken then Fender. His Uncle Caleb is out to play when it comes to the nurses.

"Jesus." I grab my lower back, freezing in the middle of climbing up on the paper cover table.

Fender gives me the eyebrow stare. Nana has been on potty language patrol, cracking down, and laying out the law.

"I meant, we should have Jell-O tonight."

"Lime. Only lime Jell-O." Fender continues digging around in my purse in search of his Matchbox cars.

"You okay?" Jed asks, helping me up on the table.

Each day he gains a bit back of his old self. The muscles and flesh filling back in. Jed was adamant about hiring a midwife to live in Moore, so I wouldn't have to travel once we found out I was pregnant. I refused to let fear control me any longer. It was a battle that I won. Once the chemo treatments ended, Jed Bryant, country music king, slowly came back to life. I'd catch him singing around the house and humming a tune when he thought no one was listening. It hasn't been easy, but with the escape of time, he's coming back stronger and better. Just like I knew he would.

"Yeah." I nod. "The Braxton things are getting more intense."

"Mom said they would. You are thirty-eight weeks pregnant though, it could be the real thing."

"And you could be Santa Claus. I'm not going early, Jed, don't try to get my hopes up."

"I do have a big package."

"Jes...Darn, I want some Jell-O." I clutch my back, but this time it's the searing paining creeping up the inside of my thighs up into my lower stomach. It's a slow burn that reveals pain I've never experienced before.

"Marlee?" Jed whispers, kissing my neck.

"I want my mommy."

The door to our small room whips open. Dr. Vandergriff walks in, face in his open laptop, hair skewed, and looking a hot mess like he always does. Once the nurses and staff on the oncology floor found out we were expecting, they set us up with their favorite OB/GYN doctor. They had warned us about first impressions and to ignore his dry humor. After six females gushed over him while Jed received his chemotherapy, I knew he was a good one.

"How are we today?" Dr. Vandergriff takes a seat on the rolling stool, still never making eye contact. "Let me guess, nearing nine months pregnant, miserable, and ready to bust that watermelon out of your lemon."

He snorts at his joke. I typically would offer up a half laugh or at least a smile but not today.

"Jell-O!" I scream, trying like hell not to.

"Lime," Fender chirps with his racecars all lined up on the floor.

"I think my girl is in labor," Jed offers.

"I am not!" I slap the paper covering on the table then dig my nails into it, battling through the pain. "You can't say that."

Warm liquid. Oh, so warm seeps down the inside of my thighs. It darkens my beige leggings and soaks into the paper.

"Oy vey. Baby Foster/Bryant is coming today." Dr. Vandergriff stands in complete confidence and walks out of the room.

"Did he leave?" My question comes out as a hiss and curse.

Jed has the phone pressed to his ear. "Mom, it's happening."

"You are calling your mom right now?" I yell, then another one hits, and I'm paralyzed with pain.

Fender's favorite nurse comes in, coaxing him out with a lab coat and set of scrubs. He doesn't blink an eye before ditching us.

"It hurts. It hurts." Once the door is closed, I let it all out. "It motherfucking hurts."

Jed is in my face, his hands cup my cheeks, forcing me to look at him as he talks slowly and deliberately. At first, it pisses me the fuck off.

"You have to calm down. Marlee, breathe. Calm down."

"You calm down, wildcat," I holler in his face. "Your vag isn't being split open by a watermelon."

"Now, now." Dr. Vandergriff walks back in followed by a team of nurses. "Ain't nobody going to be splitting anything right now, watermelons included. Marlee, the hospital is waiting your arrival. We'll get you transported over there."

"It's an elevator ride down two floors and three hallways away," I argue because the pain is turning me into a monster. It's irrational, but holy shit.

"Yeah, I know." Dr. Vandergriff reaches for the doorknob. "Would you rather hoverboard down there?"

"Fuc..."

Jed covers my mouth before I can get the rest out. A sensation that grips the base of my spine and hips takes over. Screw menstrual cramps, this is a tsunami of wreckage. I writhe under Jed's hand, wiggling around the table, battling to find some comfort. It never comes, so I bite down and ride it out.

"Son of a bitch." Jed pulls back his hand, wringing it out.

I should say sorry and I will later, but this pain is too much.

"Hang on until six in the morning and I'm the doctor on call." Dr. Vandergriff opens the door with a warm and familiar grin on his face.

The evil bastard.

"Fuck you," I reply.

Jed doesn't catch it this time. The hallway absorbs the echo of it. The nurses get me in a wheelchair, soaked leggings and all. I want to ask for a blanket, but the torture brewing inside of me is too much.

"Fender." I reach back and clutch to Jed's

forearm.

"He's with his Nana and Grams."

I open my mouth to tell Jed how big of a dumbass he is because my mom isn't here, but then I have to poop.

"I'm going to shit myself," I announce, freaked out.

"Don't," a nurse racing down the hallway demands. "Don't push. The sensation is going to be strong, but don't push. Hold on, Marlee."

"But it's a big one."

My inner Caleb. Not my fault.

"I have to push!" I scream.

I'm lifted up into bed, my leggings stripped away and the whole while Jed keeps his hand locked in mine.

"She's crowning. It's time." I hear a nurse announce.

"Don't even." Jed scowls down at me. "Don't you dare."

"How did you know I was going to say NO SHIT?" I place extra emphasis and pitch on those last two words.

"Focus on me. You've got this, Marlee." Jed keeps talking to me until I interrupt him.

"It hurts so bad, Jed. God, make it go away. It's damn horrible."

Jed doesn't answer with words but starts singing a song. "Kiss An Angel Good Morning," and I want to stab his penis. I don't, only because of the pain coursing through me. The more he sings, the more I'm grounded into his voice. I focus on it and only it. He goes through two more songs until I'm finally instructed to push.

The doctor between my legs isn't Dr. Vandergriff, but a stranger. I follow instructions and push.

"Good. A few more strong pushes. You've got this."

I roll my head to Jed. "I can't."

"You can." He gets in my face. "You will. Ready? One, two, three, and push."

I bare down on his hand and give it all I have.

"One more," the doctor instructs.

I repeat it over and over until I hear the words.

"It's a girl."

No shrill cry fills the air. It's dead silence. Jed lets go of my hand, rushing down toward the baby. I struggle to sit up, but only see a blur of movement down at my feet.

"Jed," I say.

No response, just bustling bodies everywhere.

"Jed!" I scream.

A reply of the sweetest serenade comes in the form of a high-pitched scream. It never ends.

"Want to cut the cord, Dad?"

Jed nods.

My baby girl continues to cry as they weigh and bundle her up. I never want to hear her quit. The sound is comforting knowing she's here.

"Nine pounds and six ounces," a nurse announces.

The doctor still between my legs nods. "Ran out of room to stay in there. Someone was excited about joining the world."

The doctor continues staying between my widespread legs, but I'm transfixed on my baby, watching the nurses every move. Jed is right by our girl's side the entire time.

"Here you go, Mom."

Mom.

Three letters that change my life forever. They have since I so desperately wanted a baby when Fender started calling me by it, and now as a cherub of a little girl is placed in my arms. A miracle I never thought would grace my world.

Her rosy-red cheek nuzzles into my chest. Jed pulls down my bra. In the midst of the chaos, I never got fully undressed. Big, bright blue eyes stare back at me as she works her little cheek against my skin.

"Hi, sweetie. Mom and Dad have been waiting on you for a long time."

She turns her head, suckling to find a nipple as if she's indicating the same thing. Her sweet, little lips latch right onto my breast.

"I'm speechless, Jed." I run my fingers through her baby-soft raven, black hair. She is a Fender junior, there's no doubt about it. The Bryant genes are strong.

Jed shakes and trembles above me, keeping his hand on our baby girl.

"Quinn Hope Bryant," he whispers. "Welcome to the world."

Chapter 36

"The course of true love never did run smooth."
-William Shakespeare

"Banky, it's your turn. I'm out of five dollar bills."

I peek around the corner to see Luke holding Quinn out at an arm's distance. Caleb is signaling hell no with his hands, and Fender is done with the whole ordeal.

"Is someone being mean to my baby girl?" Jed sings, striding out in his black tux pants, unbuttoned white shirt with his tie haphazardly over his shoulders.

He takes her from his dad. Our chubby ten-month-old, Quinn, begins to babble, slapping Jed's cheeks.

"Dadadadada."

Her first and only words to date. It's all about her dad. Quinn loves the boob, but once she sees Jed, it's game over. Fender rolls in at a close second, Guy a clear-cut winner at third, Nana, Papa, Grams, and my dad all mingled in there. *Me?* I'm the boob feeding the baby, and I wouldn't have it any other way.

Fender's infatuation with having a little sister wore off overnight because of poop, wet diapers, and puking. He said to hell with it and went on about his life as Fender, which includes dirt, being curious, and Guy.

I stare at my three humans with awe and love. Today is finally the day we are getting married. Jed is healthy, and I'm not big as a house. Fender fiddles with his black bowtie he insisted on having while Jed takes Quinn in her fluffy peach dress back into the room to change her diaper.

"Get back here before they see you." Martha hisses and tugs on me.

I swat her hand away. It's not like this is the typical wedding in the least. Hell, it's furthest from it. However, Mom and Martha have different plans.

"Slip into your dress. Your mom is checking in on the food. We have about fifteen minutes to show time."

"Quinn pooped," I announce. Yes, motherhood is all about dirty diapers, scraped knees, and lots and lots of loves.

"Jed will get it."

I nod, pulling down the simple yet exquisite white dress from the hanger. It's nothing fancy just a strapless white dress, fitted at the waist and flairs out, flowing to the floor. There's a slit up the side to show a peek of my leg. There's no intricate beadwork or lace. It's simple and to the point.

"Marlee, hustle up. You're going to be late for your damn wedding."

"Yeah, yeah." I wave my hand in the air and disappear into the bathroom with my dress.

I'm not concerned about being late since the only guests are our family members. Mom and Dad flew in last week. Maddie arrived last night. Then it's Jed's immediate family, so the way I see it, we can be as early or late as we want. It's the way a wedding should be. Nothing fancy or too showy with guests who attend to judge your dress, decorations, and menu selection then gossip behind your back.

Ours is an intimate ceremony with Quinn as my maid of honor and Fender the best man. Of course, they won't be able to sign the marriage license. Our mothers will.

Before slipping into my dress, I fix some of the loose beach curls with my fingers and touch up my makeup. I use the term makeup loosely as it's merely a swipe of glitter lip-gloss and eyeliner. I hear the bedroom door open and shut and get ready for the wrath of Martha. She's over the moon excited for her first wedding. She claims Caleb isn't too far behind the game, but I don't see how since he doesn't have a girlfriend or even eyeing a woman for that fact. Caleb's been quiet, behind the scenes, but our biggest support system at the same time, so he could have something up his sleeve. I'm not a fool and see the way he and Maddie get along, but then again Caleb could make friends with his own shadow.

I step into the dress and pull it up over the girls. They fill perfectly in the dress thanks to nursing Quinn.

Knock. Knock.

"Just a second, Martha." I adjust my dress in all the right places.

The door creaks open, and I turn to see Jed. White pressed button-up shirt rolled to midway up his arms, a peach tie, and dark slacks. His hair is thick, sexy, and messily styled, begging my hands to run through it.

"What are you doing here?" I ask. "Your mom is

going to kick your ass if she finds you in here."

He closes the breath of distance between us until our bodies are pressed together. He grabs me by the hips, lifting me up onto the counter. He spreads my legs, hiking the loose material up over my thighs. It pools in the center long enough for Jed to step up to me. I wrap my arms low around his waist and peer up at him.

"Are you looking for trouble, Mr. Bryant?" I kiss his jawline.

"I want nothing more than to lock us in this bathroom, tear this dress off you, and make you scream," Jed hisses in my ear. His hand is venturing to places that are going to get us in trouble because once we start, I know we wouldn't be stopping for a while.

"Marlee? Are you talking to yourself?" Martha hollers from the other side.

Jed is quick, swiveling, and locking the door.

"No!" I holler back.

"What was that sound?"

I'm a shit liar, and Jed knows it. He shoots up an eyebrow, waiting for my reply.

"I was humming."

"You have ten minutes before I'm dragging you out of there!" Martha hollers.

Jed's finger dances along my panty line, making me squirm, wanting much more, so I match his action and reach down, cupping his hard length.

"Okay, Martha."

Jed buries his face in my neck, stifling his chuckles. "You didn't just cup my dick while talking to my mom."

"You didn't just talk about your dick and Mom in the same sentence." I tug his hair at the back of his neck, pulling him in close enough our lips graze. I've never been able to resist this man from the first time I saw him. Our tongues dance around each other. Each of our mouths catches the other's moans. We are both breathless with heaving chests when we pull back.

"I have something for you." I feel each syllable with the brush of his lips on mine.

"Yeah?" I waggle my eyebrows, knowing the direction this is going. Since Jed's been back to his regular self and after the birth of Quinn, it's been on like Donkey Kong.

"Pervert." He smirks. "I'm serious. I have a gift for you."

His eyes grow misty when he pulls a square velvet box from his pocket. It happens in slow motion, but in a warped speed. I fight to engrain each movement into a bank of memories that can be viewed on repeat for the rest of my life. I look down at the simple velvet box in my hands. The material is soothing my soul with each swipe of my fingertips across the crushed material. It's a promise of forever and right now.

"Open it." Jed's full lips glide along my cheek.

As I lift up the lid, I gasp. Inside the box, on a piece of black padding, is a beautiful platinum angel wing. It's stunning with intricate details carving out each aspect. As I lift it from the box, I notice two small pearls hanging from the bottom. Both ivory in color.

Jed clears his throat, emotions thick. "I wanted

to get you something that showed you how much I love you and that represents me and our children. Your past, present, and future."

He wipes away the tears cascading down my face. "I got you this angel wing, because I know you were sent to me from God as a gift from Bentley and Hope. I had the wing made that fits with the bird from Bentley. I've always loved staring at that necklace. It made me believe in the good of the world since the first time I saw you. I was in the darkest hours of my life and that pendant on your necklace brought light back into my world."

I pull the delicate charm from the box. My fingers tremble with the simple metal once it grazes my skin. It's everything. Jed has been my person. He's always encouraged me to open up and talk about Bentley. He's been my rock even at his worst and now this. It takes me long beats of time before I'm able to string together a thought.

I clear my throat, squeeze the pendant, and dig my nails into Jed's white dress shirt. "I love you. I love it. Not a day passes that I don't believe with all I have that Bentley sent me to you. This is proof."

Jed's trembling fingers go to the back of my neck, tickling the sensitive skin. I feel the weight of my most prized possession fall away from my tender flesh. I'm naked in my wedding dress with my future husband between my legs. I'm hypnotized watching Jed lace the new piece of my life onto the intricate chain. The pendant fits perfectly with my past. Everything comes full circle. I'll never understand why and have come to terms with being okay not understanding.

Jed hooks the necklace back around my neck and leans down, kissing the complete charm set. I rake my hands through his thick, black hair. It's my go-to move. A gentle reminder he's healthy and all mine.

I push on his shoulders. "Now, you better get going before your mom catches you in here."

A sexy, devilish smirk dances on his face. "That's gift number one."

"Oh?" I tilt my head, questioning.

"I'm going to take my fiancée before the ceremony."

"No." I shake my head and push him back. He doesn't budge. "No, our mothers would stroke out."

"You." He flicks open the button on his pants.

"Are." His zipper goes down.

"Ruining." His hand disappears down his boxers.

"Our pre-wedding sex." He pulls his length out and my lacy panties off, determined.

"Holy shit," I moan out when he enters me with no warning.

"Ssshhh, baby." His palms grip my ass, pulling me down on him and spinning around. I'm pinned against the wall as he pounds into me.

"Jed." My voice is breathy and way too loud. He licks his lips before covering my mouth with his. There's nothing sweet and tender about his movements. Jed pours everything he has into thrusting into me. He keeps a steady rhythm while making love to my mouth as well. I grin against each one of his thrusts, growing closer and closer. When he growls into my mouth, I'm a goner. I bite down on his bottom lip, bubbling from the inside out with pure pleasure. Jed follows, spilling into me. He's panting harsh and hard, fighting to steady his breathing. My dress is damn near around my neck and all wadded up.

Thank God, Jed pushed down his pants because we made a mess. He sets me back down on the counter, grabbing a washcloth, and wetting it with warm water. I run my hands through his hair as he cleans me up.

"We're getting married today," I murmur more to myself than anyone.

He nods, beginning to clean himself, and then pulls up his pants, and tucks in his shirt.

"No." I pull the tails of his white button-up back out. "You're sexy as hell like this. Like I won't be able to keep my hands off you hot."

"By all means then."

"Jed." I wait for him to look up at me. "I'll never be able to explain or express how much I love you. There are no words. You saved me at my darkest of times. You gave me two children and your unconditional love every single day. I'm going to fumble my vows up out there and just wanted you to know."

Jed's eyes grow watery. "I feel the same exact way. You're my world, and I knew it from the day I saw you in the store. Never believed in love at first sight until you."

"Let's go get married." I wrinkle my nose and then pepper kisses up and down his rugged jawline.

"Jed Lucas Bryant, get your ass out here now." Martha pounds on the door, rattling the inside of the bathroom.

We both erupt in giggles. I hop from the counter and make sure my dress is smoothed out.

"Nipple." Jed reaches for my breasts, tucking them back into my wedding dress.

"Jed!" Martha hollers again.

"She's going to beat your ass," I whisper.

"Not gonna lie. I'm a bit scared for my life. You go first."

I bust out laughing. "You're going to hide behind me?"

"Damn straight."

I open the door to see both of our mothers staring at us, not amused at all.

"Out, Jed." Martha points to the door of the bedroom.

"I was helping Marlee zip up her dress."

"Oh, bullshit." My mom steps closer. "There ain't no damn zipper on Birdie's dress."

My heart beats an extra time every single time Mom calls me by my nickname from childhood. None of the Bryants use it. It's sacred.

"Never heard of a zipper screaming out Jed's name and shaking the walls of the cabin." Caleb joins the conversation.

"Yeah, no shit," both of our moms reply in unison.

"Okay." I throw my hands up in the air. "Everyone out now. There's no crime about two adults having sex before the wedding."

"Birdie..." Mom begins to warn but is cut off by Fender.

"What's sex?" He skips into the room, both hands on the edges of his bowtie.

"When a man and woman love each other..."

"Caleb!" we all scream in unison.

Jed pops him upside the head on his way out with Caleb.

"Everyone outside and take a seat." Martha grabs Caleb, dragging him out of the room.

Mom stays behind with the waterworks already dancing in her eyes.

"You look gorgeous, Marlee. I'm so proud of you."

"Thanks, Mom." I wrap my arms around her, hugging her tight. "I can't wait until Daddy retires and you guys move here."

"Five more months."

I pull back from the hug. "Are the flowers on the chairs?"

"Yes, Bentley's Army shirt is on his, Hope's pink blanket is on hers, and Papa Wally's fishing cooler is on his chair along with sprays of wildflowers. It's all come full circle." Mom kisses my cheek and leads me out to the front porch.

Dad is holding Quinn with her outrageous peach dress drowning her in tutu and frills. Dad has her belly laughing with Donald Duck talk. When he stops she squeals and claps her hands, begging for more.

"You used to do the same thing when you were a little girl, Birdie."

I walk over to Dad and Quinn. It takes some

convincing to get her out of his arms. Everyone takes a seat, leaving Quinn, Jed, Fender, Guy and myself on the porch. Quinn lunges forward, hands out, and babbling dadada over and over.

"Guess you're walking down the aisle with your little girl." I pass her over.

"I'll hold your hand, Mom." Fender races to my side, holding Guy's leash.

Jed gives Caleb the cue to fire up the music. "Marry You" by Bruno Mars begins playing. Fender pulls down his little aviators and starts bobbing his head. The song is catchy as hell, and he insisted we use it at the wedding even though he doesn't understand the words.

I glance over to Jed to find him staring at me.

"I think I want to marry you," I whisper.

Chapter 37
Eight Years Later

"We loved with a love that was more than love."
-Edgar Allan Poe

"I'm not scared of death anymore, baby, I've been blessed beyond measure. God gave me you and the best years of my life. I get to spend every single day with the ones I love. I lived my dream singing on the stage and winning awards. It's enough. It's been enough because of you and our family." Jed wipes each tear away with the pad of his thumb. "It's not the end. The chemo isn't working. It only makes me sick."

"No, Jed." I bury my face in his chest. "Don't say it."

"I want to live the rest of my days doing things we want to pain-free. We can go to Disneyland, fish, or enjoy a lazy Sunday without me being sick from chemo. I'm going to live every single day God graces me with to the fullest.

"He will take care of us. Of me. Of you. Of our children. I'll get to hold Hope and tell her how much her momma loved her and thank Bentley."

I agree with Jed, but it hurts too damn much to face the truth. Stage four cancer has struck us. Jed has battled and is exhausted. It's tarnishing his quality of life, taking away my husband and our kids' dad.

Jed kisses the top of my head. "Baby, any day that God lets me stay here and spend with you and my kids is more than I deserve."

I finally raise my head to look at Jed. The tears are hot and thick rolling down my face. "Okay, baby, let's live. I want to go to the ocean; that's my one request."

His thumb grazes over the apple of my cheeks. "I love you. Thank you."

I've lived one of the grandest love stories of history from beginning to end. I had it all. I can't be bitter or drown in self-pity because I've seen it all through the eyes of two men who loved me. They gave me the world, and that's not something to take lightly.

I'm Marlee Foster-Bryant, and I will live each and every day like there's no such thing as a broken heart. I'll fish, hum a random song, and love with all I have.

"Momma." There's tumbling and rustling coming from the other room.

Then a gorgeous blue-eyed girl rounds the corner, humming her daddy's chart-topping number one platinum song, "Only If."

"What's wrong, baby girl?" Jed sits up, patting the bed.

"I had a nightmare." Her lower lip trembles

"We need to buy you a new dream catcher."

Jed taught Quinn to hum when she woke up from her nightmares and to focus on the soothing tune of the song. My baby girl has her dad's musical talents. Her singing voice at almost nine years old is powerful and raw like her dad's.

"It was bad; a dinosaur was chasing me, and he had bloody teeth." She burrows into her dad's chest.

I hide my smile in my pillow. Quinn only ever has one nightmare, and it's about dinosaurs. I have no idea where it comes from. The girl is fearless, yet this dream gets her every single time, and the only cure is her daddy. It only takes seconds before she's sound asleep between us.

I didn't plan on falling fast. It happened out of nowhere. The force so undeniable I had no chance of avoiding it. We were a set of fools rushing in, creating a love story that will live on forever. We have a time clock counting down each second, and I'll make sure to make the best of each moment spent. We will push time together.

I barely drift off to sleep when I hear the roar of Caleb's truck pull up outside. Footsteps echo down the hardwood hallway. Then lips are on my forehead.

"Heading to football camp, Mom. Love you." Fender does the same to Jed and Quinn.

"Love you, too. Take Uncle Caleb out at the knees if you have the chance."

Fender snorts as he walks out. I can make out the silhouette of his bag slung over his shoulder. He's going to be gone for a week attending football camp at Boise State. I'm going to miss my boy.

Chapter 38

"You are my today and all of my tomorrows." - Leo Christopher

"Mommy, I think I got one."

I turn my direction to Quinn's high-pitched voice to see her hopping up and down. My is dad failing at keeping her calm and focused on reeling in the fishing pole.

"Daddy, look." Quinn waves her hand wildly in the air.

"Way to go, Popper." Jed adjusts the thick wool blanket around us.

He wheezes after hollering back to his daughter. I drop my head back on his shoulder and melt into him. I no longer ask how he's doing or feeling. I know the answer and it's not something I want to face. We are living out the rest of the days just like he wanted. I've stood by and watched my husband vanish away in the winds. The thing is we've lived every single day like he wasn't dying and his days are numbered. It's set in stone. No hope, prayers, or treatment is on our side this time, making moments like this sweeter than dripping honey.

Mom and Dad moved to Idaho, but never sold Papa Wally's homestead. It's our own personal vacation house and the one place all four of us unanimously voted to visit. Disney World, the beach, or even a luxurious cruise didn't hold a candle to the homestead.

"She is so you," Jed whispers in my ear, running his hand up and down my thigh.

Our little Popper has a beautiful rainbow trout on the end of her pole. Mom stands behind her, snapping photo after photo. Dad's chest is puffed out with pride and even though I can't see his face, I know there are tears welling up in his eyes mirroring my own.

"She's a perfect combination. Has your singing talent and my fishing skills."

"A force to be reckoned with," he replies.

"Do you think she'll follow in your footsteps?"

I feel Jed give a weak shrug of his shoulders. "If she does, I know she'll have you, Mom, and Fender right behind her as her support system."

I don't get a chance to reply before Fender interrupts us. "Dad, want to play catch?"

"You ain't tired of looking bad yet, son?" Jed rustles behind me.

I know it will take him some time to get enough energy to stand up. The cancer may be winning the battle killing him, but doesn't hold the power to touch his heart and determination. Fender beams with pride, watching his dad rise slowly and gets ready to catch the pigskin.

The boy loves, adores, eats, sleeps, and breathes all things football. He drank the Kool-Aid and found his passion. It's the furthest thing from what Jed loves, but it doesn't mean a damn thing. The two have long conversations at night cuddled together in bed about where Fender wants to play. Jed offers up advice on strategy and skill set. It's always the sweetest, loving lyrics to any song I've ever heard.

"Yours is two inches shorter, literally."

I glance back down at Quinn who has her hands on her hips, arguing with the neighbor kid. A young boy her age, Barrett. I watch the duo go after each other and can't help the smile playing out on my face. It takes me back to years and years ago. Momma winks at me, picking up on the same thing.

"You're blind." Quinn stomps over to me.

Her cheeks are reddened with heat and anger. I hold the blanket out and let her curl up underneath it. She's had her own spells of anxiety and angry outbursts coming to grips about the outcome of her daddy.

"That was a nice one." I comb my hand over her hair, pulling it back from her forehead.

"But that jerk ruined it." She crosses her arms in front of her, not ready to make nice.

"Popper, you never gloat or brag when it comes to fishing. Just enjoy the catch."

"I know," she huffs. "Papa Wally always told you that."

"He did." I smile, loving the fact Quinn knows her Papa Wally even though she never met him.

"Can I tell you a secret?" Her voice grows serious and determined.

"Of course."

She turns in my arms, wrapping her arms around my neck. "It's not really a secret."

"Go on." I rub her back.

"Barrett makes my tummy feel like there's butterflies in it. You know like Daddy's butterfly kisses on my cheeks. Then he pisses me off, Momma."

Love.

"It's okay, baby girl." I squeeze her in my arms. "This is the same place I fell in love with Bentley and I had those same feelings."

"Momma." She pulls back from me, horror in her wide open eyes. "That's disgusting."

"Your daddy makes me feel that way every day." I brush her bangs off her forehead. "It's okay."

"Yuck, I hate it and he's weird." Quinn turns her head to gaze back down to Barrett.

I smile all too well, knowing what those fluttering sensations mean. Quinn overcomes her dilemma when Barrett snags a big one. She races down to her grandpa, wanting in on the action. Jed was spot on...she's just like me.

Jed sinks next to me on the bench. The simple tossing of a football with his son has wiped him out. His chest rattles up and down. Jed's breathing rattles every pore in his body as he fights to pull in oxygen. *It's my worst nightmare.* But he wanted to live and live is what he's doing.

"Momma made fried chicken for dinner." I lay my head back on his shoulder.

"Sounds amazing." Jed wraps his arms low around my waist.

I know it's all bullshit. He has no appetite, but indulges anyway. We stay wrapped up in one another, watching our daughter fish and our son toss the football with Banky. The night floats by wave after wave. Each second ticks by and we absorb everything from our daughter who is all twitterpatted over Barrett to our son tossing the football with Caleb.

Jed nibbles on his chicken at the dinner table. He does his best to keep up with his kids and family. I don't nudge him on or encourage him to eat. Jed is doing what is best for him right now and that's enjoying his family.

"How was your day, family?" Quinn asks, stuffing a spoonful of mashed potatoes in her mouth.

It's Quinn's thing. She asks the same question every single night at the dinner table even on the days we've spent every hour together. Fender goes first.

"Awesome. I love it here." His eyes grow misty. "I loved playing catch with Dad."

Caleb scoffs, but we all ignore him. My heart is not only shattering for myself, but my nearly thirteen-year-old son who is devastated.

"I have no doubt if you keep throwing like that you'll be the starting QB your freshman year of high school."

Fender beams at that.

Momma and Dad follow suit, sharing the highlights of their day. They're all centered around my kids. I reach under the table, find Jed's hand, and squeeze it. He's cold, his fingers bony, and trembling. He leans over and kisses my cheek.

"My day was fantastic." I squeeze his hand again. "I caught the biggest fish at the pond."

"Momma, you aren't supposed to brag," Quinn warns me.

I shrug my shoulders. "Facts are facts."

My entire family shakes their heads at me, amused.

"Mom made my favorite meal for dinner, I got to watch my dad teach Quinn all of his fishing tips and tricks, and the best part was witnessing Caleb take a header in the pasture."

The table erupts in laughter. Caleb was running a play from his college days and out of nowhere went down. He nursed his shoulder for half the day. It was one of those times you shouldn't have laughed, but none of us had any self-control.

"Hey, I was just making sure you all were paying attention." Caleb takes a bite out of the crispy fried chicken. "Today was damn near perfect. I'm missing a wife, but besides that I wouldn't change a thing."

Once my plate is cleaned and Jed has picked at his mashed potatoes, Momma encourages us to leave the table. We tuck the kids in and then I follow Jed down the hall. I don't guide him or hold his back as he makes his way. I let him make it in his own time.

"Baby."

I turn to see Jed standing near the end of the bed. I go to him to be pulled into his chest. He runs his fingers over the charms on my necklace. I cup his cheek and stare into his rich whiskey colored eyes that don't shine any longer.

"Yeah," I reply.

"How does a hot bath sound?" he asks.

"Perfect." I kiss his chin and then go about starting the hot water.

Jed begins stripping out of his clothes and once he's done, he takes care of me. First my shirt goes up and over my head, his trembling fingers unclasp my bra, and then my yoga pants and panties are pushed down. I wrap my arms low around his waist, pulling him into me. Flesh to flesh; I feel every beat of his heart. I refuse to cry, ruining any moment we have left.

Jed leans down and kisses the top of my head. "My day was perfect. It couldn't have been any better, watching my two children enjoy life and having you wrapped up in my arms. It was perfect."

I peer up at him. "Mine, too."

We ease into the tub, Jed first and then I nuzzle into between his legs and relax back onto his chest. The chest that has caught me so many times over the years. It's offered comfort and protection in a way nothing else ever could. Jed laces his fingers in mine and we sit in silence just like we did so many years ago during our coffee dates. It's our love song and always will be. The silence comforts me.

Jed begins breathing heavy. I turn around to see him nodding off. I swivel in his lap until I'm facing him and cup his face. I lean forward and kiss his lips. Once, twice, and then three times before he wakes up. Tears begin to roll down his cheeks.

"What's wrong, baby?"

"Never forget I love you, Marlee."

"I won't."

"It's getting close." He snaps his eyes shut. "Can you get the kids? I want them with us tonight."

I nod and whisper, "Yes."

I get Jed in bed then get dressed in a pair of yoga pants and a Boise State hoodie. He snags me by the wrist before I'm able to get too far away, pulling me down to him.

"Kiss me," he whispers against my lips.

When our mouths meet we kiss hard and passionate, pouring everything into the simple action. Jed fists a handful of my hair, bringing me closer to him. We kiss as if it's our last one.

I pull back breathless and pad down the hall to get our kids. I let all of the tears fall, not even worrying about brushing them away. Quinn snuggles into her dad's chest and Fender climbs in on his other side. I lean on the door jamb to his room filled with so much love and sadness my body quakes.

"Everything okay?" Martha wraps her arms around me. I don't turn to her.

"Hey, I didn't know you guys got in."

"Just about thirty minutes ago. What's going on?"

"He wants his kids with him tonight." My voice hitches on the last word. "I think it's time."

My shoulder catches Martha's tears. We stand united, watching Jed kiss his kids and tell them how much he loves them over and over.

"Go be with them. I'll let everyone else know." Martha kisses my cheek and is gone.

I don't want to go to the bed. In the back of my mind, it's like if I do I'm giving Jed permission to leave. Each step is heavy and shatters my heart.

"Momma." Quinn turns her head and pats the bed. "We got you."

I smile weakly and climb in behind her. Jed reaches over Quinn for my hand and he laces his fingers in mine. The room falls silent for long beats of time. Quinn breaks it with the first words to "Amazing Grace;" it's always been her favorite song. Jed joins her, the two singing with conviction, rattling my soul. They sing song after song together until Jed's voice fades off.

It was our last kiss.

Our last night.

My heart had to learn to beat for a new reason.

Epilogue

"There is no love without forgiveness, and there is no forgiveness without love." -Bryant H. McGill

May 10th

Dear Diary,

Today Fender turns eighteen and graduates high school. My adventurous son will soon be heading to Boise State on a football scholarship, majoring in Accounting. He's crashing around the house, humming the tune to "Patience" by Guns N Roses. It makes me smile remembering my first love, Bentley. It's eerie how many damn signs there are. The universe will never let me forget.

Love gave me life. Heartache gave me a new beginning. Life has left me a battered soldier with no armor to hide behind. I don't regret any of it. My endings have never been happy, but I've learned the love stories leave me with several chapters to read over and over forever. They're mine. Imprinted on my skin. Through the darkest of days, I found God again. He gave me my son, Fender, my daughter, Quinn, and the love of two of the greatest men to ever walk the earth.

A day doesn't pass that I don't think of them and the love stories we shared. I wouldn't change a thing. They made me into the woman I am today.

Love,

Marlee Foster-Bryant

Obituary of Jed Lucas Bryant

Jed Lucas Bryant of Moore, Idaho, passed away surrounded by his family members on the twenty-third of July. He left behind the love of his life, Marlee Foster-Bryant, and their two children, Fender and Quinn Bryant.

He lost a long battle with Appendix Cancer, but cherished every single day God graced him. Jed Bryant is known to the world as the king of country music. He blazed trails for upcoming country stars. The amount of awards he received are too numerous to count.

However, Jed wanted it to be known his greatest accomplishments in life was falling in love with Marlee, building their home with his own two hands, and mostly his two children.

"I lived. Had it all. And it ended. It's now my time to fly with the angels. I'm looking forward to meeting a few of them." –Jed Bryant

THE END

Acknowledgements-

I want to thank you for taking the time to read this book. It means the world to me. There aren't enough words to express my gratitude.

Marlee's story was a very difficult one to write. The idea of the story hit me while up in the mountains at a family ranch house. Actually, it was the place where I married my high school sweetheart. The scenery is breathtaking and it's one of those places you can feel the power of the universe beat in your soul. It made me appreciate everything I have in my life and realize in the same instance how it could all be taken away.

Marlee did live two of the greatest love stories. She never grew bitter, instead cherished what those love stories left behind for her.

I'd like to thank Lydia Harbaugh. She's my best friend, sister-in-law, and pain in my ass. She loves to highjack my Facebook talking about my itchy ass. Her other past time is boning my brother. But in all seriousness, she's the best person I could ask to be on my team.

Thanks again to all!

Love,

HJB

Playlist-

Weak by AJR
Tin Man by Miranda Lambert
Mixed Drinks About Feelings by Eric Church
My Way by Calvin Harris
Heartache on the Dance Floor by Jon Pardi
Lean On Me by Bill Withers
The Ones That Like Me by Brantley Gilbert
It Ain't My Fault by Brothers Osborne
Fix a Drink by Chris Janson
Round Here Buzz by Eric Church
You Look Good by Lady Antebellum
Greatest Love Story by LANCo
No Such Thing as a Broken Heart by Old Dominion
Ugly Lights by Miranda Lambert
Tomboy by Miranda Lambert
What Ifs by Kane Brown
Pushin' Time by Miranda Lambert
This is Gospel by Panic! At the Disco
Whiskey and You by Chris Stapleton
Without a Fight by Brad Paisley feat. Demi Levato
A Little Dive Bar in Dahlonega by Ashley McBryde
All on Me by Devin Dawson
Hound Dog by Elvis Presley
Give Me Love by Ed Sheeran
When You Say Nothing At All by Keith Whitley
Kiss an Angel Good Morning by Charley Pride
He Stopped Loving Her Today by George Jones
Marry You by Bruno Mars

Slow Hands by Niall Horan

www.ingramcontent.com/pod-product-compliance
Lightning Source LLC
Chambersburg PA
CBHW072155110625
28109CB00022B/260

* 9 7 8 1 9 7 8 2 2 3 0 5 9 *